PRAISE FOR *THE LOVE CEILING*

"*The Love Ceiling* is wonderful, touching, funny. Jean Davies Okimoto writes with literary perfect pitch."

– **Christiane Northrup, MD**
Author of *The Secret Pleasures of Menopause; Women's Bodies, Women's Wisdom;* and *Mother-Daughter Wisdom*

"*The Love Ceiling* is a lovely book, full of wisdom and compassion. With keen insight, the author examines the problems of achieving fulfillment as both a woman and an artist in modern society, as viewed through the eyes of recognizably true-to-life characters."

– **Barbara G. Walker**
Author of *The Woman's Encyclopedia of Myths and Secrets, The Woman's Dictionary of Symbols and Sacred Objects,* and *The Crone*

"*The Love Ceiling*, by Jean Davies Okimoto, is a fine painting of words by a true artist. She describes, in beautiful painterly scenes, three generations of one family's women. These capable, strong, creative women go about their lives interacting with family, lovers, and friends. Love with pain, cruelty, anger, hate, anguish, and compassion color their lives. This is a book so compelling that once you begin you cannot put it down."

– **Chizuko Judy Sugita de Queiroz**
Artist and author of *Camp Days: 1942-1945*

"As Anne Kuroda Duppstaad crashes against the 'love ceiling' and realizes that the demons of the past she struggles to 'disarm' are really inside herself, she journeys from bitterness to acceptance, finally giving herself permission to create art. For a Western woman, this is a difficult enough journey. For a woman raised with Japanese values of restraint and sacrifice, the victory is even more hard won. Any woman who has ever wrestled with a difficult father will find inspiration and solace in these lucid pages."

– **Leza Lowitz**
Former Tokyo correspondent for *Art in America*, author of *Green Tea to Go: Stories from Tokyo*, and editor of *Other Side River/A Long Rainy Season: Contemporary Japanese Women's Poetry*

The Eclipse of Moonbeam Dawson

"A must read for all ages!"   *–Explorations, Barnes & Noble*

"...an endearing character whose unique upbringing has given him a quirky and amusing perspective on life...the meaning of family, first love, and friendship."
–School Library Journal

Talent Night

"A story of ethnic pride, first love and determination to overcome stereotypes. Okimoto's talents gives this book the same wide appeal as her earlier titles *Jason's Women* and *Molly By Any Other Name.*"   *–School Library Journal*

"A celebration of diversity."   *–Signal*

Take a Chance, Gramps!

"A bright, determined heroine and a snappy narrative style."
–Booklist

"Good pacing, smooth writing...and the right mix of humor, romance...make a winning combination."
–School Library Journal

ALSO BY JEAN DAVIES OKIMOTO

Plays:
> *Hum It Again, Jeremy*
> *Uncle Hideki*
> *Uncle Hideki and the Empty Nest*

Nonfiction:
> *Boomerang Kids: How to Live with Adult Children Who Return Home* (coauthor)

Young Adult Novels:
> *My Mother Is Not Married to My Father*
> *It's Just Too Much*
> *Norman Schnurman, Average Person*
> *Who Did It, Jenny Lake?*
> *Jason's Women*
> *Molly by Any Other Name*
> *Take a Chance, Gramps!*
> *Talent Night*
> *The Eclipse of Moonbeam Dawson*
> *To JayKae: Life Stinx*

Picture Books:
> *Blumpoe the Grumpoe Meets Arnold the Cat*
> *A Place for Grace*
> *No Dear, Not Here*
> *Dear Ichiro*
> *The White Swan Express* (coauthor)
> *Winston of Churchill: One Bear's Battle Against Global Warming*

Short Stories:
> "Jason the Quick and the Brave"
> "Moonbeam Dawson and the Killer Bear"
> "Next Month...Hollywood!"
> "Watching Fran"
> "Eva and the Mayor"
> "My Favorite Chaperone"

The Love Ceiling

a novel

Jean Davies Okimoto

ENDICOTT
and HUGH
BOOKS

BURTON • WASHINGTON

ENDICOTT & HUGH BOOKS
P.O. Box 13305, Burton, WA 98013.
www.endicottandhughbooks.com

Cover and interior design by Masha Shubin
Wooden Easel © 2008 Maksym Bondarchuk, Blake Island © 2008 Lawrence
Freytag, Wooden palette © 2008 Hedda Gjerpen. Images from iStockPhoto.com.

This is a work of fiction. The events described here are imaginary. The settings and
characters are fictitious or used in a fictitious manner and do not represent specific places or living or dead people. Any resemblance is entirely coincidental.

Printed in Canada on 100% recycled paper

Okimoto, Jean Davies.

    The love ceiling : a novel / Jean Davies Okimoto. --1st ed. --Burton,
WA : Endicott and Hugh Books, c2009.

      p. ; cm.
    ISBN: 978-0-9823167-3-3

      1. Mothers and daughters--Fiction. 2. Aging--Psychological
aspects--Fiction. 3. Creative ability--Fiction. 4. Japanese
Americans--Fiction. I. Title.

PS3565.K46 L68 2009   2009921057
813.54--dc22   0909

10 9 8 7 6 5 4 3 2 1

For Joe

ACKNOWLEDGMENTS

I've always had an appreciation for the constant balancing act between career and family that's demanded of so many women. And for women in the arts, the pull between self-expression and the needs of family is a theme I knew I'd eventually tackle, even though it would mean a departure from most of the books I've written over the past thirty years. With the exception of my two plays, *Uncle Hideki* and its sequel *Uncle Hideki and the Empty Nest*, and the nonfiction book which I co-authored with Phyllis Jackson Stegall, *Boomerang Kids: How to Live With Adult Children Who Return Home*, all of my books have been for children and young adults. *The Love Ceiling* is my first for my own age group and I found myself leaning pretty heavily on family members, friends, and publishing professionals for help and advice as I made my way through many drafts. My agent, Robert Astle, has a rich background in theater and his advice helped me transition from the play *Uncle Hideki and Empty Nest* to working the themes into *The Love Ceiling* and he was always wonderfully encouraging. Ali Bothwell Mancini is not only a delight to work with, but an exceptionally talented editor. One of the most experienced people I had the pleasure of working with is Ellen Kleiner. She has an amazing combination of warmth, encouragement and savvy and facilitated everything to bring the book to life. Working with Ellen was marketing and promotion coordinator Karen Riley; both of these outstanding women were *The Love Ceiling's* midwives extraordinaire.

Meeting Jeremy Solomon was a stroke of luck which resulted in my having the pleasure of working with the excellent copyeditor Linda Franklin and the talented designer Masha Shubin.

I'm indebted to Jim Devine, a.k.a. Captain Probate, who helped me understand estate law as it applies to artists, and Barbara Johns, art curator and museum consultant, was an invaluable resource. In the early drafts, the editorial viewpoints I got from Sarah Flynn, Anne Depue and Will North were very helpful. Amy Brim, Katie Klein, Margy Heldring, Catherine Johnson, Dan Klein, Barry Foster, Virginia Washburn, Julie Morser, Chris Sturgis, Roger Davies, Margie Morgan and her mother Margot Morgan were my kind readers and I'm deeply grateful to them. Katie, Amy, Dan, and Margy Heldring read draft, after draft, after draft and I can't thank them enough for going the distance with such grace. And then there's my husband Joe. Nothing is possible without Joe.

Then the time came when the risk it took
to remain tight in a bud was more painful
than the risk it took to blossom.

Anaïs Nin

1

ANNIE

The exhibition's title was splashed in blazing letters across the huge banners surrounding the entrance of the museum. *ALEXANDER GUNTHER: 1947–2007: A Retrospective.* I felt queasy the minute I saw my father's name and it struck me as ironic that as often as I toyed with the idea of inventing some ailment, something harmless and quickly curable, which would give me an excuse to skip his opening tonight, now that we were here—I actually did feel ill. Stomach cramps, which had been dormant for decades, had been my historic response to him and I could only think of the old warning: be careful what you wish for.

From the car I could see the banners had been carefully designed to reflect the palette of his most acclaimed work from the early fifties: black, white, gray with slashes of brilliant reds. Crimson and vermillion, like fire or blood, always predominated and the critics invariably related them to elements of passion. To me it looked garish, even a little obscene. The dates of the exhibition were at the top of the banners...April twenty-eighth to July fifth. How true it was, I thought, as we stopped at a light just south of the museum, that April is the cruelest month.

"Annie, what are you doing with that window?" Jack looked over at me, tapping his fingers against the wheel, impatient for the light to turn.

"What?"

"You've been fiddling with the button—it's been going up and down for the past two blocks. It's driving me nuts!"

I put the window up and folded my hands in my lap. "I don't want to go in there."

"Fine. We'll go home," he said with a smile. "And what would you tell everyone?" His tone was gentle, and it reminded me of the sweet way he would tease Cass and Ian when they were little.

"That I got sick. Which isn't far off, because he makes me sick." I looked at my hands in my lap, trying to keep from fooling with the window button. The skin on the backs of my hands was decorated with tiny brown dots as if I'd been splashed with rusty water. I can't remember when the spots first appeared. Maybe ten years ago—when I was fifty-three—and this year I'll turn sixty-four. What happened? Ten years? Where did that go?

Will you still need me, will you still feed me, when I'm sixty-four? I looked over at Jack, handsome in his dark suit. He is boyishly handsome, like Russell Baker or Tom Brokaw, although he has a bit of a chin bag, and a bald spot on the back of his head, but the rest of his hair is lovely and silver. Jack isn't vain, although he'd had a brief flirtation with Rogaine, which lasted about four days. But in spite of the fact that he's nine years older than I am, the years have been nicer to Jack than to me, and he's never had to force himself to exercise like I do. Starting with the Jane Fonda workout, I think I've tried (and quit) every exercise every invented. I'm at least ten pounds overweight, okay, maybe twenty, and it's the same perpetual poundage I've been trying to lose for the past twenty-five years. I'd also probably look younger if I did something about the dishwater gray threads multiplying explosively in my hair, but ever since my last birthday I decided I had better things to do with my time than sit in a salon with tinfoil on my head.

I felt flushed and I put the window down a few inches. "I really need some air." The evening was a little chilly, but a clear night with no sign of rain. I stuck my nose out the window like a dog. The weather had cooperated for Alexander the Great.

I turned back to Jack. "Or I could say I had a conflict—something came up that I couldn't get out of."

"Like what?" The light changed and he drove ahead toward the museum.

"Like needing to cut my toenails." I sighed, only half-smiling. "Or floss my teeth."

"Annie—" Jack glanced at me, shaking his head.

"Honestly, I do feel a little sick, sort of nauseated. Let's just go to Tomiko's and get a drink first. A little liquid courage so I can face it."

Not that Jack cared, but I'd replaced "Dutch" with "liquid" when I learned "Dutch courage" had been a British putdown of the Dutch. I'd welcomed taking Jack's name, Duppstadt. Unlike a lot of women in the seventies who kept their maiden names, I had been only too eager to dump "Gunther." I wanted nothing to do with my famous father.

"We can stop at Tomiko's— but if you want my advice,

we're better off to just get this over with and then get a drink." Jack moved over to the right lane. "Okay?"

"I still can't believe he's going through with this. She's only been dead three weeks. *Three weeks*, Jack."

"I doubt the museum could cancel a big exhibition like this, they spent—"

"Look, I'm not nuts—I don't expect that he'd act like someone dear," I interrupted, "like Mr. Rogers in a cardigan sweater with a nice little bow tie, someone soft spoken and patient. That would be delusional—but is it too much to ask for just a bit of basic decency? And I'm not saying the museum should cancel, either. But he could have rescheduled the reception—he could play the grieving widower, people would understand. It could've been changed to a reception at the show's close, in July, right around the Fourth which he'd love because, of course, he'd assume all the fireworks and hoopla were for him."

"I'll drop you off in front and then park."

"You don't have to," I frowned. "I hate going in alone."

"Just wait for me on the steps." Jack reached over and patted my hand. "There's usually space in the Ampco garage or Harbor Steps. You won't have to wait long. You might run into Cass and Richard or Kelly." He pulled up in front of the museum. "Go ahead, honey. I can't stop here for more than a second."

"Okay," I agreed reluctantly. "I'll be on the steps." As I got out of the car, two young women walked by; both had cleavage that rivaled a produce display at the supermarket and one of them had a swatch of bare stomach peeking over the top of her pants. I thought they were regular people, not prostitutes; they walked along as if they had a specific destination, wearing these really stupid shoes—high heels like pencils. Weren't they afraid they'd fall on their fannies? I can't fathom for the life of me why this trampy look is fashionable. But at least Cass hasn't gone in for it. I glanced up toward the museum entrance, hoping I might see her and Richard. She said they'd both be coming—he didn't have to be on call at the hospital for once. She sounded happy, which was reassuring because Cass hasn't been herself lately and I've been worried about her. It's nice for her that he's coming, but I have to admit that I'm never too excited about seeing him. In fact, I sometimes wished she'd dump him and find some guy who could commit. Not marriage to any old person, not to some creep. I just wish Cass could have a reasonably happy marriage, a good enough marriage. The main thing that bothers me about Richard Matsunaga is his reluctance to marry my daughter, and I'm pretty sure he's the one dragging his feet. I can't see or talk to him without just wanting to goose him.

I stood on the steps waiting for Jack, looking up at the banners heralding my father's lifetime achievement. They say all children are artists, they create freely, naturally, without reserve or inhibition, and I certainly wanted to be one from the moment I first opened a box of crayons and knew to draw with them rather than eat them. I think my mother knew this, but in our house there was only room for one artist. She infantilized and indulged my father—probably partly out of fear, but everything he did was tolerated and the result was that he was the only one allowed to be a child. The great Alexander Gunther took up all the space, all the air, even the light.

Annie, you have a gift. An unusual sense of color. An intuitive feeling for light.

5

Mr. Fillinger had penciled his comments on the back of my pastel. I remember staring at the words and memorizing each one, breathing them in, holding them in my heart.

He'd taken our class on a field trip to Seward Park to learn to work outdoors. It was a crisp spring day and we sat on the grass in the upper picnic ground facing south where Mt. Rainier rises over Lake Washington. I was fifteen; it was the first time I'd ever worked in oil pastels and I loved them. The mountain was so beautiful and it was exhilarating trying to capture it, the deep green firs and the light dancing on the surface of the lake.

That day after school, I stood tentatively in the doorway of the studio at the back of the house. "Dad? Are you busy?"

"What is it?" He looked up from the issue of *Art News*. "I'm sure whatever even you have to say is better than this asshole critic." He hurled the magazine across the floor.

"Maybe I should leave." I pulled the pastel close to my chest.

"No," he barked, "go ahead, what is it you want?"

"I made this in my art class. My teacher, Mr. Fillinger, said—"

"Mr. who?"

"Fillinger. He also teaches at the community college, he's had shows in galleries and he said—"

"He said something you did was good."

"Yes and he wrote on the back and I just thought—"

"Bring it here." He adjusted his leg brace and pulled himself up and limped to an easel in the center of the room. "Give it to me."

I handed it to him and my father read the comments on the back, and then clipped the little pastel to the easel.

My stomach began to cramp and I was almost afraid to breathe as he stared at my delicate rendering of the mountain. His jaw was clenched as he walked with his awkward gait to a table where tubes of paint, brushes and palettes were scattered. His back was to me and I couldn't see what he was doing. After a few seconds he turned and returned to the easel.

"Now, what I'm about to do is for your own good." His eyes narrowed as he looked down at me. "This Fillinger is just trying to get in with me. He's using you." He motioned to the easel as if he were brushing away a gnat. "This work is Sunday hobby painting and pedestrian." He spat out the words, "it's representational, decorative crap. You'll never be a serious painter—you don't have it. I'm doing this so you'll never forget this moment, to save you a lot of pain." He paused, holding the palette knife poised over the pastel. "The art world is filled with rejection and betrayal and you're far better off if you learn now to stay away from it." The palette knife was loaded with brown paint and he gouged at the pastel, pulling the dark pigment from one corner to the other like smeared feces. I fled from his studio, my stomach roiling. The onset was so violent that when my mother heard me in the bathroom, she thought it was food poisoning.

The night air was cool and brisk and I hunched my shoulders against the chill. I placed my hand over the silver pin near my collar, running my fingers over it like a talisman. It was a silver frog, designed by Bill Reid, the Haida artist, and had belonged to my mother. The frog, a reproduction she'd gotten at the museum store in Vancouver, had been one of my mother's favorite pieces. My dear, sweet, sad mother. She was the only reason I was here at all, and if there was any consolation I could find about losing her, it was that after tonight I'd never have to deal with my father again. At the most the future might hold a courtesy visit at Christmas, and I suppose I could stomach that, if it was short. Hello Dad...Merry Christmas...Good-bye.

I didn't see any sign of Cass and Richard or Kelly, my daughter-in-law. What if they never came and I just turned around and left? How wonderful, I could just picture the pompous old rooster looking around the crowd, making excuses for us, and then finally realizing that he, the great Alexander Gunther, had been stood up. Too bad, you jerk.

Cass and Ian always liked these openings, although Ian was in Chicago on business and wouldn't be here tonight. I sometimes wished my kids felt the way I did about my father: the same conflicted, retaliatory mess that would make it equally impossible for them to spend more than ten minutes in the same room with him. I'd never say so directly, because I knew it was childish and I felt stupid about it, after all he was their grandfather—not their father—but I always felt slightly betrayed when they made more than a token appearance at one of his affairs.... Affairs. How many would show up tonight? Art groupies crawled around my father like ants at a picnic, the only question being how many would appear.

"Annie! We're over here!" Kelly shouted from the steps near the main door.

I turned and waved, my spirits lifting when I saw Sam. With my mother gone, my grandson was like oxygen. Kelly, as usual, looked perfect in her essential little black dress, and Sam, who had just turned three, looked like a miniature adult in gray pants, a navy blazer, white shirt and tie.

From the distance, where I stood at the bottom of the steps, I was struck with how strongly Sam resembled Stan Bailey, Kelly's dad. I'd always wondered what narcissism or wish for immortality made us search for ourselves in our grandchildren, hoping the roll of the genes would come up with our eyes, or mouth or any one of our assorted features in this new little member of the tribe? It seemed shallow and vain to me, and my mild disappointment that Sam looked more like Stan Bailey than my family embarrassed me. When I thought about it, if you went far enough back, everyone in the human family resembled Curious George anyway, so what was the point of all this effort to identify whose nose showed up on the baby?

I climbed the steps and held out my arms to Sam, who in spite of his dressy attire bolted from his mother and cuddled with me as if he were wearing his snuggly pj's.

"How handsome you look." I held him close and leaned over to peck Kelly's cheek. "Hi, Kelly. You look beautiful, as always."

"Thanks. This is quite the event isn't it?"

"Yes, quite." There's something about the way Kelly tosses her head and runs her hand through her long blonde hair that reminds me of Ann Coulter. Kelly's personality isn't junkyard dog vicious; it's only the little head thing she does that seems similar. And of course, this is not an observation I would make to anyone, not even Jack. I have tried to like her. Truly, I have.

"I have a tie." Sam said proudly, lifting it so close to my face I had to look cross-eyed to see it.

"It's a fine tie, Sam." I laid my cheek against his. "Have you seen Cass?" I scanned the steps of the museum as more people began arriving. The guests attending tonight's

opening reception were my father's family, friends, colleagues, museum members and members of its board,
donors to the museum, the academics, art critics, collectors,
and one other group: a selection of students he'd invited
from his teaching years. How many of the ones he'd been
screwing would show up, I couldn't help wondering again
as I watched more guests arriving. Wouldn't he have the
decency to resist the attention for once? I always picked up
on it and had from the time I was fifteen. You'd think by
eighty-three he'd try for some statesman-like dignity, but
he'd just become a lecher emeritus, strutting like a peacock
oblivious to his aging, tattered tail.

"We just got here." Kelly looked around. "We thought
Cass would be with you."

"We decided to come separately, we're not going to
stay long."

"I thought Sam and I should just come alone, too."
Kelly smiled. "I never know how long he'll hold up."

I tipped my head back to look at Sam. "I'm with you,
Sam. I never know how long I'll hold up." Sam giggled and
I gave him a little kiss.

"There's Jack." Kelly waved and I turned to see him
mounting the steps. He really did look handsome in that
dark suit. His gray hair added dignity to his lined, boyish
face—Mother Nature was certainly kinder to her sons than
her daughters. Although to look at Jack, you'd never know
that lately he'd been kind of lost. At the height of his
career he was one of the country's leading researchers in
hematology, but his latest grant wasn't funded and he was
slowly being forced out. I knew it had been eating away
at him, but Jack was a master at acting like everything's
fine. He fit in easily with this kind of tony, well-heeled

crowd, whereas I invariably felt awkward, as though I'm ten years out of style, in a dress with underarm pit stains beginning to seep into the fabric, while my slip is showing (even though I was wearing a black pants suit).

Jack held out his arms for Sam and I passed him over.

"Hi Grandpa." Sam grabbed his tie and held it under Jack's nose. "I have a tie."

"That's quite the tie!"

"Hi Jack." Kelly kissed him, then stood back and looked at Jack and Sam appreciatively. "I wish I had a picture of you two. I didn't bring our camera, I was sure you'd have one," she said to me.

"Actually, no." I watched the crowd again. "I suppose Cass will find us. Maybe we should go in."

A table was set up near the coat check with a guest book and the exhibition catalogue. Young men and women in crisp white shirts and black pants, the staff from the Bon Appétit Company, which catered all museum events, circulated among the guests with trays of champagne and hors d'oeuvres. The food was exquisite: polenta squares with pesto, caviar and crème fraîche in a buckwheat blini, smoked salmon in cucumber cups, chicken kabobs with spicy mango sauce, and my favorite, tiny Vietnamese spring rolls with shrimp and avocado. We each took a glass of champagne while we waited to sign the guest book.

"I'll get some orange juice for Sam, they should have some at one of the bars." Kelly left Sam with Jack and me and went to the closest of the three open bars stationed on the mezzanine.

I noticed a fourth bar on the Grand Staircase. They certainly haven't spared any expense. I wonder which collectors had helped underwrite the exhibition? I sipped my champagne, then noticed the people next to me turning to look at the Grand Staircase. There was a buzz and a scattering of applause, as my father, so recently a widower, descended from the gallery above, like a monarch about to greet his subjects.

"He looks good," Jack whispered.

"Yes," I said with indifference. "This is his moment. He lives for this."

Age had robbed him of some height. He was less than six feet now, but still commandingly elegant in his gray silk jacket and the creamy, ivory silk turtleneck carefully chosen to complement his glorious white hair. The years didn't seem to have left a mark there; it was still thick and full and was beautifully cut to just graze the top of his shirt collar. His cobalt blue eyes had lost little of their intensity and the laser surgery he'd had fifteen years ago—always a risk taker, he'd been among the first to have the procedure—still made glasses unnecessary. He had theatrical looks, most closely resembling Peter O'Toole without the traces of dissipation. He moved slowly down each stair, not for effect, although that was a welcome by-product, but out of necessity. Polio, when he was young, had left him with his left leg atrophied and misshapen. Aided by a brace, he'd been able to walk, albeit a halting and uneven gait—but he could do it. When he was in his sixties, the stress on his good leg caught up with him and he needed to use aluminum crutches with arm pieces enclosing his forearms. He couldn't walk without them.

When I tried to be objective, I could say that Alexander Gunther was a passionate man, charismatic and possessing great warmth. It's a warmth that radiated, captivating people who drew in its heat and light, then reflected it like mirrors with a glow that fueled him. He had very little interest in other people as separate beings in their own right, with a separate orbit. They were important to him only in this fueling, mirroring capacity, temporarily feeding the hollow, stunted need of the pure narcissist. I've always thought his hunger for reflection actually made him a surprisingly good teacher. It was a venue he loved: all eyes on him, students lapping up his every word like kittens with cream. His teaching had been compared to Hans Hofmann; in fact he studied with Hofmann at Hofmann's school on Eighth Street in New York from the late forties into the early fifties. Like Hofmann, my father was robust, enthusiastic, expansive, and assured. But unlike Hofmann, he could never treat his students like colleagues. He always had to be one up and have power over people. So he was limited to the less confident and more worshipful students who outgrew him and left after a few years before the next crop took their place.

He stopped a moment on the Grand Staircase, smiling and nodding to the crowd milling about below until he saw me, Jack, Kelly and Sam and lifted one of his crutches in a little salute, holding the pose, milking it, I thought, before proceeding down the steps. His progress was slow and laborious. He would stop briefly to chat and receive accolades from well-wishers while continuing to make his way to us, his beloved family. It was a charade I knew well.

"Annie," he smiled, leaning heavily on his crutches as he bent down to kiss my cheek.

"Hi, Dad. Congratulations." My tone was wooden as my guard went up automatically, but I was not impolite. My mother and her Japanese civility were too much a part of me for that.

13

Jack shook his hand. "Great achievement, Alex. And a wonderful turnout."

"Thank you." He smiled, and then turned to kiss Kelly. "I'm delighted you brought this little guy."

Kelly beamed, tossing back her head. "Never too early to see art!"

"I have a tie," Sam announced.

"I never wear them myself..." Alexander touched the top of his turtleneck.

Of course the subject goes back to him. I only half listened as he expounded on why, when, and how he'd come to give up ties.

"...you know, I was just a young squirt myself when my mother first took me to an art exhibit, it was..."

Naturally. More about him. It would always be about him. I stared blankly just to the right of him, so I appeared to be listening.

"...my mother took me to the Northwest Printmakers Show when I was eight. It was a professional show, Ken Callahan was one of the judges and George Tsutakawa had a print in it, and he was only in high school. Can you imagine? And then she took me to the Northwest Annual when I was nine. It was at the Henry Gallery and although most of the paintings were representational..."

A little sneer here. Detectable only to me.

"...some were rather expressionistic, as well, even back then..."

Like he really knew this at age nine. Oh such genius.

"...and then of course, when I was ten, the Seattle Art Museum opened in Volunteer Park just a few blocks from me, where I grew up on Capitol Hill. So I was a frequent visitor." He smiled down at Kelly as if she were the only person in the room. "So it's a good thing you brought the little guy tonight."

Sam. Your great-grandson, you turd. Did you forget his name? I took a long swallow of champagne and the bubbles stung my nose.

"Do you think that influenced your decision to go into art?" Kelly asked, ever so eagerly attentive.

"I think it was in the genes. It always is..."

Except for me, which you made quite clear. I took a smaller sip this time.

"...my Aunt Anne, Annie's namesake, was curator of a museum in Philadelphia. She died before I was born, in the flu epidemic of 1918. But she had great influence on my mother, and therefore on me. And the polio, you know..."

Oh here we go. The old polio bit. It got 'em every time. Another swallow, this time a big gulp. I wiped my nose. Kelly's eyes shone with admiration.

"...when I was thirteen, I was bedridden for almost a year and spent most of my time drawing. It saved me from despair. I had been quite physical and athletic up to that point. People often think these things are diametrically opposed—the artistic and the athletic—but often they're not, as it was in my case."

I continued to gaze slightly to the side, tuning most of it out. But then I saw her. I didn't know her name but the type was unmistakable. This one was a little closer to his age, perhaps ten years younger, in her early seventies. Thank goodness for that. Someone his granddaughter's age, like Cass, would be obscene. Her hair was pale silvery blonde and she was tall and slim in a stunning light sage pants suit, probably Gucci, with a large gold and emerald pin worn just below the shoulder. She approached him steadily, like a ship heading for port. A collector, no doubt.

"And this must be your family, Alex." She slid next to him, casually laying her hand on his forearm with familiarity.

He smiled and kissed her cheek. "Hello, dear. This is my daughter and son-in-law, Annie and Jack Duppstadt, and my grandson's wife, Kelly. I guess you'd call her my granddaughter-in-law."

Kelly beamed. "And this is Sam."

How nice. She's saved him the embarrassment of forgetting Sam's name.

"I'd like you all to meet Leslie Meldon. She's loaned the museum a piece from her collection for the exhibition."

"I'm delighted to meet you." She shook hands with me first, then paused and said softly, "I'm so sorry about your mother."

Oh please. It took you all of five seconds to pounce on my father.

"Thank you," I muttered, wondering if I'd managed to sound civil.

Then she shook hands with Jack and Kelly. "And how do you like being here?" she asked Sam.

"I have a tie," Sam announced, mantra-like.

"And which painting comes from your collection?" I seized a bridge to an exit.

"It's titled *St. Helens*, it's on the center of the left wall after you enter the gallery.

I turned to Jack. "Let's go look, we haven't seen the exhibition yet."

"I'm sure you'll enjoy it. It's truly splendid," she said with pride. "It was good to meet you."

"We'll catch up with you in the gallery." Kelly said, obviously still enjoying standing next to the great one, I noticed, as Jack and I made our way through the crowd.

On our way to the exhibition in the Northwest Galleries, I kept looking around for Cass and Richard, but there was still no sign of them. "I wonder if Cass and Richard got caught in traffic," I said. Jack always reminds me that the kids are adults. He says I worry too much. He's probably right, but Cass really hadn't been herself—she'd been strangely distant and it started even before Mom died.

I put my hand on Jack's arm. "Would you mind going back down by the entrance to see if they've just arrived? Maybe they're at the bar? There was a big group around it."

"Sure, I'll meet you in the gallery."

I watched Jack weave through the crowd and then I went on to the gallery. This was the first opening of my father's that I'd ever attended without my mother and I missed her terribly; my heart ached for her. I hesitated just outside the wide doorway and leafed through the exhibition catalogue, ALEXANDER GUNTHER: 1947–2007: A Retrospective. It recorded the recognition my father had received throughout his career, most notably his solo exhibitions at the Museum of Modern Art in New York, his Guggenheim International Award, and his election to the National Institute of Arts and Letters. All his glory and fame—the acclaim for his great talent. His great talent. The only one allowed to have any.

I looked up to see *Paris Recollection* opposite the entrance. He had painted it when I was in high school, when he'd returned from Paris filled with a bitterness towards us that went far beyond his usual resentment, the same spring he'd destroyed my pastel of Mt. Rainier. The

huge painting dominated the wall the way he had dominated my mother's life and diminished any ability I had.
This time with the stomach cramps, tears came, and I frantically looked back at the crowd hoping to see Jack, hoping
that he'd found Cass and they'd be there.

2

ANNIE

I can't remember how old I was when I learned to translate my mother's language. I don't mean that she spoke Japanese. She was a Nisei, the first generation to be born in America, and she always spoke English. The translation was in knowing that when she asked if I wanted to do something, it meant she wanted to do it. It was a kind of opposite-speak, because my mother was culturally incapable of being direct. She could never say, "I want to go to Adams Lake, will you take me?" Instead she had asked, "I wondered if you'd like to go to Adams Lake?" I also understood that I was the one she asked because quite clearly, as usual, my father had other priorities. This time he was in Los Angeles, lecturing at the Getty.

"I'd love to take you. I'm sure I can leave work Friday morning so we can get an early start."

"Do you think they'll have room?" Her voice was raspy, almost a whisper as the cancer had metastasized and gotten to her lungs.

"I'm sure they will, it's the off-season. But I'll call and check."

One of the great things about the Adams Lake Resort is that they allow dogs, and I could bring Daisy, which I knew Mom would want. I love my dog. Jack enjoys her, perhaps feels some affection, but it is not love. A big, dark, furry bear of a dog, a rescue from the Seattle shelter when she was two months old, Daisy is a creature of uncertain heritage. But whatever she is, this beloved animal brings comfort, and she's a professional. Most of the patients at the hospital know me as either the Pet Lady or the Craft Lady, never by my title, Art and Occupational Therapist, and rarely by name, but they all know Daisy. It's fine with me to be upstaged by a dog, my work at Woodside Psychiatric Hospital is not the stuff my dreams had been made of—I'd always been afraid to risk being an artist in any serious way and I'd settled for the Craft Lady.

The hotel had plenty of room and I made our reservation for one of the old cottages—I knew without asking that's where Mom wanted to stay. We both loved Canada; I probably even had a tendency to idealize the Canadians, their decency and values, lower key and so not "in your face." When we were kids, she had taken my brother David and me to Adams Lake at least a dozen times during our spring vacations. I can't remember a place or time in my childhood when she had ever seemed so relaxed. It had been only the three of us.

The Adams Lake Resort had pools fed by hot springs near the lake and I threw in a bathing suit as I packed. It was one I got last summer from the Land's End catalogue. Each suit had a shape-rating icon next to its picture to show what figure type it best enhanced. I noticed that most of the suits had a triangle icon indicating that the hips were wider than the bust. Big surprise. And each suit came with your choice of "high," "modest," or "most coverage" cut depending on how much upper thigh one wanted to expose or how much fanny one would care to have hang out. As little as possible, thank you, I'd decided and I ordered the black Tugless Tank with the "most coverage" cut. It had been a toss-up between the Tugless Tank and the Miraclesuit in the Norm Thompson catalogue, which trumpeted a tummy-hugging device made of Miratex™ that'll give the appearance of trimming ten pounds off the torso. Look ten pounds lighter in ten seconds! The claim was pretty compelling, but since it didn't say anything about leg coverage, I was afraid the ten pounds trimmed from the torso of the Miraclesuit might squish out the bottom like the open end of a roll of sausage.

I got ready for bed and opened the window, letting in the cool night air. The new sheets I had bought at Macy's made me smile. The color was called "Sunlight." A creamy yellow, the weave smooth as satin, their purchase had been a large dose of retail therapy. It was an extravagance unusual for me, as I hadn't waited for a white sale, instead I snapped them up—something, anything, to brighten my darkening world, one that I knew would soon reel with the finality of the loss of my mother.

There was a thump as Daisy settled down on the floor next to my side of the bed; she soon began to snore and I said a prayer. Prayer is not something I am very good at. Historically, I seem to mess it up with concerns of why my prayer deserves to be heard in the midst of the constant cacophony of prayers sent up to the heavens from all over the earth. Supposedly everything is heard, but I could never totally grasp that. I didn't imagine my prayer up against the prayers sent from the Hamptons, Scottsdale, or Beverly Hills, just places like Iraq and Darfur, and this comparison usually served to put the kibosh on my efforts. But not lately. I was in foxhole now, or more accurately, my mother was, and I prayed for a miracle. Simple prayers like Please, and Please let her live, or sometimes just Help.

Jack was in his study, writing something—probably a new grant, although I hoped it wasn't. I didn't want him to set himself up for another blow. The top post-docs and graduate students were flocking to younger researchers with big labs and big budgets and the invitations to speak at professional meetings were becoming rare. He's clearly being cut from the team but he acts like a gambler on a losing streak who's sure this one last hand will win it all back.

I glanced at the clock—it was after one when I heard him come in. He lay close, slipping his hand under the creamy yellow sheet to caress my back, then the curve of my hip. I stirred and turned to him and we made sweet, creaky love, less vigorous than the encounters of our younger selves, but an act of exquisite dearness that brought no small measure of comfort and joy. Afterwards, I held on to him—and to the tenderness, a refuge against the gathering storm.

The next morning, when I arrived at my mother's house, there was a cab in the driveway and the driver, a dark-skinned man wearing a white turban, was putting my father's bag in the trunk. My father stood by the door to the back seat, leaning on his crutches, waiting for the driver to open it. Damn. If I had been just a few minutes later leaving Woodside, I could have avoided seeing him. As an adult, I had carved out a very limited relationship with him. My mother often came over to my house, we talked on the phone, and we went out to lunch frequently—I saw a lot of her. But my sparse interactions with him were characterized by an empty civility, the harvest of years of neglect and contempt. At family gatherings, if my father came at all, Jack acted as a buffer and there were enough of us that I could usually avoid him.

He looked a little frail, but undeniably handsome, all decked out in a gorgeous camel hair blazer and gray slacks. I wonder whom he'd be meeting in Los Angeles. There was always someone.

"Hello, Annie." He waved to me as I got out of the car. "I left the number where I'll be by the phone in the kitchen."

"Fine." Do you want a medal for this heroic gesture?

"My trip's been planned for a year, you know." Amazing. He sounded almost defensive.

"I'm sure it has been," I said, icily. I tried not to glare at him, but wasn't too successful and alone with me, without our usual buffers, he quickly pulled out the knife.

"And it's easy for you to leave that little job." He smiled a Cheshire cat smile and got in the cab, then waved as the cab backed down the drive. The smirk on his face was undeniable. That little job. My insignificant, unimportant work. It wasn't a surprise. He had been somewhat hostile lately, a shift from our empty civility, and I was sure it was because last month my mother had given me and not him medical power of attorney. It was logical on her part because he continued to travel so frequently, but a choice I imagined he found insulting, even though it was a responsibility I was certain he didn't want. When Mom first became so weak and exhausted from the chemo, I'd hired Rose Tibonga to be their housekeeper, and as long as

23

there was someone to wait on him, my father didn't much seem to care, or even know the difference if it was Rose or my mother.

At first my mother protested when I brought up the idea of having someone to help her. "I don't need any help, Annie. I'm fine."

"I think you should consider it. Won't you just think about it?" I asked.

"I don't want a stranger in the house."

"She's not exactly a stranger, Mom. Her cousin's a nurse at Woodside, I know her."

"Oh." She softened a little.

"Look, here's the situation. Rose has just left her marriage after twenty-five years. All she knows how to do is keep house and she needs work."

"This would help her?

"Yes, and she could just start out on a trial basis."

"Three days.

"Three days what, Mom?"

"Three days trial."

By the end of Rose's first week, Mom was affectionately calling her *imooto-chan*, little sister; and Rose, who had come from the Philippines when she was ten, was teaching my mother a few words in Tagalog. I suspected it became a kind of code for them, a way to circumvent my father.

In the house I talked to Mom about her medicine and asked her if I could check her bag.

"Rose helped me." My mother looked hurt. "I have everything."

"I know, and I'm sure you do. I'm just worried and want to be sure we'll have all the medicine, please let me have a look. I know it's silly, but just for my peace of mind."

"*Shikata ga nai*," she mumbled, nodding with resignation and a sad acceptance. It was a phrase I'd heard often as a child, "what can you do?" or "it can't be helped." I'm not sure she ever told me the exact literal translation, but I understood it.

Looking in her bag was heart wrenching. Rose had put in the few things Mom could wear: sweaters, and the pants with elastic waists I'd helped her get when I saw she was taking in her clothes with safety pins just to keep them from practically falling off. But on top was one of her beautiful silk scarves. She was wearing another one of them now and I found it disturbing, like a shiny balloon on a skeleton. I don't know how much weight she'd lost, but it was considerable, and she wasn't a big person to begin with. My mother had been beautiful, and the years had been kind to her as they are to most Asian women—until she got sick. Her dark eyes now were dull, almost a slate gray, and her honey skin was sallow and blotchy. I thanked Rose for her help and got the car so I could pull up in the drive and Mom wouldn't have to walk far. She seemed so weak, I wondered how she'd ever walk anywhere in the resort.

Mom slept almost the whole way, waking up only for a few minutes as we crossed the Canadian border when she had to get out her passport. It looked bleak as we headed north. We got to the hotel late that afternoon. Snow still covered some of the peaks of the Monashee Mountains and Adams Lake was desolate. The summer cabins dotting the shore were boarded up without a trace of welcoming wood smoke and all along the beach, rafts rested upside down like matchstick card tables. The only lights came from the south end of the narrow lake where the old Adams Lake Resort was brightly lit.

In March, the hotel gave special discounts to conferences and tour groups and advertised mid-week packages and weekend specials to entice people. But when we arrived, the hotel, in spite of its bright lights, was two-thirds empty. The whole place reminded me of a gym at the end of a high school dance when the lights come on and only a few stragglers are left with the clean-up committee. Having Daisy would be a comfort, I thought, reaching in the back seat to pat her.

Mom waited in the car while I checked in and then we drove to the cottages, which looked very much the way I remembered. Mom smiled as I helped her out of the car, taking it in. "The air is so fresh here, Annie." The cottage was pleasantly furnished with acceptable Best Western type furniture, a slight cut above Motel Six. An Emily Carr print of the Haida totems in the Queen Charlottes hung on the wall over a slightly lumpy looking wing chair. The cottage had a sitting room and one bedroom with twin beds, with a small bathroom in between the two rooms.

I called Jack and let him know we'd made it. We were good about checking in with each other, and I wanted to hear his voice, an anchor I always needed, but especially now.

"Any hassles crossing the border?" he asked. His voice was low and quiet and he sounded depressed. I'd been afraid it would catch up with him after I left.

"It wasn't that bad, and Mom slept most of the way. So did Daisy."

"Good," he mumbled, attempting to sound cheerful—but it didn't come off. I think when I'm not there it's harder for him to keep it all at bay. And this past year, whenever I've said anything about retirement, he gets a look of something between dread and panic, then quickly laughs like it's a joke, but the laugh sounds hollow.

Cass had asked me to call her when we arrived and I got her on her cell phone right after I hung up with Jack. "Can I say hi to Bacch?" she asked. Baach, short for *Obaachan*. Grandmother. Cass and Ian adored her. I had yet to tell either one of them there wouldn't be any more treatment. Maybe denial on my part, or simply cowardice—trying to avoid their pain because of the way it would rip into mine. I gave the phone to my mother, who smiled at the sound of Cass's voice, and I had to turn away from the pain of too much tenderness, to hide my tears.

After they hung up, I unpacked for both of us. "When do you want dinner, Mom?"

"Later. They should get married, Cass and Richard."

"I'm sure they will." Three years they'd been living together and not even a scent of marriage in the air. Not a whiff. Nothing. Nada.

"Richard's a good boy."

"Yes."

Except for the way he sits on his butt and lets Cass wait on him, the way he seldom shows an interest in other people and only talks about himself, the way he seems apolitical and indifferent to what's happened to this country—to name a few.

"They should have children."

"I'm sure they will, Mom."

Hopefully before her eggs decayed or dried up or whatever happened to them when the clock ran out.

"I want to see the lake tomorrow when it's light. I'll rest now."

I knew she meant she was saving her strength. She

didn't want to waste her energy walking to the dining room when it was getting dark and she wouldn't be able to see the lake or the mountains.

"I should take Daisy for a walk since she's been cooped up in the car, but I won't go far." I was reluctant to leave her.

"Go ahead. I'll be fine." Mom sat on the edge of the bed and took off her shoes. She pulled down the spread and carefully folded it on the end of the bed, and then she lay down. She put her head back against the pillows and closed her eyes. "When you come back with Daisy, go to the spa."

"Are you sure?"

"I'm sure. I'm fine here."

There was a hot spring near the resort that fed the spa pool and the hotel touted its healing properties, and I wished it could ease the ache I felt about my mother. When I came back after taking Daisy around the grounds, I pulled my suit out of my bag and grabbed a towel from the bathroom. Wouldn't it be nice if the hot spring water could do something for my rubber-jello jiggly stomach, crows' feet, sagging jowls, or notorious upper arm dingle-dangle. Sam had brought it to my attention last summer when I was driving him home from our outing at the zoo. It was a really hot day and I had on a tank top. Sam, strapped in his car seat in the back on the passenger side, was unusually quiet. From the rear view mirror, it looked like he was intently studying something near the steering wheel or the dashboard, when he asked, "Gran, who took the air out of your arms?"

In the spa pool, the hot water crept up my body and I sighed and lowered my eyes, watching it stop just below my armpits, submerging all but the straps of my Kindest

Cut Tugless Tank. In spite of the matronly cut suit, I actually felt almost like a teenager, practically a nubile nymph, and it had nothing to do with the so-called healing of the hot spring water. It was because I was sharing the pool with a half dozen members of a German tour group, and these were not a hardy fortyish, stylish lot that exuded European cynicism and nonchalance. They were old, large Germans. A few were pushing the envelope on obesity. They were blowzy, red-faced and blotchy, with bulbous noses and beefy upper arms. I had to smile, thinking of the many "b" descriptions, all with the "b" derivative of beer. The Germans were quite zonked out, having just come from the Victoria Room where they had enjoyed the all-you-can eat prime rib buffet, and now they were all blissfully submerged, soaking in silence.

Driving up to Canada, I'd noticed a billboard just south of the border advertising the hotel, trumpeting bargain rates for mid-winter romantic getaways. It displayed a glamorous silver-haired couple lolling about this very spa pool. She: a flat stomach and long, cellulite-free legs. He: glistening biceps and washboard abs. She: well-defined upper arms, no evidence of underarm dingle-dangle. He: a firm jaw, no trace of a chin bag resting on his throat. No one in the spa at this moment quite fit that profile. If Mom were here we would have laughed about it, I realized with a twinge of sadness. I closed my eyes, feeling the tension ease from my neck as the water, fed by hot springs buried deep in the earth, seeped around my shoulders. Then one of the largest of the German women heaved herself from the pool, causing a spa-sized tsunami. The water sloshed back and forth across the spa and I sat up, waiting for it to settle.

"Pardon, Madame?" A bald man with lumpy jowls

inched toward me. I gave him a blank look. It's Mr. Potato
Head. The minute his heifer wife leaves, he makes his
move. Of course. Men are dogs.

Mr. Potato Head slid closer, staring at me with red-
rimmed eyes, his large beer belly protruding from the pool.
He cleared his throat. "Madame? Quelle heure est-il?"

It was so lame, I could hardly believe it. Did I look
like I was wearing a watch? In the spa pool? He must have
decided I was French or French Canadian and this was the
only phrase he could come up with. Surely, he must speak
a little English. But it was no big surprise. With Mom
being Japanese American, and my father claiming German,
Dutch, Irish and Mohawk Indian, although I questioned
the latter and thought it was his attempt to appear more
interesting, it all added up to "a creature of uncertain race"
like the dog in the Madeline story Jack and I used to read
to the kids, confusing Mr. Potato Heads everywhere.

Mr. Potato Head inched closer and this time addressed
me in Spanish. "¿Senora, qué hora es?"

I stifled a laugh and Mr. Potato Head grinned, dis-
playing several gold teeth. "I don't have on my watch so
I'm afraid I can't tell you." Duh, I wanted to add but I
found it difficult to be rude, often even when a situation
called for it. Shades of Akiko, I guess, my mother's legacy
of deference and civility.

"So you are not French or Spanish?"

I shook my head.

"Very well, then." He sank back in the water and a few
minutes later rolled out of the pool like an old walrus and
lumbered off to the sauna.

The hot moist air with its slightly medicinal smell, the
combination of chlorine and sulfur, for a moment reminded

me of the hospital, all the trips to the oncology clinic. He
never took her, not once. The anger I felt was like a dead
weight in my stomach and I leaned my shoulders back
against the edge of the pool and tried not to think about
him, but memories continued to intrude, and the spa pool,
which was supposed to bring relaxation, brought anything
but—instead, a hot summer day when I was about seven
and David was five.

Mom had just filled a small plastic wading pool for David
and me, and was nearby watering the flowers. My brother
started the splashing frenzy and we giggled and squealed.
Our father was working in his studio with the windows
wide open. Within minutes he charged out, limping across
the lawn with the fury of an injured bull.

"God damn you! How the hell can I work!"

Mom dropped the hose and David scrambled out of
the pool and ran to her. She scooped him up and scur-
ried, running as fast as she could to the house, while I sat
weeping in the little pool, terrified and unable to move.

"I'll give you something to cry about!" He pulled out
the knife he used to cut canvas and slashed the sides of the
pool, making long gashes like the gestures in his paintings.
The water spurted, then gushed out until all that remained
was a flat circle of plastic lying on the grass.

In the morning Mom slept late, and we had room service
bring breakfast. She had hoped we could go to the restaurant in the hotel for lunch, but she fell asleep after breakfast and I couldn't bear to wake her. While she slept, Daisy
and I walked along the trail that went to the hot springs.

Daisy stopped to sniff every few minutes and I ambled

along, feasting on the quiet, the silence broken only by the sound of dry leaves crunching under my feet and the dee-dee-dee of a little chickadee coming from one of the tall firs bordering the trail. That morning, the pure white peaks of the mountains looked like they could have been painted on the ice blue canvas of the sky and for a second I wished I had pastels to make a quick sketch. I often had these thoughts when I was struck by something breathtakingly beautiful. And the thoughts always lasted the same amount of time, a nano-second, if that.

It was close to four-thirty before we slowly made our way across the grounds for an early dinner. Tiny lights in the shrubbery next to the hotel had come on and sparkled like rhinestone buttons on a shabby coat. The promise of the morning had held; it had been a sunny and golden day, but a stiff breeze had come up over the lake. It was so windy that the seagull we watched from the restaurant window flew against the wind with no forward momentum, like a soldier marching in place. He looked like a prop in a school play that was suspended from a cloud by an invisible wire. After we finished eating, or after I had, as Mom was only able to manage some broth and only a few sips at that, we waited to see if the wind would die down, as it often did in the evening. When the leaves on the trees were only faintly moving, and the lake was smooth, we ventured out. The wind was tranquil, now just slightly more than a gentle breeze, but we walked along the hotel promenade with forward progress not much better than the seagull had made in the strong wind: Mom leaning heavily on my arm, the two of us stopping every few steps to rest.

We came to a bench. Carefully, as if she were made of a thin sheet of glass, I helped my mother sit down. It was the time of half light. Over the lake we could see the moon, the setting sun, and a sprinkling of stars, and as if on cue, about two hundred yards to the east of the promenade, a deer and her fawn emerged from the trees and walked gracefully through the brush to drink at the edge of the lake. It was as wondrous and perfect a scene as the inside of an Easter egg.

We watched, not moving, not daring to speak, afraid almost to breathe until the deer had finished and ambled back into the brush and the sky deepened and the sun dropped below the mountains, turning the jagged peaks to indigo. We sat in silence watching the lavender, pink and silver lake, like the iridescence within a large shell, fade in the gentle twilight and become the darkest blue as night fell.

"What are the words to 'Taps'?" Mom tried to hum, then struggled for breath and stopped, squeezing her eyes shut. I didn't know if she was fighting pain or sadness, or both.

"What song, Mom?"

"Day is done."

"Day is done. Gone the sun?"

Mom nodded.

Softly I began to sing. My mother reached for my hand and held on tightly as my voice rose in the early evening air, like a prayer at Evensong.

"Day is done...Gone the sun...From the lakes, from the hills, from the sky.

"All is well, safely rest...God is nigh..."

Mom looked out over the lake. "Gone the sun, now. There's just the moon."

"Stars, too."

"Yes. So beautiful."

Her hand was thin and cold, the veins in her wrist bruised and weakened from the repeated assault of needles. I covered first one hand then the other, cupping my warm hands around them as tenderly as if they were baby birds. Mom sighed, watching the stars gleam brighter and brighter against the darkening sky.

"When you see this, do you...want to paint it?"

"Always." It was a whisper, as much to myself as my mother.

"I thought so." Mom grabbed both my hands, turning her head to look at me. "You must do it."

"Maybe someday. You know how it is, Mom."

"You must do it." Direct, unequivocal, this time almost a command, while she tried pathetically to squeeze my hands. "Promise me, Annie."

"I promise," I whispered.

She continued to hold on, staring straight ahead at the lake, her breathing slow and labored. After a long while, forcing herself, the words barely audible, she finally spoke. "I'm sorry. I'm sorry about him."

I couldn't remember a single time, not once in my entire life, that my mother had ever spoken to me about it, so that those few words...I'm sorry about him...those few hard-fought, rasping, tortured words meant she understood. And she was deeply sorry she'd been helpless to do anything about it. What more was there to say? That's all there is. There isn't any more. It might have saved me a lot of shrink bills if she'd said that about forty years ago, but the thought was only a wry observation and was free of bitterness. My mother's remorse was not "too little, too late," and not even "better late than never." To me it was an unexpected gift from my precious mother whose limitations I'd accepted and forgiven years ago, for the most part—or as much as one can.

"But he will know," she added.

"Know what, Mom?" Her remark seemed odd and cryptic, but she wouldn't explain. Or perhaps I'd misunderstood.

"There's something else." I had to bend near her lips to hear her.

"I want to last until your father's show."

I nodded and stroked her hand. God knows why this was important to her, but for her sake, I hoped she'd have her wish.

"And then, Annie, one more thing. No more hospital, promise me." Her eyes were pleading. "I want to die at home."

"I'll try, Mom. I'll do my best."

3

CASS

Cass wanted to hang up on Richard, she was so sick of it. Instead, she flipped the bird at the receiver, waved the phone around and made a huge Munch silent scream face.

"Cass?"

She brought the receiver back to her ear and stared at the photo on the desk. Taken last August on their bike trip to San Juan Island: the two of them after a sultry afternoon of love-making, freshly showered and smiling in the summer sun. And on the wall above, the two photos from their trip to Tuscany the summer before that. Richard had taken the one of the Ponte Vecchio in Florence. In the other, they looked like tiny elves standing in front of the huge Campanile di Giotto. A man selling flowers in the square had taken it, laughing good-naturedly at them as they tried to speak Italian, leafing through a pocket dictionary, gesturing as if they were playing Charades. When they were first framed, the photos had looked vibrant, perking up the space over the desk. Now they seemed to hang on the wall tentatively, almost drooping, like the petals of a tulip gone by, reminding her of a time gone by when she and Richard couldn't be together in the same room for five minutes without touching.

"Cass? Are you there?" Richard's voice was impatient. "Didn't you hear me? I said, 'I won't be home until later.'"

"New?"

"What?"

"So what else is new?"

"Look, this is what I do, okay? I never pretended to be some nine to five bank teller."

"Fine. Whatever."

"One of the admissions last night had some complications, and it'll take longer to brief the next shift. What's wrong with you, anyway?"

"Nothing. Forget it," she snapped. Cass took a deep breath and regrouped, trying to hide her frustration. "I'm walking with Lena, so I guess I'll see you whenever you can get away. Any idea when that'll be?" She pressed her fingertips to her temples, trying to ease the throbbing that had been there ever since she woke up.

"No." His voice was tired.

Had he always sounded so depleted? She went to the kitchen and pulled open the café curtains. She'd been used to his exhaustion, but this seemed different, although she didn't exactly know how. The bright morning sun that streamed in the east window, a departure from March's typical gray drizzle, would usually be a gift she'd welcome, but this morning it just hurt her eyes and she quickly yanked the curtains shut.

At least she'd made plans. She loved walking with Lena and her partner Valerie, too, when Val could join them. Their walks around Green Lake had become the highlight of her week, which aside from work and her softball team, had lately been marked by a gnawing emptiness and the ache of longing.

Cass poured a cup of black coffee. Fair Trade, a brew for progressives. She'd taken it home from work; one of the bonuses of managing a Starbucks. Holding the cup in both hands, she raised it to her lips and drank two big gulps, hoping it would help.

"Shit." She felt even worse, her head throbbing more, if that was possible. And then it came. Quickly trumping the wave of nausea was a wave of remorse tinged with self-disgust: hung-over. Again. And no one to blame but herself. She told herself it was temporary, just a phase, that she'd get back on track when he was through residency, when nights wouldn't be lonely. She never drank during the day, she reminded herself—just nights. That's when she enjoyed a good bottle of cabernet. Or chardonnay. Or pinot grigio. Red, white—she wasn't picky. Although she could do without the guilt. And the hangover. Compazine should fix it. Their medicine cabinet held a mini pharmacy, one of the perks of being with Richard.

It had been windy the night before and alder pollen covered Cass's blue Prius with a light dusting of chartreuse powder, giving it an iridescent sheen, a color that reminded Cass of the head of a male mallard. There were four other cars like it on just this one block. She loved her Capitol Hill neighborhood, the gay hub of Seattle, with a lot of artists and actors. Two blocks from the apartment was the playfield where her softball team practiced, and it was only a five-minute walk to the Taj Mahal, her favorite Indian restaurant. When Cass and Richard decided to live together, he wanted to move in with her rather than keep his place or find a new apartment. It was close to the hospitals and he said they'd have more time together. She remembered him joking, "We'll have more time in bed." Except that lately he was hardly home, and when he was, he was in bed...dead to the world.

At Green Lake, Cass spotted Lena jogging towards her from the west side of the lake. She was wearing her old "Bulldogs" sweatshirt from Garfield High School, and with her Michelle Kwan smile and her dark hair held back with a scrunchie, she could have been a teenager. Cass thought it was a hoot that no one ever pegged Lena for a physician at University Hospital, as if she had a secret identity.

Cass and Lena Choi had bonded in the seventh grade honors program when they discovered they were the only two kids in the class whose parents hadn't been divorced. They didn't count the fact that Cass's mother had been married once before, only that their own parents weren't divorced. They immediately trusted each other at a time when the pre-teen backstabbing and treachery had emerged. There was a brief exploration of their budding young bodies at a slumber party spring vacation of seventh grade, but Cass woke everyone up with a fit of hysterical giggling. The juice for her had always been with guys— but she loved Lena. It was balanced and reciprocal, not a relationship where one person was the star and the other the audience, or where one person's transmitter is stuck on send and the other's is always on receive.

"Sorry I'm late," Lena apologized as they hugged. "My mother called just as I was leaving."

"No problem. I just got here."

"She's having a melt-down."

"The wedding?" It was a dumb question, Cass knew.

For weeks it had been their main topic of conversation ever since Lena's brother announced his engagement to Sandra Wong. Mrs. Choi was ecstatic. She'd all but given up hope that Doug would marry a Chinese girl after he'd dated a succession of blondes all through high school and college. Lena thought Sandra was okay. She was fourth-generation Chinese-American from a wealthy family in Portland, a bit of a princess, but okay. And she seemed good for her brother, which Lena said was the main thing anyway.

"It turns out the Wongs are pillars of their church in Portland. And my brother is classic for avoiding stuff, if it even occurred to him that they'd have a problem with me." Lena and Cass walked quickly, passing a couple strolling leisurely in front of them. "But it's hit the fan because they're getting married in the Wongs' church and my mom doesn't know how to explain me and Valerie." She stopped and bent down to tie her shoe, then looked up at Cass. "Mom just regresses with the whole Chinese thing. She's disintegrating about Mr. and Mrs. Wong, the rehearsal dinner, Mrs. Wong's church friends, the showers. All that stuff. I think she wants to stuff me back in the closet for the wedding and have Valerie just disappear."

It was always explicit what Lena and Doug Choi were supposed to do. There were three expectations: excel in school, excel in a career, and marry Chinese. When Cass compared her mother to Mrs. Choi, she always thought the messages she got from Annie seemed goofy and contradictory. Annie encouraged her to do things she hadn't been able to do when she was young: travel, meet lots of different people, experience different cultures, explore, have fun, and not be in any hurry to settle down. Then somehow magically, Cass was also supposed to have a good, well-paying career of some kind. Something she cared deeply about. And this was all supposed to be done in her twenties. How the great career was supposed to happen while she was traveling around having the adventures was never quite explained. And by thirty, Cass was sure Annie expected her to be married and on her way to having kids. And it was supposed to be a good marriage. She was supposed to improve on Annie's track record and get it right the first time. Even though Cass acknowledged she had more breathing room than Lena did, Annie's expectations seemed a lot weirder to her than the three Mrs. Choi had for Lena.

"Enough about my brother's wedding. What about you and Richard?"

They passed the refreshment kiosk at the north end of the lake. Weather-beaten and in need of a coat of paint, it was still boarded up from the winter, although the pedestrian and bike paths were beginning to fill with joggers, cyclists, walkers, parents pushing strollers, and kids on tricycles and bicycles, wearing shiny, colorful helmets. It was Cass's turn to be silent.

Lena smiled. "You know I'm the only one that can get away with asking."

"Marriage?"

"Yes. I believe that was the subject." Lena rolled her eyes.

"Oh, that subject. You're right. You are the only one who can get away with it. My mom's learned not to bring it up, but my dad still does and I wish he'd just shut up. I've told him I don't want to talk about it, so now he starts calling it the "M" word. He thinks it's funny."

"And?" Lena persisted. "Are there any plans?"

41

Cass didn't say anything.

"And?"

Cass sighed. "Well, I think there's sort of an understanding. When he's through residency."

"That's another two years. Are you okay with that?"

"I guess I'll have to be. Richard's mother let me know they were in no hurry for a wedding. Not until he finished his residency and I think that's how he's programmed."

"Hard wired, I'd say. " Lena's voice had an edge to it. She'd never said so directly, but Cass suspected she didn't really like Richard. And she was right. Lena had sized up Richard Matsunaga early on, and saw him as fiercely ambitious, clever and competent, moving through life with a restraint and charm that she was quite sure obscured a highly calculating nature. He was also breathtakingly handsome and she worried that Cass's usual common sense had been swept away in a hormonal torrent when she jumped into the relationship so soon after they'd met.

"You still get along with his family okay, don't you?" Lena asked.

"They seem to approve. I think the Matsunagas always liked that my grandmother is Japanese and I look sort of Asian."

"Remember how people were always getting us mixed up?"

Cass laughed. "They knew you were Asian, but they never were quite sure what I was."

They reached the parking lot and Cass glanced over at the houses which bordered the lake. The lawns blazed with azaleas like living jewels, bursting with the most vibrant shades of red, coral, magenta and the deepest ruby. Near some of the homes there were rhododendrons with blossoms big as basketballs. Everywhere, a thousand shades of green; and the new young leaves emerging in front of the evergreens looked like finely wrought lace.

"My grandmother loved spring—she had a wonderful garden. I usually love spring, but this year with Baach being so sick, everything seems off to me." Cass looked at Lena. "Was it high school or college when your grandmother died? '*Puu-puu*,' isn't that what you called her?"

"Not poo-poo!" Lena cracked up. "*Po-po*. In Chinese it's *po-po*."

"Oh yeah, *puu-puu* are those things they eat in Hawaii."

"She passed away right at the end of my first year at Stanford. Has your grandmother taken a turn for the worse?" Lena asked quietly.

"Mom didn't say so, but I'm pretty sure she has. You know, Baach is the one person in my life where I've felt unconditionally loved. Cherished. There's no other word for it." Cass squeezed her eyes to stop the tears, and dug her keys out of her pocket.

"Are you okay?"

Cass nodded, brushing away the tears.

"Call me, day or night. Anytime, Cass. I mean it."

"Thanks." They hugged again and headed for their cars.

"Oh, I almost forgot." Cass called, turning around. "We need a sub for softball Tuesday night, can you play?"

Lena shook her head. "I've got a meeting, but ask Val. She'd probably love to."

On Tuesday when Cass left Starbucks, the misty drizzle that had appeared on and off for most of the day had started up again. A low ceiling of cement gray clouds covered the sky, reminding her of the roof of the old Kingdome stadium, and by the time she got home, the rain was coming down in a steady sheet. She'd called the league rain-out hot-line from work, but there wasn't any information. Scurrying into the apartment, she threw her parka over the doorknob and went to the computer to check the Underdog Softball website. Then she phoned Valerie to tell her their game hadn't been listed.

"Do you think they'd really play in this?" Valerie asked.

"I doubt it, although it could be another night of soggy softball if it lets up a little. Games are canceled if the field's closed by the city, or if the league's site supervisor thinks it's unsafe. If it's not on the website or the hot-line we're supposed to go to the field—it means a last-minute decision."

"Works for me."

"Really?"

"No problem," Val said, cheerfully. "I'll see you at the field."

Big rolling clouds blew in from the northwest and the temperature took a sudden drop as Cass was getting in her car. They were bluish gray thunderclouds, dark and ominous, and the game looked even less promising. Five minutes after she got to the field, the sky opened. Rain pounded the pavement, sewer drains surged with water and swirling leaves, and the street was instantly littered with scattering debris of twigs and broken branches.

She waited in the lot until she saw Valerie's car, then drove alongside her and put down the window a crack.

"This is wild!" Cass grinned as lightning streaked across the dark sky. "Did you see that?"

"I think it's kind of fun. Reminds me of the Midwest, we had these all the time."

"Even if this stops soon, the field will be a mess." She looked at the parking lot; there were only three other cars. "There's not much point in waiting until it's official. Want to get a beer?"

"Sure. The Harvest Moon?"

"Right. See you there."

When Cass got to the tavern, she stopped to chat for a minute with David and Sean, two guys from the team who had also ended up there. Then she spotted Valerie waving from a corner table in the back near the fireplace. Her cloud of strawberry blonde hair had gotten even curlier in the rain and lay in damp ringlets around her face. Valerie was about five foot-seven, taller than both Cass and Lena, with creamy skin and vibrant blue eyes, and always stood out in any crowd. Guys (usually drunk) would hit on her even when she was obviously with Lena. (The old "if you'd ever had me, you'd never want a woman" refrain.)

Cass took off her parka and slid into the seat across from Val. "That's David and Sean from the team. They called the rain-out hot-line and it's listed now, so they came straight here."

"I thought they looked familiar. Did they play the last time I subbed?"

"Probably. They've been on the Beans since the beginning. They work at Adobe, and when we were trying to get a name they wanted us to be called Synergy. But there are four of us from Starbucks so they were overruled."

"Battin' Beans is cute." Val looked around for the waiter. "They're sure busy tonight, you'd think people wouldn't want to go out in this weather. I had trouble finding parking. Where'd you park?"

"In front of the Harvard Exit. I lucked out, someone was leaving just as I drove up." I pulled my chair closer to the fire. "It's a great old theater. In high school, Lena and I used to go there to *The Rocky Horror Picture Show*. One time Mrs. Choi practically went postal because Lena raided her bag of Cal Rose rice to throw during the wedding scene. Then for the fifteenth anniversary of the film, she went as Riff Raff the butler, and I was the maid, Magenta. I toasted bread at home and stuffed it in my backpack." Cass laughed, remembering. "That was my favorite part, throwing it when they shouted, 'Toast!'" She held out her hands to the fire. "Am I glad you got a table near this fire. I'm freezing."

"Maybe we should get coffee nudges, or something hot instead of beer," Val suggested.

"Good idea." Cass looked out the windows lining the north wall of the tavern. "It's let up a little, but not all that much. Want popcorn, too?"

"Sure."

"You said it reminded you of the Midwest, I forget where? Somewhere in Michigan, right?"

"Traverse City."

"Everyone in Seattle's from somewhere else, it's hard to keep track."

"Everyone, except you and Lena." Val laughed, "Native daughters."

"I've heard Traverse City is beautiful." Cass tried to catch the eye of the waiter.

"It is. It used to be rather red-necked, but that's changing. Although the killer winter is the same."

"How's Lena? I haven't talked to her in a few days."

"Same old, same old. You know, her mother."

"Weddings seem to bring out the worst in a lot of families," Cass said, remembering her brother's wedding.

"A lot of pathology. Lena says latent dysfunction rears its head with the scent of orange blossoms." Valerie nodded. "I guess what got us was that we didn't expect it from the Chois. For one thing, as you know, Lena had been with women since her sophomore year in college, so they'd had some time to get used to the idea before we got serious."

"I remember the summer she brought what's-her-name home—"

"Kathy. They're still friends." Val looked for the waiter. "Don't they see us back here?"

"Looks like somebody didn't show up for work. There's only that one guy for the whole place."

"Want to go up to the bar?" Val asked.

"I don't mind waiting." Cass had a lot of empathy for people in restaurant work. She knew how obnoxious people could be, especially at five A.M., frantic to get their hit of caffeine before work. So whether it was a tavern or a restaurant, she tried to be patient and leave healthy tips; she always said anyone who waited on her would practically have to be stoned and stumbling around spilling stuff on her before she'd complain.

"The thing is," Val continued, "her parents really had been okay about us. Especially Lena's dad. So we just weren't ready for this crap from her mom. It's easier to deal with things if you see them coming."

"Like a garbage truck."

Valerie laughed, but it faded quickly and she sat back and became quiet.

"What's Doug say?" Cass asked.

"Doug? I don't think he's even aware of it. He seems to be sort of disengaged, like it's Sandra's thing and he'll just show up and do what he's told, sort of a little robot that marches to the altar. I'd be surprised if he knew his mother was putting this pressure on Lena to get me out of her otherwise perfect picture."

"Lena's always had a hard time bucking her mother."

"I know. And it's not like I don't get it. My family's Catholic and my coming out wasn't exactly a walk in the park. Frankly, I'm glad to live this far away from them. But in my heart of hearts, I would like to see Lena stand up to her mother." She looked away again. "For us."

The waiter finally got to them, harried and apologetic. Cass tried to be nice about it, but Val was slightly less friendly. They ordered drinks and popcorn and Cass watched the bar in amusement, as a young guy in a Mariners shirt seemed to get up enough nerve to approach a woman sitting two tables from them. Blonde and pretty, she was sitting alone and didn't seem to be expecting anyone because she'd obviously gone ahead and ordered; the waiter had just brought her a burger and a basket of fries. Cass was a people watcher, and pointed out the scene to Val, careful not to actually point. They strained to hear the conversation, but couldn't make it out over the music and the tavern noise. They saw the blonde pause, holding her burger, while the guy stood chatting at her table, casually sipping his beer. Then she smiled, and he smiled and took the seat across from her. She offered him some fries.

"She's thinking 'Maybe my prince has come,'" Val whispered.

"Yeah. And he's thinking 'Maybe I'll get laid.'"

They were still laughing when their drinks and popcorn arrived. "This will help." Cass cupped both hands around the hot mug for a few minutes before taking a sip. "It'll definitely warm me up."

"How're things with you and Richard?" Valerie's blue eyes were intense. She was so direct that Cass found it hard to get away with her usual deflection, making a joke, bobbing and weaving so she wouldn't have to admit anything. Something about Val seemed to strip away her guard.

"I haven't said anything to Lena, but actually...things at home aren't that great." She grabbed some paper napkins from the dispenser.

"What's going on?" Val took a handful of popcorn.

"That's just it. Nothing. I never see Richard and when he is there, it's like it's just his body. His physical presence. He's somewhere else."

"I went through that with Lena. They just get consumed, but it doesn't last forever. Residency eventually ends—trust me, it really does. What rotation's he on?"

"The VA."

"Cass, that one's hideous. They've got all these kids back from Iraq, smashed up, their lives ruined. It's the worst. Absolutely the worst."

Cass took a big gulp of the coffee nudge. "It didn't matter that we marched against that fucking war. They were going to do it anyway." She eyed the popcorn. "Want another bowl? "This one's almost gone."

"No, I've had enough. Go ahead, finish it."

"Richard will never take the last one of anything. I think he thinks I'm a little uncouth when I do. But why let something just sit there?" I smiled. "Sure you don't want anymore?"

"No, really." Val shook her head. "How's your family? Lena said things aren't good for your grandmother. I was so sorry to hear that."

"Thanks. My mom took her to a resort in Canada and they got back yesterday. She probably doesn't have too much time left. Mom goes over every day and my brother and I, at least one of us will be stopping by every day, too. Mom said we didn't have to stay long, that it might tire her too much, so we're just popping in for a few minutes." Cass cleaned the bowl, slowly chewing the last of the popcorn. Then she grabbed more napkins from the dispenser, wiping her mouth and hands. "I'm glad you could make it tonight."

It was hard for her to talk about Baach and they sat in silence, a quiet island in the noisy tavern, with its din of conversation, ringing cell phones, the Huskies game on the huge television and cheers exploding when they scored.

Cass glanced over at the blonde and the guy she'd picked up and stared into her drink, then she looked up at Val. "It gets lonely at home."

"It's time limited, really." Val said, reassuringly.

"I'm not so sure, Val. Even though Richard has time off in the summer and our trips have been fantastic, when we get back home, he just disappears again into his work and I miss him. Once, I wondered if it would've been better if I were a doctor, too. But I almost flunked chemistry and the sight of blood grosses me out. I guess if I just had something I was really passionate about, you know—more of my own thing—I could handle it better."

"You seem passionate to me." Val looked surprised. "You have a lot of interests—who says everyone has to have some all-consuming appetite for one thing?"

"Maybe, I don't know. My job is fun. I enjoy travel, music, books, hiking—oh, and softball," Cass smiled, "I'm on a roll...then there's restaurants, especially Indian...riding my bike...and Sam, my nephew. I'm in love with him."

She lifted her water glass, taking long swallows. The ice clinked against the glass, pressing against her lips as she emptied it. What she didn't say was that the one thing she imagined she could be passionate about was kids. Her own. She treasured Sam. But he wasn't hers.

The rain had stopped by the time Cass got home, although the street was covered with a sheet of water which spread from a small river that ran along the curb where leaves and fallen debris had clogged the storm drain. Getting out of the car, there was no way to avoid it, and her shoes were wet and soggy by the time she got to her building.

When she came in the apartment, she saw the message light blinking on the phone on the desk. Snapping on the overhead light, Cass took off her parka and shoes, then went to the phone to check the name on the caller I.D., hoping it was Richard, calling to say he'd gotten through early, that he'd be coming home. But it wasn't. It said, "Jack Duppstadt."

She must be mistaken. Cass turned on the desk light to get a better look. Her mom always called...not her dad. But it was her father, there was no mistake, and she knew in her bones something was wrong. With a feeling of dread, she sat down at the desk and picked up the phone.

4

ANNIE

I went straight to my computer when I got home from Adams Lake. I didn't even unpack. After checking my email, I googled "art school Seattle." If I was going to keep the promise I'd made to my mother, and most importantly to myself, I knew I'd need the structure of classes. And I knew also that if I didn't get going on it, I'd put it off. It would be something I'd do tomorrow and the tomorrows would pile up like old newspapers, with self-doubt once again the victor.

I went on the links to each school and studied them carefully and finally narrowed it down to two: Pratt Fine Arts Center and Gage Academy of Fine Art. They each seem designed for people like me—with classes for every age and every level of ability. That was reassuring. But on the Gage website it said, "...courses offered with some of the leading figures of Northwest painting," which immediately triggered a cramp in my stomach. My typical fear response. It was more than annoying—by this age, I thought I'd have outgrown it. Wouldn't it be nice if there were a menopause of "issues" so that old baggage at a certain age would cease to be fertile ground? But there it was, a painful knot, set off by the idea that the teachers most likely knew my father. They might even have been his students. When they found out I was his daughter, they would have expectations and I would, of course, fail miserably to meet them—any pitiful painting I produced would be laughable.

But then I heard my mother. Promise me, Annie.

I screwed up my courage, and emailed both schools to ask for information, taking, at least, that one small step.

The great Alexander Gunther was still in Los Angeles when I'd dropped Mom off. He wasn't expected back until late that afternoon, so I had asked Rose to stay. She had our cell phone numbers: mine, Cass's, Ian's and Jack's, and the number of the hotel where my father had been staying. My father refused to get a cell phone. I don't think it's a reaction to technology, I'm quite sure he just doesn't want anyone to be able to track him down easily.

Mom seemed so determined to make it until his show and had rallied enough after being at Adams Lake that it encouraged me to believe she could make it. The show was in another three weeks, and for the most part, she still had strength to get to the bathroom, bathe, and eat on her own. Occasionally, Rose had to help her, but Mom was still managing, although it exhausted her and there was little else she could accomplish. From her bed, she looked out the window at her garden, watched some television, but mostly slept. On the way back from Adams Lake she told me if she didn't have the strength to walk, she'd go to the museum in a wheelchair. She didn't have to explain that she wanted to wait until after the show to arrange for hospice care. I knew that would be the time. And I was beginning to believe she would make it to his opening. When she makes up her mind, my mother can have a steely determination.

I had called Jack after we'd crossed the border to let him know when I thought we'd get there and he told me he'd be at the lab. He seemed to be in a good mood.

"I'm leaving in a few minutes and probably won't get back until late this afternoon; there's a guy on the faculty of a new medical school that's starting in Cambodia—Dr. Phriep. He's a first-rate researcher. He wants to consult with me."

"That's great. He's lucky you want to help him," I said. "Then I'll just go ahead on over to see Sam."

Jack had sounded so depressed when I'd talked with him from Canada, I'd been worried about what he'd be like when I got back. But it was really reassuring to see him perking up about consulting with this guy and I hoped he could figure out that going from player to coach would be a good thing at his age. Maybe we could go to Tomiko's for dinner, I didn't feel like cooking. It was our favorite place, we've been going there for years, I can't even remember how long—at least ever since Cass was a baby. Mom would baby-sit so Jack and I could have a night out and we'd bring her back some of her favorite gyoza. So it has to be at least thirty-two years. Oh my—thirty-two. Where did it go?

Then I unpacked and went to see Sam. I have to say, Jack doesn't seem to need to see Sam as often as I do. When more than a week goes by, it literally feels like I begin to crave the little guy. It seems visceral, almost the way I used to crave Mom's soba noodles, or the sun after too many dark days.

Ian and Kelly live on Hunts Point on the east side of Lake Washington. It isn't too far from Microsoft, where they met. After a few years, they both left to give birth: Kelly to Sam, and Ian to his own high tech start-up, which he began with several young men from Microsoft. When the tech bubble burst and the venture capital dried up, Ian's company stayed alive with whopping cash transfusions from Kelly's trust fund.

I just don't worry about Ian the same way I do Cass. With Ian, for the past five years since that ridiculous wedding—ten bridesmaids, a twelve-piece orchestra, and a trumpet heralding the arrival of the bride—the struggle has been to conceal my dislike of his wife. Maybe Jack's right when he accuses me of thinking no one is good enough for our kids. But my only real complaint is that I don't get to see enough of Ian. He travels constantly.

I drove in the circular drive and parked in front of the house. It's on a three-acre wooded lot with a sweeping view of Lake Washington and Mt. Rainier to the south. Supposedly, according to its previous owner, it had been featured in *Architectural Digest*, a little factoid Kelly loves to cite.

Sam was waving madly from an upstairs window and by the time I got to the front door, I only had to wait a moment before Kelly opened it and he came bounding down the stairs and into my arms.

"Gran!"

"Sam!"

I hugged him and he clung to me like a little monkey and I put my face to his soft hair and breathed in the smell of him. Peanut butter, wet grass, the outdoors: it was the smell of the dearest innocence and I took it in like oxygen to my lifeblood. Had it only been a little over a week?

"Gran, come see what I made." He wiggled to get down and took my hand, eager to escort me.

"Ian's watching basketball." Kelly said as we hugged. "How's Akiko? Ian said he stopped in to see her right before you left for Canada."

"It seems to change day to day, it's hard to predict," I said, as Sam tugged on my hand.

"Come on, Gran."

"Let me say 'hi' to your Dad first." We went to the den where Ian was watching the basketball game on the "entertainment center," the screen almost the size you'd find in an old movie theater in a small town.

"Hi Mom," he put his beer down and started to rise.

"Don't get up, honey." I bent down and pecked his cheek. "Is the team you want winning?"

"No, and I should be working anyway, but I thought I'd just try to catch a little before the half. Did Kelly tell you someone from the museum called about Grandpa's opening?"

"Oh yes, the reception."

"Unfortunately, I've got to be out of town—"

"But I'll represent us," Kelly smiled. "I'd love to go."

"I'm sure you would." I took Sam's hand. "Sam, I don't think I can wait another minute to see what you want to show me."

Sam's room looked like something out of FAO Schwarz. The bedspread and drapes were coordinated with the wallpaper, everything done by Kelly's designer: an amazing contrast to the bedroom Ian and Cass had shared in the early years of Jack's career, a stunning example of Late American Garage Sale.

"Look Gran," Sam pointed to his creation, a collage of animals Kelly had cut from magazines. He'd pasted them on construction paper and colored around them with crayons.

"It's wonderful." I put him on my lap and together we examined his project. I studied each animal carefully and the colors he chose for what looked like a lot of scribbling. "I like having the elephant in the middle. I think it was a good idea to put him there." I pointed to the scribbles in the left hand corner, "I think the blue there is a nice choice with the blue sky behind the parrot. It kind of ties it together."

"I'll put more blue."

"Good idea."

Sam grabbed a crayon and began coloring with serious intent. There was something about the way he held his head, and the determined expression of focus and total concentration that reminded me of Ian. So strong a resemblance that I found myself swept with the current in a river of years to a place that had rushed by as fast as the beat of a heart, and I'd have to stop myself from calling him Ian.

"That's beautiful."

Sam beamed and melted into me like syrup, snuggling his head on my shoulder, resting the top of his forehead against my chin as I lifted him on my lap. I was holding him, wondering how long I could get away with keeping him on my lap, when Ian came in.

"Mom, Grandpa just called. He's at University Hospital, Bacch is being admitted. He says she's taken a turn for the worse." Ian came to me and bent down in front of me, squatting on his heels, while I clung to Sam. He put his hand on my shoulder. "Mom, come on, I'll drive you."

Kelly stood in the doorway. "Gran and Daddy have to leave, Sam," she chirped in a cheery voice. "Come with me and we can watch Big Bird!" What fun, what enthusiasm. I wanted to strangle her. Of course I knew she was trying to distract him, of course I knew that she didn't want him to see his grandmother weep or fall apart, of course I knew that. I still wanted to strangle her.

I kissed the top of Sam's head and Kelly came and unfolded my arms from around his narrow shoulders. She took his hand and they left while I sat hunched over at his little table.

"Mom..." Ian stood up and held out his hand and helped me up, then put his arm around me. "Let's go. Leave your car here and come with me, we can worry about your car later."

"Does Dad know? And Cass?"

"Grandpa asked me to call them. I called Dad and he said he'd call Cass and they'd meet us at the hospital."

It was easy to let Ian take charge; he has a calm strength that is much like Jack's and as I watched him driving through the traffic, fast, but not too fast, I saw the striking physical resemblance he has to his father. Both tall and lanky, Ian has Jack's boyish good looks although Ian's cheekbones are high like my mother's. The only trace of his Japanese grandmother though is his long, silky straight eyelashes. Ian's hair is lighter than either Cass's hair or mine; his is more chestnut. He adored Baach, both kids did, and I think they brought her more joy than anyone or anything ever had. I prayed as we drove over the bridge across Lake Washington to the city. That I would be there at the end. That we could transfer her to hospice care, that she'd make it for his show, that she'd get her wish. That she wouldn't die. Not yet. Please not yet.

At the hospital we went straight to intensive care. Ian

took my hand as we left the elevator. A man on a gurney was being pushed toward the elevator by two orderlies, but other than that, the corridor was empty. We didn't need to stop at the nurses' station to ask which room. We saw Jack and Cass. Jack held Cass, who was quietly weeping. In my mother's room my father stood with his back to us, looking out the window as the nurse unhooked the respirator and the IV from my mother's body.

Jack held out his arms and Ian and I went to him and the four of us clung to each other, awash in our grief.

5

CASS

The memorial service for Akiko Koroda Gunther was held on Thursday of the following week. It would only be the immediate family, Annie was adamant about that. Cass and Ian couldn't help overhear her talking on the phone to their Uncle David, she was practically shouting.

"No David. I mean this. Otherwise it will turn into a big production and the whole thing will all revolve around him!"

David Gunther, Annie's brother, had lived in England at least thirty years, ever since graduate school, when he went to the London School of Economics. He'd married a Brit and he and Edwina had two boys: Trevor and Carl. When Cass and Ian were younger, they used to call their aunt Mr. Ed behind her back, because she had a long horsey face. David and his family had visited Seattle just six weeks before, and with that in mind, decided it made more sense if only David came for the service.

It was held at Golden Gardens Beach in a beautiful waterfront park north of the Shilshole Bay Marina. Akiko had been cremated and Annie and David had decided that her ashes should be in Puget Sound, where they could merge with the Japanese current and go out to the Pacific. They chose a weekday, Thursday, and decided to go early, almost at dawn, when they were sure there would be few other people. Akiko had loved first light, as did both her daughter and granddaughter. Annie told Cass she could remember as a child waking early, tiptoeing downstairs to find her mother sitting alone on the back deck. Huddled in a blanket, cupping her tea, she would watch the garden slowly emerge in the pale light. Annie said it was about the only time her mother seemed at peace.

Richard took the morning off to be with Cass and when they drove in the parking lot at Golden Gardens, she saw that they were the last to arrive. Ian, Kelly and Sam had come in their van and picked up Annie and Jack. Cass's grandfather came with David, who was staying with him.

"It's a three-car funeral," Cass said as they pulled in next to Ian and Kelly's van.

Richard gave her a tender look. "Ready?"

Cass nodded. He looked especially handsome this morning, she thought, as he came around to open the door for her. Baach would have liked the green Tommy Bahama shirt. Her grandmother once told her Richard looked like a famous Japanese movie star, Toshiro Mifume. He had the same high cheekbones, a strong, masculine face and a beautiful seductive mouth.

"I'm glad you're here." Cass whispered, getting out of car.

"I liked your grandmother."

"She liked you, too." Cass realized it was a bit of an understatement. Her grandmother had adored Richard, who could be charming when he wanted to, and he'd been very

charming to Akiko. He had a powerful effect on women of
all ages, Cass knew. She remembered one softball game last
summer when he'd subbed on her team.

They were playing a Microsoft team and the score was
tied in the ninth and Cass, who was second in the line-up,
had just grounded out. She returned to the bench and sat
next to Sherrie Williams, the Battin' Beans Beans short-
stop; and they watched Richard, who was up next, go up
to the plate. Richard didn't swing on the first two pitches,
both balls. Sherrie commented that he had a good eye. The
next pitch was right over the plate and when she heard the
crack of the bat, Cass knew it was out of there. Walk off
home run. She and Sherrie screamed, hugged each other
and the bench emptied, cheering Richard as he rounded
the bases, his gorgeous smile flashing in the sun. Sherrie
put her arm around Cass. "You better hang on to that one,
honey. He's hot."

They got out of the car and Richard took her hand. She
loved his hands, his fingers were slim and delicate, perfect
for a surgeon, and she held tight to him as they walked
toward her family. He was present, not just physically; Cass
felt Richard was truly with her, and she hoped it meant
things would be better between them, that this wasn't just
fleeting closeness or a temporary gift of compassion that
had washed in with her loss, soon to disappear with the
next tide, like a piece of once valuable flotsam.

Everyone hugged, and then they walked across the sand
to the edge of the water. There was hardly any wind and
the air had the tang of salt and seaweed. It was hard for
Cass's grandfather with his crutches, but her brother and
her uncle walked on either side of him to help steady him

over the sand. Cass didn't think her grandfather had much to do with planning the service. Both she and Ian had the impression that their mother and Uncle David had told him how it would be and there wasn't any negotiation.

They stood in a circle and as Cass looked around it struck her how her grandmother's DNA had powered down the generations to show up in the women. Annie and Cass looked quite Asian, whereas Uncle David and her brother had only a trace of Asian features and you had to really look for it, especially with her brother. Ian and Uncle David stood on either side of Cass's grandfather; her mother was between Uncle David and her dad; Cass was between her dad and Sam, and Kelly was between Sam and Ian.

David took a paper from his pocket. "We're here today to remember and celebrate the life of Akiko Kuroda Gunther," he said quietly. "Annie and I chose this poem to begin this morning. It's an anonymous poem, but well-know and we think Mom would have liked it." He put on his glasses, then cleared his throat and began.

> *Do not stand at my grave and weep/I am not there. I do*
> *   not sleep*
> *I am a thousand winds that blow/I am the diamond glints*
> *   on snow.*
> *I am the sunlight on ripened grain/I am the gentle autumn*
> *   rain.*
> *When you wake in the morning hush, I am the swift*
> *   uplifting rush*
> *Of quiet birds in circling flight. I am the soft stars that*
> *   shine at night.*
> *Do not stand at my grave and cry. I am not there. I do not*
> *   die.*

Then it was Ian and Cass's turn. Annie had asked them to read "Seeds of Silence" by Hiroko Kobayashi, a poem their grandmother had loved. They had decided Ian would read it first in English, followed by Cass reciting it in Japanese. Cass smiled at Sam; he was leaning against Kelly's leg, scuffing the sand with his toe, while Ian read.

Cherry trees blossom, crane wings soar
Wind whispers.
Autumn fog
The moon of winter
Early spring evolves to summer
Love endures.

When he finished, Ian looked at Cass, who held tight to Richard's hand. Unlike her uncle and her brother, she didn't need to read, she had memorized the words and knew them by heart. Cass had taken a couple of years of Japanese in high school, and although she'd forgotten most of it, she was still more comfortable than Ian in pronouncing the Japanese words, especially the "tsu" sounds which Ian inevitably said as "zoo" whenever he tried.

Sakura ga saita, tsuru ga tobu
Kaze ga sasayaku
Aki no kiri, fuyu no tsuki
Haru wa natsu ni nari
Ai wa tsuzuku.

"We'll sing a song for Baach now." Kelly bent down, "Are you ready Sam?" They'd decided to sing something everyone knew, something each generation had sung with her. Cass wished it had been a Japanese song, but the best they could do was "The Itsy Bitsy Spider." Sam and Kelly started and they all joined in. The sun was higher now, and except for her grandfather, who leaned on his crutches, on the verse "Out came the sun and washed away the rain," they all looked up at the sky and made a circle of their arms to the delight of Sam. Then Annie and David walked to the edge of the water with the ashes and the woman who had been a wife to Alexander Gunther, a mother to Annie and David, a grandmother to Cass and Ian, and a great-grandmother to Sam became part of the sea.

After they left the beach they went back to the house, where Rose Tibonga had brunch waiting for them. On the way there Richard told Cass he thought it was a really nice service.

"'The Itsy Bitsy Spider' has great symbolism when you think about it. About the web of life, the cycle of nature, and the persistence of the spider, the force of life," he said.

Cass nodded, but didn't say anything. She wasn't in a mood to intellectualize about the depth of "The Itsy Bitsy Spider." All she could think about was Baach, and how she thought her grandmother would have liked what they did. But she reached for his hand, grateful he'd been a part of it.

After brunch, Cass found Annie in the kitchen trying to help Rose, who resisted her efforts and kept shooing her away, urging her to go back in the living room. But her mother wouldn't leave; she insisted on rinsing the dishes, explaining to Rose that she needed to keep busy. Cass also suspected Annie didn't want to be near her grandfather. On the beach, he'd been unusually quiet, almost subdued, but now back on his own turf, her grandfather was holding court in the living room, true to form.

"It's nice Richard could be here," Annie said, grabbing a handful of silverware and holding it under the faucet.

"He really liked Baach, I think he was close to his grandmother, too."

Cass could tell her mother was trying to be nice, mentioning Richard. Her parents had always been polite to him, but from early on Cass had picked up on some kind of weirdness when it came to Richard. It was especially apparent with her mother and Richard, and Cass really didn't want to talk to her about him. She went to the dining room to get the last of the dirty plates. Her grandfather was leaning against the fireplace, talking with Richard, Kelly and her dad, gesturing, as if he were lecturing about something. They were in one little group in front of the fireplace, while Ian, Sam and her Uncle David were still sitting at the table.

Ian helped collect the plates and followed her to the kitchen. "Too bad Mr. Ed couldn't come," he whispered.

"Sh-sh, Ian," she said, laughing, remembering how he always used to crack her up about their aunt when they were kids.

"Your Japanese sounded pretty good. Baach would have been impressed." He looked at her empty glass. "Want another drink?"

"Sure, thanks." Cass watched her brother go to the bar that had been set up in the living room. Kelly's lucky, she thought.

Ian came back with their drinks. "I can still count though—ichi, ni, san..."

"Excellent." Cass sipped her drink. "Remember when she taught us 'rock, paper, scissors'?"

"Jan, ken, pon...." Ian was quiet, then he said, "Here's to Baach." He lifted his glass and they toasted.

"To Baach," they said together. Ian took a sip, then looked out the window at their grandmother's garden. "I can't believe she's gone, Cass."

"Me, too." Cass nodded, her eyes filled with tears. "I'm glad you could be around these past weeks. I miss you, you know."

"There's not much I can do about the travel—at least for now."

"Not just that—just our lives now, we're in really different places, I guess."

"I suppose—but Sam sure loves it when you come over. We all do." Ian looked over at their grandfather where Richard, Kelly and their dad were still gathered around listening to him. "It's good to see Richard, we missed him at Sam's party."

"Yeah, well, I think he traded call with someone so he could be here." Cass looked in the kitchen. "I better help Mom."

Cass glanced over at Richard listening attentively to her grandfather, with Kelly and her father, and was struck by how no one who was related by blood to her grandmother was hanging out near her grandfather. Just the in-laws.

She joined her mother in the kitchen and put the plates on the counter next to the sink. "Mom, why don't you go in there, I can do these."

Her mother didn't look up from the sink. "I'm okay, thanks."

"You know when I think about grandparents, I hardly think about Grandpa," she whispered, "in fact, I don't think I remember anything from him that felt like love. It was always Baach. I think I felt loved unconditionally from her."

"You give unconditional love to an infant," Annie bristled, "but not to an adult." She turned on the water and quickly began rinsing the dishes. "Love has conditions and responsibility, and one of the conditions is that you'll make every effort to treat the person you love with respect and kindness. I think the idea of unconditional love between adults is just an invitation for abuse and masochism. If someone kicks you in the stomach repeatedly are you just supposed to take it and love that person unconditionally? I think that's crap."

"I was talking about Baach, Mom."

Where had *that* come from? Cass didn't know but she didn't want to stick around to find out. She and Richard left soon after and at home she slept the entire afternoon. She was exhausted. They'd gotten up so early to go to the beach, but it was grief that drained her. Cass kept picturing her mother and Uncle David at the edge of the water, putting Baach's ashes out to sea, knowing she'd never see her beloved grandmother again.

In the days after the service, it wasn't long before Cass felt the distance between her and Richard slowly seep back into their relationship. Although initially he had been sweet and supportive, his attention to her began to wane, becoming thin and intermittent. Intermittent rewards. How Pavlovian, she thought without amusement—his sporadic affection only strengthening her attachment to him as if she were a little lab monkey. By the end of the second week, the loneliness she felt was a malignant ache. So she was pleased when Richard mentioned that they'd been invited to a wedding shower for a medical school classmate of his, Bob Starkey. He'd gotten his April schedule and said he'd be free the night of the shower and he wanted them to go. Cass was looking forward to it; other than getting a few quick bites to eat in the neighborhood, it seemed like they hadn't been out together in ages.

Friday morning Richard called her at work and asked her if she could pick up a present—he said he'd left the wedding invitation at home which listed the wedding web-site. He was on call and Cass didn't mind doing it. Fred Meyer's was open late; she could probably buy something there unless the couple's list was too picky and specific.

When she got home from work and went in her building, Cass caught the scent of curry drifting from Mrs. Sidhu's apartment across the hall. Mrs. Sidhu and her hus-band kept to themselves, they were polite, but reserved. But the aromas emanating from their apartment were seductive and tantalizing; they never failed to arouse Cass's taste for Indian food or her wish that they were her friends and would invite her to dinner.

She decided to check the wedding website, then head to the Taj Mahal for some take-out. She could pick up the present after that. Cass hoped she could find the invita-tion. Richard was a bit of a slob, although she had to admit he had come a long way. Other than a pile of medical jour-nals next to his side of the bed, and his jeans on the chair, the apartment was reasonably neat and reflected his prog-ress. When he'd first moved in with her, Richard had been sharing a house with four guys and never picked anything up, so her apartment looked like a rabbit cage. And the bathroom. Cass couldn't believe what happened after just a couple of days: towels all over the floor, shaving cream stuck on the sink, and toothpaste that looked like it'd been put in the Cuisinart and the lid had flown off. And then there was the toilet seat. Richard had gone fishing with his father the week before he moved in with her, and Bob Matsunaga, a not very verbal Boeing engineer, in a rare father-son moment had given Richard some advice about living with women. Richard really laughed when he told her. "My Dad said, 'Tell them they're pretty, don't yell at them, and leave the toilet seat down.'" Richard used to tell her she was pretty, and he wasn't one to yell. But after living in a house with guys for so many years, the toilet seat accommodation had taken a while.

Cass looked by the phone, on the table next to the bed, and on the kitchen counter, but she couldn't find the invitation, and figured Richard had left it in his car or it was stuck in his briefcase or something. She didn't remember the name of the bride and was in no mood to mess around on the Internet googling the groom's name. She was, quite frankly, sick of going on these wedding websites, picking something from the happy couple's list, buying it, wrapping it, schlepping it to the wedding, only to hear about the divorce seven years later. It would be much more efficient to just give every couple a gift certificate for marriage counseling, or a list of names of good divorce lawyers. Although she didn't think she was as cynical as Troy, from her softball team. One night at the Harvest Moon, he'd said, "Why bother getting married? Just find a woman you hate and buy her a house."

At least her brother and Kelly were still married. Their wedding was a huge production. Cass had been one of the ten bridesmaids and had worn the dress to an Ugly Bridesmaid Dress Halloween party last year and won third prize. The whole wedding had a six-figure price tag. Kelly's dad was one of the largest apple growers in Eastern Washington, and her stepmother had let the number slip to Cass and Annie.

"It just got out of hand," she complained, but then smiled proudly, her bleached toilet bowl white teeth and her Puerto Vallarta–tanned face making her look like a dried apricot with pearls stuck on it, Cass thought. Weddings. Was she just so cynical because she wanted one?

Cass decided she'd better give Richard a quick call at the hospital to get the name so she could see what they'd registered for and get the stupid present. Cass went to the desk and looked through the drawer for the list of hospital numbers and called the VA.

"Could you page Dr. Matsunaga, please?" She waited, twirling the phone cord. Seconds, then minutes went by. Cass sat down at the desk and doodled on the note pad by the phone. Maybe she should just hang up. It was his friend anyway. He could get the present.

The operator came back on the line. "Dr. Matsunaga isn't on the schedule. He's not on call tonight."

"Are you sure?"

"That's what it says."

"Could you check again? There must be some mistake."

"He'll be here in the morning, if you'd like to leave a message."

"But he's not there tonight?"

"No, ma'am."

"You're sure?"

"Yes ma'am," irritation crept into her voice. "Would you like to speak with another doctor?"

"No. Thank you."

Cass looked at the list of hospitals and their phone

numbers. Could he have been assigned somewhere else? Had she gotten it mixed up? Maybe she should try them all.

But she didn't try them all. She went to the kitchen and poured a glass of wine, then returned to the living room taking the bottle with her. She could still smell the curry from the Sidhus' apartment, but she'd lost her appetite. Cass opened the drapes and sat facing the street watching the cars, staring, looking for his. The headlights of the cars had a hypnotic, numbing effect and all the events she had attended without him the past months flashed like a montage in a PowerPoint presentation. New Year's Eve. Click. The Mostly Mozart concert. Click. The Fun Run for Leukemia. Click. The cross-country ski weekend at Leavenworth. Click. The Battin' Beans potluck. Click. Sam's birthday party. Click. Click. Click.

She was asleep on the couch when Richard got home, then she heard him as he crossed the room to put his briefcase by the desk. Cass opened her eyes and saw the empty wine bottle on the floor. The street light outside the apartment created an eerie half-light and she watched him in the shadows. He moved, as always, with cat-like grace. It was three A.M.

"Late night, huh?"

"What are you doing up?"

"Just waiting. Must have been a rough night."

"Yeah." He unbuttoned his shirt and walked toward the bedroom. "You should be asleep."

She sat up, swinging her legs to the floor. "A lot of emergencies, I suppose."

Cass followed him into the bedroom, where he sat on the edge of the bed, taking off his shoes.

"Where the hell were you, Richard?" she shouted.

"What do you mean?"

"I said...where the hell were you!" She spit out the words, her face inches from his.

"Oh, for God's sake."

"Who is she?"

"I'm really tired. Do we have to do this now?" He sounded aggravated, resentful.

"I called the hospital last night."

Richard sighed, resigned. "Okay—"

"Okay what?" she hissed.

"So I wasn't on call." He sounded casual, like she was making a big deal out of nothing.

Cass stood over him staring and he stared back coldly. Finally he said, "I'd like to get some sleep. Do you mind?"

"Who is she?" Her voice caught in her throat.

He stared at the floor, his voice barely a whisper. "Cass—"

Cass went to her side of the bed and faced the wall, turning away from him as she wept. She bit her lip, then blurted, "I have to know!"

Richard stood up, leaving the bed, and went to the chair, throwing his jeans on the floor before he sat down. "Okay, okay."

But he was silent, sitting in the chair in the dark while she lay on the bed, crying. Cass rolled over, facing him again, tears spilling down her cheeks. "I have to."

"Really, what does it matter?"

She sat up. "You shit! It matters!"

"Just tell me why." His voice was dry, authoritative.

"I have to know and I don't have to give you any goddam reason."

Richard was silent. After a while he said, flatly, "Her name is Linda Hargrave."

They sat in the dark room, staring at each other in agonizing silence. Cass was the first to speak.

"A nurse, I suppose."

"I'm sorry," he said quietly, his voice tinged with remorse. But an odd tone, because it was also defensive, as if he was resisting the role of someone who could cause such pain. "I'm sorry I hurt you."

"I said, a nurse I suppose."

"No, she's a resident in my program."

"Oh, I see. Bonding like war buddies on the front lines of medicine together. You and Hot Lips Houlihan."

"She was a nurse."

"Who?"

"Hot Lips Houlihan."

"You're so cute, you fucker."

"Say whatever you want, I didn't plan anything. It just happened."

"And when were you going to tell me, Richard? How 'bout that? I suppose you were just going to keep going like this, screwing both of us. Or didn't she think we were still having sex. Or maybe she didn't care, as long as she got hers."

"She's married."

"Oh, Christ. A paragon of virtue and fidelity."

"You're such a purist, Cass."

"Fine, so now it's time to attack me. I suppose I drove you to it, by having a few expectations, by not absolutely loving every single thing you do."

"I didn't say that."

"How long has it been going on? I can't believe you didn't go to my family's party for Sam so you could be with that bitch."

"She's not a bitch."

"Fine. Defend her. How long has it been going on?"

"What difference does that make?" he said, coldly.

"Don't you think you owe me anything?" She shouted.

"All right. Since January."

"Is she better?"

"What?"

"Is she better in bed?"

"Oh, for Christ's sake, Cass."

"What do you want to do?" her voice was almost a whisper.

"I don't know."

"Then get out." She began crying again. "Just get the hell out!"

6

ANNIE

My heart ached for my mother. When she was alive she'd never miss one of his openings, and not just because it was expected of her and she was, at her core, conscientious and dutiful. It was because she was Mrs. Alexander Gunther. His glory reflected on her and gave validation to her long-suffering and sometimes hideous marriage. I'm sure it was her devil's bargain.

Jack was still looking for Cass and I stood near the entrance, still not finding the nerve to go in more than a few feet, waiting for the cramps I'd felt to settle down. The place was packed with strangers admiring my father's work and I really wanted to turn around and leave. But he was still holding court at the base of the staircase and I couldn't stomach being anywhere near him without Jack—I felt queasy enough as it was.

Holding court was my father's default position. When he was home for dinner, which wasn't that often, we ate together as a family and he always dominated everything, expounding about art. He might engage my brother a bit, asking about school and sports, but everything else was about the great Alexander Gunther—my mother and I might as well have been invisible.

I looked around at the paintings. The exhibition hadn't been hung chronologically. On the first wall next to the gallery entrance were several of his smaller pieces. Next to the first one, the plaque read, "Alexander Gunther, San Francisco No. 6, 1948," Hirshhorn Museum and Sculpture Garden, Smithsonian Institution, Washington, DC. It had been done when I was four years old, but other than the fact that my brother had been born in San Francisco, I didn't have any memories of those years.

I stood in the back of the crowd imagining I was a docent giving a little description...The painting has a vigorously brushed quality with richly textured small shapes suggesting energy in conflicting components. It has vivid, dissonant colors, which surprisingly somehow still gives a feeling of openness and airiness. Unlike Gunther himself, who's a rigid, self-centered creep.

I joined the crowd in front of the next painting "Paris Recollection, 1960, from the collection of Mr. and Mrs. T. Worthington Jones of Boston." This one had stirred up a lot, but I didn't want to get phobic about the damn thing and decided to stare at it, like it was just so much graffiti on the side of a building that had no connection to me.

The color was dominant and the crimson and vermillion shifted toward pink, black to indigo and royal blue, ochre to yellow and it had a light hazy feel to it. It was a stunning painting and in spite of my best efforts to think of it as graffiti, I felt a wave of disgust.

I was sixteen when it was featured at his solo show at the Henry Gallery.

Paris Recollection had been on all the posters, brochures, and postcards. He had completed it in the fall when he had spent the first quarter of the academic year in Paris with a select group of exchange students from the Northwest. My father had gone to Paris without us and his absence provided a peaceful oasis. I treasured the time he was in Paris, just as I had any time he was away.

The night of the opening reception, my parents had decided to take two cars. It was a school night and Mom needed to leave early to take David and me home after we made our appearance. I always felt shy and clumsy at these events. David and I were uncomfortable in our dress-up clothes and unless the eighteen- and nineteen-year-old art students at the University were counted, we were always the only teenagers. That winter when the show opened, Kennedy had recently been elected President and all the women wore dresses like Jackie, princess-style narrow sheaths, with hems falling just at the knee. My mother looked lovely in pale aquamarine silk with shoes dyed to match. My dress was emerald green, much like my mother's, only I wore black patent leather high heels with a rounded toe. I was still trying to master walking with a natural gait, and as I clunked along in the bright green dress, I felt like a tottery green bean.

My mother, who was usually demure and gracious, seemed unusually tense that evening. She rarely drank more than one glass of champagne; like many Asians, alcohol affected her chemistry so that her face became quite red after just a few drinks. But that night Mom had more than several glasses and flitted nervously from guest to guest, darting around like a little bird, while making frequent trips to the ladies' room.

David and I stayed together, not venturing more than

a few feet from the gallery entrance, as we watched the guests mingle and circulate and pay homage to our father. Occasionally someone would notice us and stop briefly to chat. The remarks were always the same: "You must be very proud of your father..."Isn't it a wonderful show?" Sometimes a person would ask if either of us were artistic and had gotten some of our father's talent. David always told them that I had, and I always blushed.

We were relieved when after about a half hour, Mom made her way through the crowd and told us she was ready to go.

"Shall we tell Dad we're leaving?" I asked.

Mom looked across the room where he was holding court, the center of a large crowd. "It's not necessary. He's quite occupied."

The three of us slipped out of the gallery into the starless night and walked quietly across the parking lot. A few feet from our car, Mom stopped abruptly. "Oh, no."

"What is it?" My brother and I asked, almost in unison.

"I've left my purse." Mom looked at me, her eyes anxious with a flicker of what seemed like desperation. "It must be in the ladies' room. Get it for me, please, Annie. I'll wait here with David."

I walked quickly back to the gallery. Mom was acting weird, so distracted and unnerved. It wasn't like her to lose or misplace things. She was organized and efficient, the one who held everything together in our family. I hurried into the gallery and down the corridor to the right of the entrance to the restrooms. When I entered the ladies' room I saw my mother's beaded clutch purse resting on the edge of the sink closest to the lavatories. I grabbed it and as I pushed the door open to leave, I heard a rustling sound and a muffled laugh, then breathing in the shadows a few yards from me. The light from the ladies' room fell across the corridor to the alcove of the museum office and as the door opened wider, I glanced to my left to see my father passionately kissing a young blonde woman. Her blouse was open and his hand caressed her breast and her arm was pressed against his leg, her fingers laced across his crotch. I froze. My father turned to the light and saw me before I ran from the gallery.

I turned away from the painting sickened by the memory and looked around frantically for Jack. A balding, white-haired man was walking towards me. He was of medium build, on the stocky side. His dark suit was a bit rumply and he appeared to be about my father's age. It looked like he was coming over to talk to me, maybe to offer condolences. Probably some friend of my father's I'd be expected to recognize...hopefully, I wouldn't get stuck talking for long. I looked at my watch—I really wanted to leave, Jack or no Jack.

He approached me and smiled. "You must be Annie."

"I am. Annie Duppstadt." I offered my hand. "And you are? I'm sorry I—"

"I'm Fred Weiss," he interrupted, "and I don't think we've met, so don't apologize. You look so much like your mother, I was sure you were Alex and Akiko's daughter. And I wanted to tell you how sorry I am for your loss."

"Thank you." His eyes were kind and I was surprised at the rush of gratitude I felt at the mention of my mother.

"My wife died last year; it was cancer, like Akiko."

I held his gaze. "I'm sorry."

"Thank you," he paused, "I know you understand how it is."

"Yes," I said, looking away.

"Are you enjoying the show?"

"It's a great tribute to my father's work," I said, carefully.

"Yes, it is indeed."

"How did you know my parents?" I studied his face, taking in his soothing, grief-softened presence.

"I was actually Alex's student, even though we're not that far apart in age. I'm seventy-nine, actually, I'll be eighty next week. I was in the Korean War and decided to study art when I got back so I studied with your dad for a year. He gave me an entrée to Hans Hofmann and my wife and I moved to New York. But Sylvia didn't like it, she missed her family. She had an aunt in Chicago, actually Evanston, so I went to the Chicago Institute of Art, did a little teaching. But the winters were dreadful. I ended up teaching at Gonzaga in Spokane and retired in 1993." He laughed. He had a low voice, somewhat wheezy with age, but his laugh was deep and hearty. "I'm sure that's more than you needed to know. The older I get—the longer my stories, I'm afraid." He smiled at me.

"The main thing," he continued, "is that Akiko and Sylvia were quite friendly. I suppose they could commiserate about being married to artists. When I had shows in Seattle, your mother always came." He hesitated, then said quietly, "I appreciated her support. She was a lovely woman."

"Yes, she was. It's good to talk to someone here who knew her. Are you still in Spokane?"

"No. My daughter convinced me to live closer to her.

She and her husband live on Vashon Island. They have five acres and their kids are in college, but they're still around quite a bit. I live in a yurt on their property. I love it."

"A yurt. That sounds like Vashon. I haven't been there in years, but I'm sure it's still beautiful."

"It's an amazing place, really. 'Awesome,' as my grand-kids say." He smiled. "When I moved over here I couldn't believe it was just a twenty-minute ferry ride from Seattle, but still so rural—an entirely different world. Melissa and Mike have an old chicken coop on their property that I've renovated and turned into a studio. I've been wanting to do a little teaching there, but so far I've just got one student during the day. Although there are six in the evening. I haven't gotten around to advertising in the local paper, although I did put up a notice at the coffee stand and then it blew off and that was the end of my marketing campaign. But the studio is dandy and I'm doing my own work, of course." Fred paused, "I'm talking too much again. It's a problem with an aging brain, I think. I seem to ramble on and on. Now tell me, what do you do?"

"Well, we have two grown kids and one grandchild." I looked around, "My daughter-in-law and my grandson are here somewhere, and our daughter's supposed to be here. My husband went to track them down. I guess I define myself first by my family," I said. "And I work part-time as an occupational and art therapist at a psychiatric hospital."

"So you're an artist, too."

"Well, no, I mean, not there—not really," I stammered, suddenly self-conscious. "I help them with crafty things, not really what you'd call art. But I've been looking into taking some classes." I tried to make it sound casual, but

I felt ridiculous the minute I'd said it, and I looked nervously around the crowd for Jack.

"Who's to say what real art is?" Fred pointed to the *Paris Recollection* painting. "When Alex painted that, the critics were saying the abstract expressionists were caught in a creative crisis when all the Pop art, minimalism business came on in the sixties. It was a big hullabaloo. It had a huge impact on him—he was in quite a snit, as if he were in a crisis. We were at a dinner party with them around that time and I remember your mother whispered to Sylvia that Minidoka was a crisis. I don't know who else heard her, but I knew she meant World War II when her family was sent to the internment camp. I guess I'm wandering, so bear with me because the point is, why give a few people who make pompous statements like that 'crisis' business the power to decide what is real art?"

"You have quite an attitude." I smiled. "Unusual."

"I don't know about that, but I just never played the game."

I thought I should find Jack, see if Cass had come yet, and touch base with Kelly and Sam. "It was wonderful to meet you." I held out my hand. His hands were bony and blue-veined but his clasp was firm. I looked into his warm, brown eyes beneath their bushy white brows.

"Why don't you come over to Vashon? I'd love to show you the set-up I have—our daytime student-teacher ratio is pretty good," he said, laughing. "It wouldn't be as convenient for you as a class in the city, but you can't match the quiet and beauty of the island." Fred took his wallet from his back pocket and carefully pulled out a business card. "Give me a call, Annie," he said, handing me the card. "Anytime."

I thanked him and opened my purse and tucked the card inside. I still didn't know if I'd have the nerve to follow through on taking classes anywhere, but I hadn't been to Vashon in years and it might be fun just to go see him. Most of all, I appreciated what he'd said about my mother. And I liked him.

I left the gallery and ran into Jack. He was coming up the stairs with Kelly, and carrying Sam, who had fallen asleep. "There's no sign of Cass anywhere," he said. "Kelly even checked the women's room—"

I pulled my cell phone from my purse. "Maybe's she left a message. It's not like her to just not show up."

7

CASS

When she woke up on the couch, Cass's throat ached from crying. A dog was barking somewhere down the block and she heard the whine of an old car as the engine turned over. A pearl gray light filled the room as dawn rose behind the dark shapes of the trees lining the street in front of her apartment. Sitting up slowly, she saw her wine glass on the carpet, tipped on its side next to an empty bottle of cabernet.

"Shit." Her head throbbed and tears came again. Under the glass was a blue-red stain, the shape of a small leaf. She felt as if he'd toppled her like the glass and she had bled on the floor. On the floor with her guts all over the place. Well, maybe that's a bit dramatic, she thought. A drama queen. That sucks. She left the couch to go to the kitchen. But it was exactly how she felt—like she'd been stabbed. In the back and the heart, the fucker.

In the kitchen, Cass fumbled through the junk under the sink until she found a spray cleaner and a scrub brush. She yanked a bunch of paper towels so hard the whole roll came off its holder, which set her off again. Everything was falling apart.

In the living room she went to work on the stain. She sprayed it with the cleaner, then laid a few sheets of paper towel over it while she went to the bathroom to get some aspirin. It's only temporary, she told herself. She wouldn't be always drinking like this.

Scrubbing and blotting the stain, Cass was obsessed with memories of Richard's lies. That fucking asshole, did everyone in his residency program know?

At the Christmas party was she there? This Linda Hargrave. Which one was she anyway?

The lovely Asian woman married to the white guy?

The voluptuous earth mother with the shiny brown hair?

God damn him.

"God damn him!"

After a very cold shower and a Compazine, she actually made it to work, which she decided had to be a major triumph—although her concentration was totally shot and she moved through the day on some zombie-like autopilot. Sherrie Williams asked about the game the other night, when Val had subbed for her, and it took Cass a while to even remember they'd been rained-out.

She tried not to think about Richard, but the demons of rejection and betrayal had taken hold, intruding even when she took over while Sherrie was on break and the regulars came in from the Rowene Olive Brown Clinic next door. Cass knew them by drink, not by name.

"Double tall non-fat latte?" She forced herself to smile.

Where had he spent last night? Not at her house,

the bitch was married. Unless her husband traveled or something. That would be cute. Classic.

"What will it be today, chai tea?"

Husband of bitch comes home a day early and shoots Richard. His blood splatters all over the wall in a nice polka-dot pattern.

"Which bagel? Plain or the sesame?"

Or maybe the blood decorates the walls like an abstract expressionist painting, like Grandpa's. Oh shit. His show. It's tonight. Cass looked at her watch; it was close to the end of her shift. She just didn't know if she were actress enough, or resilient enough or whatever the hell it would take, to pull off this thing at the museum. She was exhausted, totally tapped, and the idea of having to get dressed up and chat up a bunch of people was overwhelming. Ordinarily she really liked his openings. They were glamorous, and there was a certain prestige that she had to admit she rather enjoyed in being the granddaughter of Alexander Gunther. He liked to show her off. He acted like she was a work of art he'd created, and although she recognized that his attitude bordered on annihilating her parents and all her ancestors, Cass still couldn't help being flattered. Unlike her mother, who she was sure would be happy to spend the rest of her life in jeans, Cass loved to get dressed up.

She'd been avoiding her parents, not answering the phone when they called, and calling them only when she knew they were at work to leave a message which she hoped sounded normal—whatever that was. But she could tell from the sound of Annie's voice on the messages she left that her mother was starting to worry. And tonight, it was guaranteed they'd ask about Richard. They always did, and she seriously doubted she could handle it without falling apart. She was afraid she wouldn't be able to stand their sympathy, or just as bad, the I-told-you-so refrain that would hang in the air. They wouldn't come out and say it, but Cass knew she would feel it, and the humiliation that went with it.

On the way home from work the thoughts about Richard continued to plague her like a swarm of mosquitoes. Where had he spent last night? Richard didn't have that many close men friends. He was too competitive to really get close to anyone. To be close you had to expose your soft underbelly and he'd never do that. Maybe he didn't have one. Maybe the prince in the family grows up without one, with the protection of all that mommy adoration. She thought about the guys Richard hung with when she first met him. Brent and Rory, his college roommates, and Sean, his high school buddy. Sometimes he'd have a beer with them, and he played golf with Sean from time to time, but Cass couldn't imagine him going to stay with any of those guys last night, showing up at their door like a stray dog. He'd gone to the hospital to sleep, she was sure of it. There was always a bed for residents. That just had to be it; he was too cheap to get a hotel room. Did they screw in the hospital? Or when he went to that rural clinic east of the mountains, did they go together? Were there times he fucked us both in the same day? Oh, he would have loved that—what power.

And that was something that really bothered her: the idea of him still having power, still being able to derail her now that she'd finally found out. Cass had always been a firm believer that success was the best revenge and God dammit, she would just not become some pathetic victim who crumpled in a fetal position, unable to cope, opting out of life, giving up, letting him take away something she really wanted to do—like her grandfather's show tonight. It was a big deal and she'd been looking forward to going to the museum, in spite of her mother's weirdness about it, and she decided that even if she looked like she'd had a bad hair, face, and body day (which she'd had) or could be mistaken for one of her mother's patients at Woodside, she would damn well show up. No way would she let him keep her from going.

Getting ready, as Cass was washing her hair in the shower, she remembered watching an old musical with her mother, probably when she was in middle school. Her dad loved musicals, too, and this was one of his favorites, *South Pacific*. Annie confided she had a thing for the leading man, some handsome Italian dude, an opera type singer, Cass couldn't remember his name. But it had surprised her, seeing her mother all dreamy eyed when he sang and she reached for her father's hand and snuggled next to him. Obviously, by that age Cass was aware her parents had sex, at least she had some abstract concept of it with the evidence of her existence and her brother's, but to realize her own mother could get turned on by a singer was quite a surprise. From watching her, it dawned on Cass that it was probably not too different from the way she'd felt about Prince at the time when he sang "Purple Rain," and the revelation had been jarring. But there'd been this great song in the movie, "I'm Gonna Wash That Man Right Outa My Hair," which had been filmed on a beach with a lot of soapsuds. She scrubbed her head, wishing she knew the lyrics or even the tune. Cass smiled at the memory of the movie scene as she rinsed out the suds and then poured more shampoo, washing her hair a second time. After she rinsed her hair, she washed her body and as she did, the memory of the movie scene faded and Cass was swept with longing for Richard. Memories of him, of the two of them together, engulfed her. His gentle caressing hands as they showered, warm and wet, lather foaming and sliding over each other with growing urgency until he couldn't wait and they made love with her back against the cool tile, drenched in the warmth of the cascading water. She closed her eyes, lifting her face to the spray, hoping it would stop hurting, and finally, as her breath became more even, the tears that had come so quickly began to subside.

The phone was ringing as Cass was getting out of the shower. As she dried herself she knew that not that long ago she would have run, clutching the towel, to see if it was Richard, hoping to hear his voice.

Calmly, she picked up the hair dryer and began drying her hair, consciously drowning out the ringing phone. She looked like hell; there was no doubt about it, but maybe she could manage to at least be presentable. If she spent extra time on her hair, and put on some make-up, especially covering the dark rings under her eyes. And some bright lipstick. That might help. She moved slowly, exhausted and spent with emotion and feeling weak, thought she'd better eat something. But nothing appealed, not even the wonderful aromas from the Sidhus' apartment, which always set her mouth to watering. In the kitchen she grabbed a banana, forcing herself to at least get something in her stomach.

Is that a banana in your pants or are you just glad to see me?

The dumb joke she and Richard used to laugh about

popped into her head. Wasn't there anything she could see or do or think that wouldn't remind her of him?

For crissake. Just get dressed and get out of here.

Automatically, she reached for her go-everywhere black dress, but then she put it back. Better wear something to perk me up, she decided, taking out her red silk pants suit. Cass was trying to figure out jewelry when she remembered the perfect thing: the red, gray and black scarf that had belonged to Baach. She went to the bedroom closet and brought down the box Annie had given her. Carefully, she opened it and unwrapped the tissue paper, which held the beautiful pieces of silk. The one she had thought would work with her red suit was on top and she tenderly lifted it from the box. As Cass arranged the scarf around her neck, letting it drape over her shoulder, an onslaught of grief she was helpless to stop came again like a sudden and fierce storm, rolling in, flooding her with sorrow. She curled up on the bed and her grandmother's beautiful scarf absorbed her tears. I'm sorry, Baach. I'm sorry I couldn't give you a great-grandchild that looked like you.

8

ANNIE

My cell phone rang just as I was pulling into the Woodside parking lot and for a split second I thought it was my mother, it was her ring: the faint strains of the Moonlight Sonata. Ian had programmed my phone with a distinct song to ring for each member of our tribe—he'd chosen the Moonlight Sonata for my mother. It had been the perfect choice, sad and beautiful like she was. For weeks after she died, I still sometimes found myself going to the phone to call her, a reflection, I suppose, of my inability to truly comprehend that she was gone. And then I'd remember, as I did now, and would be slapped with another wave of sorrow. I shut off the engine and fished in my purse for the phone, assuming it was Rose Tibonga.

"Annie." My father's low gravelly voice was icy. "I've just heard from my lawyer, and it seems Akiko recently made a new will. Do you know anything about this?"

I was shocked it wasn't Rose. I hadn't spoken to my father since his opening. I was disgusted by the way he reveled in the attention that night, untouched by grief as if my mother had never existed.

"Annie," he barked. "Are you there?"

"Yes."

"Well, do you?"

"Do I what?"

"I just said, I've learned Akiko made a new will. Do you know anything about this?" he repeated, raising his voice.

I felt assaulted and I just wanted to get off the phone. And as far as anything about a new will—I was sure he had to be confused. "Do you mean a list of personal possessions or something?"

"Did you hear me say list?"

"No."

"What did I just say?"

"Look, Mom never said anything to me, okay? I don't know what you're talking about."

"Are you sure?" he said, accusingly.

"Of course I'm sure. There's got to be a mistake."

"Bob Dennison doesn't make mistakes. I'll call you after I meet with him." And that was it. He hung up without bothering to say anything else, and of course, not so much as good-bye.

I had thrown myself into work in the weeks after Mom died; it was my salvation, keeping me upright like the keel of a ship. And that morning I was especially glad to be at the hospital so I could just forget that he called. I couldn't stand having to deal with him—with my mother gone I had predicted my so-called relationship with my father would go the way of most dysfunctional families: at the most, we'd gather at Christmas, compelled at that jolly time of year to connect with our family of origin in a ritual of denial. Besides, he had to be mixed up, it was ridiculous—unfathomable really, that my mother would do something on her own like make a will he didn't know about.

My office was at the end of the hall between the day room, where the patients and staff assembled twice each day for group meeting, and the smaller art room next to it. The art room was my domain. I shared the space with a rotating cast of borderline personality disorders, schizophrenics, patients with bipolar disorder, major depression, and since the Iraq war, a growing number of young men with post traumatic stress disorder. It was the closest thing I'd ever had to a room of my own.

Lauren Thomas was the first patient I was scheduled to see that morning. Her diagnosis was abnormal grief reaction. Her son had been killed in Iraq just before his twenty-first birthday. A member of the National Guard, he had worked at the same lumberyard in Tumwater, Washington, where Lauren was the bookkeeper. A divorced, single mother, she had a daughter and a grandchild. After the death of her son, she stopped going to work, stopped selling Mary Kay cosmetics, something she'd enjoyed doing part-time for years, and stopped going to church. For the past ten months she'd been living with her daughter in Seattle but had shown diminishing interest in her grandchild, the one relationship her daughter had been convinced would pull her out of her despair.

I brought Daisy into the art room where Lauren Thomas was sitting quietly at the table. Her brown hair was fastened in a ponytail and she wore a pink sweatshirt and navy blue cropped pants. Although her face was lovely with a small, straight nose and large blue eyes, her pale skin had a grayish cast. I thought she looked a lot older than forty-five, but that was nothing new. I'd often had the experience of reading patients' charts only to learn they were much younger than I'd assumed, another one of the ways the anguish of psychiatric illness took its toll.

I slid into a seat next to her and opened a bag of beads I'd brought and dumped them into a dish "This is a fun project. It's for Daisy."

"The dog?"

I nodded. "Aren't these beautiful? I got the whole bag for a dollar at a garage sale. We're going to make a necklace for Daisy." I'd discovered it was non-threatening for people to make a necklace for a dog, a creature that wouldn't judge them or their efforts. The spirits of even the most severely depressed patients would often begin to lift a little as they strung each bead, seeing and touching something tangible that they'd accomplished, the growing necklace a sign of forward progress.

Daisy sat between us, her head level with Lauren's lap. "Do you like dogs?" I stroked Daisy's head.

Lauren nodded.

"She'd like it if you'd pet her."

Lauren put her hand on Daisy's head, letting it lie there for a minute before she slowly began to move it. She petted the dog and I took a thick cord and a needle from the bag. "Here, I'll get you started." I knotted the cord, then threaded the needle and strung the first bead.

"I like Daisy to wear a necklace on Dog Day Afternoon. It's next week, when I bring a few dogs from the shelter to visit." I strung several more beads and held it up.

"She wears a necklace when the other dogs come so they'll know she's top dog."

It looked like my corny jokes had brought a flicker of a smile, at least I thought I saw one, so I handed the cord to Lauren. "Could you finish this for Daisy, while I sketch the two of you? I like to make a sketch of everyone with Daisy."

Robot-like, she picked up the first bead her fingers touched without examining the dish to choose any particular color, then strung it on the cord, followed by another, then another. It was the smallest step, but it meant a crack in her crippling apathy, and I felt the way my mother must have when she saw a tiny sprout poking up from the earth after a long winter.

We worked quietly, Lauren slowly stringing beads while I sketched with pastels. Daisy's dark head, as she sat next to Lauren, made a striking contrast against the pink sweatshirt. I commented on that and Lauren asked if she could take a look.

"Of course." I smiled and turned the sketch to her. It was good to see a spark of curiosity, and I hoped it meant that the terrible weight that had blunted her spirit might be beginning to lift, even a little.

Lauren stared at my pastel for a long time. "It's good," she said quietly.

"Thank you."

"I guess you make lots of pictures, being an artist and all."

"Not really. These little sketches are just things I do here for fun."

"Why?"

"Why? I'm not sure I understand, I mean—"

96

"Why just here? Why not anywhere else?"

"Oh, well—I guess I always thought that someday I'd get serious and really work at art, but I don't seem to get around to it." I thought about the information the two art schools had sent which still lay on my desk at home.

"You don't know if you'll have someday," she said sharply, her grief opening in a stab of pain. "There were things Robert wanted to do someday."

She looked at the clock next to the cupboard. "I have to go to group now." Lauren held out the string she had beaded, then put it against Daisy's neck. "Do you think this is long enough?"

"Yes, it's perfect. She'll look beautiful. I'll put it on the bulletin board until it's time for her to wear it."

The sun was streaming in the windows of the art room as Lauren left. The morning fog had all burned off, and as I went to the cupboard to put away the beads and the box of pastels, I could see the top of Mt. Rainier in the distance. When the clouds covered it, Mt. Rainier could disappear for weeks. Sometimes it seemed you could almost go for months without seeing it and then, on some clear, sparkling day it would reappear, and even though I'd lived here my whole life—I'd be startled all over again by its beauty. Every time I saw the mountain, I wanted to paint it.

I had about fifteen minutes before the next patient so I went back to my office. I grabbed my purse from the bottom drawer of my desk and found Fred Weiss's card where I'd stuck it that night at the museum. I hadn't done anything about the information I'd gotten from the art schools. The biggest hurdle was the fear the teachers would find out I was the daughter of the great Alexander Gunther, expect real talent, and discover I wasn't any good. But Fred Weiss knew I was the daughter of the great Gunther and he seemed kind, I reminded myself—and, he knew my mother. When Lauren Thomas said, "You don't know if you'll have someday," it could have been my mother's voice, and remembering that last evening with her at Adams Lake, and before I lost my nerve, I picked up the phone and called Fred Weiss.

The phone rang a few times and I looked at my watch, thinking I should get back to the art room, when he answered. The same low voice, somewhat wheezy with age.

"Fred? This is Annie Duppstadt—"

"How nice to hear from you," he said, "I hope you're calling to take me up on a visit to Vashon." And the same laugh, deep and hearty.

"I really would love to come, I thought it'd be fun to see your studio, and learn about the class." I tried to sound casual in spite of the fact that I was twirling my reading glasses and wiggling back and forth in my desk chair at a speed that would have delighted my grandson. But Fred was easy to talk to and we agreed I'd come over on Friday afternoon when I was through work. After he gave me directions, right before I was about to hang up, I thought I'd ask about Daisy.

"Would it be okay to bring my dog? She has very good manners."

"Absolutely, it's dog heaven over here."

On Friday morning before I left for work, I'd told Jack I was going over to Vashon. On Friday nights we typically ate at Tomiko's around five-thirty, the fuddy-duddy hour we share with many seniors.

"I'm not sure what time I'll be back from Vashon, but we can eat later."

"How late?"

"You never know about traffic, I can call you when I'm on the ferry. But we can probably can get to Tomiko's by seven-thirty."

"Who are you going to see over there again?"

"Fred Weiss. I told you that I met him the night of my father's opening."

"The guy with the art class. Well, if you're too late we might not get our table," he said, gloomily.

"What?"

"Never mind." He reached for his briefcase, and started out the door.

"Look, it won't kill us to sit at another one for a change." I called after him.

"Fine," he said, sounding dejected, then got in his car and was off.

The past few days Jack had fallen back into a funk. I was pretty sure it was because the researcher who had consulted with him had gone back to Cambodia and Jack was struggling with feeling like he was on his way out again. I worried a lot about him, but I also knew there wasn't anything I could do about it. Jack really did have to figure out retiring, or cutting back at least, and how he's going to spend his time. As much as I'd like to help him, I couldn't do it for him.

I called Cass before I left for Vashon, but she wasn't there, so I just left a message. There had been a voice mail message from her when we got home from my father's opening, apologizing for missing it, saying things had gotten crazy at work. I assumed someone probably hadn't shown up and Cass had to fill in. All week we'd been playing phone tag, and I figured things must still be pretty hectic since she never seemed to be home. She'd probably call when she had the chance, but it bothered me—going this long without talking. I suppose you have to be senile to stop worrying about your kids. I tuned into every nuance, every inflection and underneath the false cheer on the messages she'd been leaving, I couldn't help detecting the sadness in Cass's voice. It was wrapped in an armor of nonchalance, designed to keep me from probing. When I talk to my children, I often find myself calling on my better angels to help me keep my mouth shut, while above my head I imagine a comic strip balloon filled with words, often advice and concern, and yes, sometimes, God forbid...criticism. Lately it's been concern. Cass, how are you, really? was the message I wanted to leave, but instead it was my usual benign, "Hi honey, just wanted to say hi. Call me when you get a chance."

At the Fauntleroy dock where I waited for the ferry to Vashon Island, the anticipation lifted my spirits as nothing had since my mother died. Ferries on Puget Sound were a common scene, but when I saw the boat nearing the dock and could read the name, *Issaquah*, it evoked more than the promise of a safe passage to the island and I felt a rush of excitement. At first, I had tried pretending to myself that this was a casual visit, but even though Fred said there was only one other student, I knew it wasn't. "It's a step, Mom," I said, silently. "Maybe a first step."

I took a seat toward the front of the boat where I saw a rack of pamphlets. Fred told me I'd find a brochure with a good map of the island. He lived on the west side between Paradise Cove and Reddings Beach. The road he lived on, Margot Road, was a small dead-end that turned south from Klein-Pfeiffer Creek Road. From the map, it looked easy to find. I leafed through the pages of the brochure; there were ads for island businesses interspersed with an article on kayaking and island boating on forty-four coastal miles; one on Vashon Island festivals, especially the Strawberry Festival in mid-summer; and descriptions of horse trails, alpaca farms, organic farms and lavender farms, with names like Big Dog Lavender and Crowsfeet Lavender Farm. Every description of the island made some reference to the artists. An excerpt in the back of the brochure from a Seattle newspaper said, "Musicians, actors, writers, painters, potters, glass blowers, tile makers, furniture makers and carvers find the solitude and community support to flourish on Vashon."

To flourish. Could I? Would I be one of them? All my adult life I'd accepted my father's version of my ability; what if it was too late to change it?

Up ahead, the deep green mat of cedars and Douglas firs woven against the hills became more distinct. People began leaving for the car deck and I followed them, remembering Fred's craggy face with his warm brown eyes beneath the bushy white brows, picturing him like a refrain whistled in the dark, as I made my way down to the car where Daisy waited. Moving with more assurance than I felt.

Driving off the boat, I noticed there were no sidewalks or streetlights anywhere along Vashon Highway, the main road that ran the length of the island. Fred wasn't kidding when he said it was rural—all I saw were horses, sheep, chickens, goats, and geese. About a fifteen-minute drive from the ferry, I came through the little town of Vashon.

Only about three square blocks, it was the kind of place you'd miss if you blinked. It could have been any small town from the forties or fifties. Except for signs for massage therapists, yoga instructors, and organic produce, it looked like it had been frozen in time.

At an intersection I saw an unattended flower stand conducting business on an honor system. About a dozen bouquets in large plastic cups were marked with various prices and customers were instructed to put money in the slot of a small locked metal box. It wasn't fastened to anything. It was just sitting on the table. When I drove through the little town, I felt as though I'd experienced a time warp. At the flower stand, I thought I'd landed on another planet. Farther south on Vashon Highway I saw another honor system establishment, a vegetable stand that also sold fresh eggs.

As I turned off the highway on Margot Road, the gravel crunched under the weight of the car on the rutted country lane. A mile down, on the waterside, I saw the bright yellow farmhouse Fred had described. At the end of the drive next to the green mailbox, was the sign "Foster" and "Weiss" hanging from a piece of driftwood. I drove past the house up a hill to the studio, a small, cedar shake building that was situated next to a meadow lined with alder and fir. It overlooked Colvos Passage, the wide channel between the west side of the island and the Olympic peninsula.

I got out of the car next to the studio and held the door open for Daisy. The quiet wrapped around me and I inhaled the fresh country air with reverence, slowly filling my lungs.

Daisy bounded out, her tail waving rapidly as her large

paws slid across the gravel. Fred emerged from the studio and greeted me with a quick hug.

"Good to see you, Annie."

"It's great to be here." I inhaled again. "Absolutely great."

Fred dropped his arm to let Daisy sniff his hand.

"This is Daisy."

"Hello, Daisy." Fred leaned over to pat her.

I looked at the meadow and sparkling water beyond it. "This is just beautiful."

"Indeed, it is." Fred nodded. "Any trouble finding it?" His low voice seemed more robust out here than it had in the museum. Everything seemed more vivid. He wore faded jeans and a flannel shirt and seemed a little taller, too. Or maybe my father's immense canvas dwarfed anyone who stood next to it.

"No, your directions were perfect." I smiled. "I can't believe how quiet it is."

"I notice it, too. Every time I return from the city. The minute I drive off the ferry, I'm sure I feel my blood pressure go down."

An old dog, a black and tan lab mix with a gray muzzle, slowly sauntered from the side of the studio and Daisy galloped over to it.

"It's really okay to just let Daisy loose?"

"Oh, sure. That's Pablo, he loves company." Fred beckoned to me as he opened the door. "Come on in, I'll show you the studio."

It was hard to believe the structure had ever been a chicken coop. Only the studio's long and narrow shape hinted at its history. The shed roof had obviously been raised and now enclosed four large skylights. Large French windows rose to the ceiling and faced the meadow to the west, while the south wall was entirely glass with tall, narrow casement windows on either side. Wide shelves covered the east wall, and a wood stove in the corner rested on a small hearth tiled with blue-green slate. All the walls were unfinished, giving off a woody aroma of cedar, which mixed with the smell of paint. For me, it was a heady concoction, like enticing perfume. A door next to the stove led to an outdoor utility sink and several shelves filled with turpentine and various cleaning compounds.

Overstuffed easy chairs were grouped in front of the woodstove, and a small sink near the door was set in a counter that held a microwave, coffee and tea pots, various cups and mugs, and housed an under-counter refrigerator.

"It looks like you have everything."

"Except a bathroom. I hope to add one before the end of the year, but I've gotten hung up trying to get a permit. I'm also looking into an electric toilet that burns everything up, called an Incinolet." Fred laughed. "My daughter calls it a turd toaster."

"Sort of a high-tech outhouse, hopefully not shocking." I laughed with him.

"In the meantime, folks use the one attached to my yurt." He ran his hand over his thick bushy eyebrows. "The permit thing is a real hassle. Don't get me started," he sighed. "Would you like some coffee, or tea?"

"Love some coffee, thanks." I sat by the stove. The old chair was a little on the ratty side, but very comfortable. Out the French windows I could see Daisy and Pablo in the meadow, circling each other and sniffing, their tails wagging.

"Cream or sugar?"

"Black—thanks."

Fred sat opposite me and sipped his coffee, smiling at the sight of the dogs in the meadow. "Looks like they're getting along."

"I love to see Daisy get to run free—it's a wonderful spot here."

"This place really saved me. Back in Spokane after Sylvia died, I was well on my way to becoming a weepy barfly. More accurately, Melissa saved me. My daughter. She told me to pull up my socks and then she got me over here."

"Has it worked out well, living so close?"

"I doubt it could have worked as well without the yurt, if we were all under one roof. Having my own separate place is important to all of us. And I'm lucky that we get along—we see most things the same way and our temperaments are compatible. That doesn't always happen with parents and children, as I'm sure you know, sometimes the apple falls far from the tree."

"We've been lucky that way with our kids, too."

Fred leaned forward, putting his hands on his knees. "Now tell me, why do you want to paint? It may seem an obvious question, but all the years I taught art I always wanted to know what a person's expectations and needs were."

I sighed. "Is there more coffee?"

"Sure. Help yourself."

I went to the counter behind our chairs and refilled my cup. "I've thought for so many years about what's stopped me from painting, or how I've allowed myself to be stopped, that I haven't thought as much about why I want to do it. It's a good question," I came back and sat across from him again. "I suppose it's a form of worship. At least to paint the beauty I see, maybe as a counterpoint to the ugliness in the world. For the beauty of the earth…" then I laughed, feeling a little embarrassed. "Although these days, I'm sure the plein aire landscape painter, or the impressionist, is probably considered a cliché."

"If cliché is supposed to mean something's been done so much it becomes predictable, and so overused that it's not original, it's only the competitive who are afraid of cliché and I'm not of that tribe."

"I don't know if I'm competitive, but I admit I'm scared I'll find out I'm an ordinary, Sunday hobby painter."

"If you make a serious expression, you always create what has meaning to you. If the same subject matter has meaning to other artists, so be it. No one will see it or create it exactly your way." He leaned forward again. "One thing I've learned over the years is that if art has any authenticity, it's always going to be a reflection of that separate individual. We're each of us unique."

I smiled. "That could be liberating." But I felt cautious, not quite believing him. "How are the classes structured?"

"The main structure you and I would adhere to is the ferry schedule." He laughed and it surprised me how comfortable I felt with him. Because all along, like a little hum in the background, was my awareness that he was a colleague of the great Alexander Gunther.

"I'm serious," he continued, "I don't really have a structure. I'm available for painting and drawing, and using all kinds of media from charcoal, pen and ink, pencil, watercolors, pastels, acrylics, to oils. Although before oils, I think it helps to get your feet wet with acrylics. They're more forgiving and faster. Basically, I make myself available for four hours a day, every afternoon from 1:00 to

5:00. And evenings from 7:00 to 9:30, which is when most folks are here. I think I mentioned, there's only one person coming in the daytime now. But I leave the studio open all the time. The fee is fifty dollars a month and—" he paused, "you look surprised—"

"You're right, I am surprised. It's so reasonable."

"It doesn't include any materials, just access to the space...and to me. I'm like an old reference book you can take off the shelf when you need to."

"I'd say you were a lot more than that."

"There is one expectation though, and that is that all students work on something for our show." Fred didn't notice me wince. "Creativity is a communication. It has two parts. The first is the solitary exercise of creating what you want to express, and it's imperative that this endeavor be one that's truly sustaining—that when you are most autonomous and alone you can be absorbed in it, and that it's deeply satisfying. Not that it doesn't have its agonizing moments, but the whole of it has to feed and sustain you."

"When you're by yourself and you're fulfilled by doing the work," I echoed.

"Exactly. But the second part of the process is to then connect what you've expressed in order to communicate with others, to connect with them and transcend our existential loneliness, to touch others."

"This is very philosophical." I looked down at my coffee.

"I suppose. But one has to master a fear of criticism, of rejection, if you're ever going to create anything and realize this second facet of art. And I've found no better way than to plunge right in by making art to be shown. That way we can immediately flush out all the demons and begin to disarm them." Fred got up and refilled his coffee. "Of course, Annie, we never get rid of them," he said, quietly. "We all have demons, but it is possible to disarm them so they don't defeat us."

I watched Daisy and Pablo exploring the meadow, with Daisy in the lead. I felt terrified and exhilarated. And, I had to pee. A lot of coffee had taken its typical morning toll. "May I use your restroom?"

"Sure, there's one in my yurt. The door's open—just go on in. The whole place is only about 700 square feet, so you won't have any trouble finding the bathroom."

I was struck again by the quiet. Gravel crunching under my feet, leaves rustling in the trees, birdsong, and the tapping of a faraway woodpecker were the only sounds that I heard. Fred's yurt was nestled near a grove of madrones about twenty yards to the east of the farmhouse. Perched on a platform above the ground, it featured four wide steps that led to a small covered deck at the entrance. The Douglas fir door had inset cedar panels and its brass doorknob gleamed in the sunshine. Opening the door, I expected the dim interior of a tent. Instead, the natural light that streamed through a skylight in the center of the domed ceiling made it seem like entering a cloud. The soft light was also filtering through the ivory colored fabric of the walls. I loved the simplicity of the small space, made to seem larger by the top of the dome that had to have been twelve or thirteen feet high. Two tall bookcases enclosed the pie shaped bathroom, and I was surprised by its comfort and sense of space, a lot roomier than the head on any boat I'd ever been on.

The yurt had everything: a kitchenette, a small dining area with a round table and two chairs, a couch that I assumed was a sofa bed, a wood stove on a small hearth, and five windows opening it up to the outdoors. They were made of strong, clear vinyl with sewed-in screens. A yurt of one's own. A piece of heaven.

As I was leaving the yurt, my cell phone rang. It was the lovely strains of the Moonlight Sonata, but this time I knew there could be another possibility. It might not be Rose Tibonga. It could be my father calling me and I couldn't stand the thought of talking to him, especially now, especially here. I waited to see if a message would be left, just in case it was Rose, and when I heard it, heard the sound of his voice, I might as well have been fifteen.

"Annie. Call me immediately!" he shouted, his voice filled with rage.

I went back and used the bathroom again and then came out to the deck of the yurt. Daisy and Pablo were there waiting for me, wagging their tails, creatures so happily in the moment. I took my time patting them, comforted by their pure hearts. I looked over at the studio where Fred waited by the door. Dear Fred Weiss. He seemed to be a person who was so much at peace, it was hard to imagine him plagued with demons, even though he'd made the point of saying everyone had them. I tried to collect myself, waiting for the cramps and burning knot to subside, and when I was sure I was ready, I left the yurt and went across to the studio, fast-forwarding forty years.

"I lust after your yurt." I said, somehow managing to laugh as I joined Fred. "What a wonderful way to live."

"All the girls say that. Seriously, the women all do seem to have that reaction, much more than the men."

"I'm not surprised."

"Well, what do you think?"

"It's incredible here." I leaned down and patted Daisy. "But truthfully, I wonder if I have any business trying to move beyond the crafty things I do at work. Maybe being the craft lady is my true calling." I continued stroking Daisy's head, looking down at the ground.

Fred leaned over to scratch Daisy's ears. After a few minutes he said, "It must have been hard to have been his daughter."

The elephant in the room, in the yurt, had been named. "Yes," I said, quietly. "It was."

"I try to create an atmosphere that isn't pressured. I've always liked Kahil Gibran's great quote about teaching. Now here's cliché for you," he winked, as he inhaled, lifted his head and recited in his wheezy voice. "The teacher...if he indeed be wise, does not bid you to enter the house of his wisdom, but rather leads you to the threshold of your own mind." Fred smiled. "I like to think of it as leading folks to the threshold of their own talent."

I might have laughed, his oratorical pose in his rumpled flannel shirt was close to being comical, but he was so kind I felt only tenderness and gratitude.

"Thank you for that."

"I hope you'll come out to paint here."

Remembering my mother with a leap of faith, and feeling quite like I was about to jump out of an airplane, all the while holding on to the hope that this dear old man would be a parachute, I was able to answer, "I'd like that very much."

9

CASS

"My butt's freezing," Lena said, as she stood. "Aren't you cold?" A layer of fog hung over Green Lake, and the grass on the banks was wet with dew. The sun, which usually burned off the fog by mid-morning, had yet to make an appearance and the bench where Cass sat with Lena was damp.

"I don't seem to notice much." Cass stared across the lake at the fog lying on top of the water like a gauzy comforter. "Most of the time I feel numb."

Lena grabbed her hand, pulling her off the bench. "Come on. We're going to the café."

"I need this." Cass managed to smile.

"Need what?"

"Someone to tell me what to do."

"Cass, you look terrible. Are you sleeping?" Lena always said she didn't like to look at her friends or family with a clinical eye, but admitted there were times she couldn't help it. Cass supposed this was one of them.

"I know I look terrible, but did you have to say it?"

"You're beautiful. Even messed up you're beautiful, that's not what I mean and you know it. But you seem to be disappearing right before me. You're so thin! And you didn't answer my question."

"What question?"

"Cass are you this spacey, or are you just trying to avoid me?"

Cass didn't know what to say, or what was true. She just didn't know.

"We'll get our coffee, and then we'll talk." Lena slowed her brisk pace to stay abreast with Cass, who walked with her shoulders slightly hunched and her head down.

The café was deserted except for an elderly couple that sat at a table by the window, sharing the paper. Twos. Cass noticed them everywhere. At work, in cars, on the street. Couples, and people with babies, they seemed to be all over the place. Lena and Cass got their coffee and sat by the fire.

"Cass, are you sleeping?" And what about your appetite?"

"I sleep alone."

"Come on." Lena put her hand on Cass's arm. "Talk to me."

Cass leaned back, running her hand along the leather arm of the chair. Outside she watched two squirrels chasing each other up a tree. Even the squirrels were a pair.

"Cass?"

She took a sip of her coffee. "I wouldn't call it sleeping, exactly, or at least not much. I have trouble getting to sleep. I toss and turn, and then maybe I sleep a few hours. But I wake up about four and can't get back to sleep. I lie there until the alarm goes off. Then it's time to go to work."

"Are you eating?"

"Not really. Nothing appeals. I just don't have any appetite. I make myself drink some juice, or milk for energy, I guess. But what's really weird is that I don't even want my favorite chocolate bar. You know, that Divine dark chocolate."

"That's serious, when you don't even want a hit of chocolate." Lena smiled, but it didn't hide her concern. "You've got to get this turned around, Cass. I think you're heading for a really shitty depression."

"Exercise is supposed to help, so I'm trying to walk every day."

The last thing she wanted was for Lena to think she was just folding her tent, hanging it up, caving in like some wimp. And she had been walking. Long solitary excursions, but she was losing focus and lately it seemed like she was just wandering around like a lost dog. She woke every morning with a feeling of dread, a shroud of despair so heavy that just getting up to face the day took every ounce of will she could muster. She had made it to work each day, which, in itself, seemed a bit of a miracle and she functioned as well as she could. But her concentration was shot and it was beginning to catch up with her.

"I'm going to call in a prescription for sleeping pills. But it's just temporary and not enough to kill you." Lena tried to sound matter-of-fact. "Are you having any thoughts like that?"

"Suicide?" Cass shook her head. "No. I feel apathetic about everything. Like I don't care what happens. I just don't give a shit about anything. The only person I want to kill is Richard."

Lena laughed. "That's a good sign, as long as you don't do it."

"Look, I may be messed up, but I'm still Cass. Remember? I'm the one who won't kill bugs."

"You still catch and release spiders?"

"Sure. Some things never change. They might be the reincarnation of somebody's grandmother." Cass's reverence for bugs was an inconsistency that amused Richard. But she never found it inconsistent that she loved tandoori chicken, lamb curry, barbecue ribs, pepperoni pizza, and the occasional Big Mac. If a chicken, sheep, pig, or cow wandered in her house she wouldn't kill them either.

She looked at Lena. "So you really think I need drugs?"

"You've got to get some sleep and stop this downward cycle, and if you don't start sleeping and don't begin to feel a little better, I want you to promise me you'll see someone."

"A shrink?" Cass asked, a little annoyed.

"Anti-depressants usually help and you'd need a doc to manage the meds. Richard can't be your drug connection—and I can't be, either, Cass. I can give you some names."

"You know I didn't want to be this way." Her eyes filled with tears, she couldn't help it. "I didn't want him to be able to knock me over."

"Look, break-ups are gory and humiliating. There's no way you don't get very, very wounded. It can't be helped," Lena said, "unless there was nothing there to begin with." Lena's cell phone rang, she checked the number then put it back in her bag.

"Do you need to make a call?"

"No, it's fine. I'll return it later." Lena sipped her coffee. "Have you told your folks?"

"No. I keep dodging them—I don't feel ready. I don't think they ever really liked him that much. And not only my folks—" Cass wiped her eyes, and took a sip of her coffee. "I've been dodging Richard, too. Although he's been at the apartment getting his clothes and stuff, but always when I'm at work."

The first time she'd noticed was when she saw the closet door open and some of his shirts were gone. Later, it was his shoes. After that, books. At first it was as if the apartment had been robbed and it frightened her, she was so anxious she never slept. Later it just felt predictable; losing him bit by bit, like a tree losing its leaves before the onset of winter.

"Last night he called," Cass said, quietly, "and for some reason I picked up."

"What did he want?"

"He said he wants to talk and I said 'okay.' I guess he got me in a wimp moment. He's coming over this weekend."

"Why give the fucker the time of day? You should just get rid of the jerk, slam the door and never look back. Hang up on him, for God's sake. Cass, you are fun, energetic, carefree—not this zombie."

She did not want to cry in front of Lena.

"I'm sorry. This is why you can't help your friends, I mean, intellectually I know what depression does to people, but another part of me just can't get what's happening to you, you've always been so feisty, and Richard is acting like a total jerk. Oh, Cass," Lena leaned forward and put her hand on Cass's arm. "You wouldn't go back with him if that's what he wants to talk about?"

"I don't think that's it. Really, I don't. Besides, how can you be with someone you don't trust? Not after this."

"People do it though—I just hope you don't."

Cass looked out the window. "I think he probably just

wants to divide up our stuff, although I don't know if I can deal with it. I feel like I'm running on empty, I hardly have the energy to wash my hair. I'm so tired of this shit." She watched the squirrels, which were now chasing each other around the trunk of the large maple. "Enough of my little drama. How're you doing?"

"I'm fine with talking about your stuff."

"No really, I want to hear how you are. I can't stand the idea of turning into some drama queen."

"I'm okay. I guess. But my brother's wedding, or should I say my mother's obsession with it, is really grating on me. There's really not a lot to say about it." Lena finished her coffee, draining her cup, then smiled, "And you don't need to worry, you'll never be a drama queen."

"So what's up with the wedding?"

"There's a stalemate because I told my mother I'm not going if Val's not invited, and we both attend the rehearsal dinner like the couple we are—Sandra's new sisters-in-law. My mother is avoiding talking about it, trying to wear me down, working her usual guilt thing about how it's my brother's one big day. But it's her one big day and she wants us in the closet for it."

It was great to be with Lena, but Cass hadn't been able to exactly tell her everything. When she listed what she'd been consuming (juice and milk) there'd been one little omission: wine. She'd been going through almost a bottle every two days. Last weekend—one a day. When she got home she went straight to the kitchen and got an open bottle of pinot gris out of the refrigerator. As she poured a glass, she noticed the recycle bin overflowing with empty green and bronze bottles, some toppled over onto the floor.

"Damn." She felt disgusted at the sight and kicked one of the bottles back toward the bin. She should just empty the damn thing, but the thought of carrying them behind the building to the dumpster was overwhelming. Instead, she went back to the living room, slumped on the couch and drank.

What did Richard want? Could it be that he missed her? Even a little. Or a lot? What if what's-her-name wasn't all he'd hoped for and he was going to come crawling back. On his belly, like a worm. Cass refilled her glass. And he'd be flooded with remorse, wanting her. And they'd make love all afternoon. She remembered his skin, how it felt like cool silk and how once inside her with her arms around his smooth back everything else fell away and he belonged to her. And he'd beg her to take him back and she'd move away, telling him she needed time to think about it, and there he'd be, left dangling like a leaf in the wind or a puppet on a string, or a mouse held by its tail. The images were quite satisfying. Cass drained her glass. Especially the picture of Mouse Richard with a tiny stethoscope around his furry little neck, swinging back and forth while she squeezed his little tail.

10

ANNIE

At Tomiko's, Jack and I were still able to have our favorite booth, the last one on the west side with its stunning view of Elliott Bay. It was good to be in our usual booth, if it were taken this late I worried Jack might be even more sullen than he had been that morning. The smallest thing seemed to get to him lately. I slid across the seat toward the window, the familiar soft gray leather enclosing us felt like a tiny harbor in a safe port. I had decided not to return my father's call until after Jack and I had dinner. The great Alexander Gunther would just have to wait. He'd be poison on an empty stomach, and I needed the comfort and familiarity of our Friday night ritual of dinner at Tomiko's.

"How you doin' tonight, folks?" Tommy, the owner, smiled and handed us the menus even though we knew them by heart. His first name was Kizamu and for a brief period in the early seventies he'd tried to shed his Anglo nickname but had met with little success. A few conscientious customers like Jack and I had tried to show respect by switching to Kizamu, but the name never really took with most customers and it wasn't long before Tommy seemed fine with being Tommy again.

"Great." I returned the smile. And Jack smiled, as well. He seemed to be trying.

"How's that grandson of yours?"

"Growing like a weed. How's your family, Tommy?" I asked.

He beamed. "We've got another one coming. Number four. You gotta catch up with me."

"We'd like that," I sighed. "But we don't get a vote."

We ordered, our drinks arrived, and then sat there like those couples that have been married forever and have run out of things to say when Jack finally asked me how things had gone on Vashon. "Who did you go see again?" he asked.

"Fred Weiss. I met him at the opening. I told you about him and his classes."

"And he's trying to get you in his garret?"

I almost spilled my drink. "He lives in a yurt," I said, brightly, deciding to ignore Jack's weirdness.

"Garret, yurt—same thing—"

"A garret and a yurt are not the same," I interrupted. "A garret is an attic and a yurt is a circular tent. Yurts were first used by nomads in Central Asia, they were covered with animal skins and—"

"It doesn't matter if he lives under a rock. He wants to show you his etchings and we all know what that means."

"Jack, he's eighty years old," I said, calmly.

"You think I'm overjoyed at the idea of you hanging out on Vashon Island with some artsy-fartsy, horny old toad?"

Tommy brought our orders, shiyoki salmon for me and

kasu cod for Jack. Jack tore the paper off his chopsticks and put rice in the small bowl next to his plate, and began shoveling the rice in his mouth with quick strokes of his chopsticks.

"I'm sorry, but this is ridiculous. Look, I know you've had a hard time ever since that guy went back to Cambodia, but this is important to me and I want the space to be able to see about it. Literally—I'm pretty sure I'm going to want space here in the house, for a studio. Probably Cass's old room...and the space, my own space—emotionally to commit to—"

"And there'll be a lecherous old fart in the space."

"He's not a lecherous old fart!"

"How do you know?" Jack glared at me.

"Because I just know."

"Your father's eighty-four and he hasn't quit."

"Oh, this is really getting us somewhere." I took a long sip of my wine. "You know, Jack. I just wish you had something you really cared about. So you'd be looking forward to having more time for interests and things you'd like to pursue since there's less to do at the lab."

"I don't plan on retiring."

"Well, as things slow down, that's all. You'll have more time—if you want it, and I just think you should be considering what you might like to do."

"I'm not going to build birdhouses like my brother-in-law."

"Who said anything about birdhouses? I didn't say you were supposed to build birdhouses."

Jack was struggling and I felt sorry for him. But that nonsense about Fred Weiss took the cake. It was just ridiculous. Not that I think it's easy to get older. Aging, as they say, is certainly not for sissies, but I wondered if men had a harder time than women leaving the stage, not being a player. Although I'd never been one, so how would I know? I wanted to start a career, begin taking myself seriously—before it was too late.

But I also wanted to age with grace. Grace...Grace who? How 'bout a Grace resembling Cinderella's fairy godmother, the Disney version, who would pop into my life with a nice bibbity-bobbity-boo complete with a few harp flourishes and a sprinkling of stardust to accompany me on my journey to cronehood. Or maybe she could show up for Jack, that would be nice. He could use the help.

The rest of our dinner, we were politely distant, and when we got home Jack went straight to his study, and I couldn't help hoping that he wasn't working on trying to get another grant. Daisy followed me upstairs after she'd greeted us as usual with her little four-legged boogie-woogie, rump gyrating, tail swinging in large arcs, nails clicking as her paws slid over the tile floor. She lay down next to me on the floor beside my bed, where I sat looking at the phone. The message light was blinking, and I sat on the floor and hugged Daisy as I listened to it.

"Annie. Didn't you get my message? Call me immediately. I met with Bob Dennison today. As I told you, not only is there another will, but you've been named the Personal Representative." He sounded furious.

Could this be true? What had my mother been up to? I found it almost impossible to believe she'd taken some kind of action that he had no knowledge of. It was incomprehensible really.

My father's anger had always frightened me and instead of the phone, I picked up the remote for the TV and clicked it on. PBS was having one of those doo-wop fund-raisers, I loved the sweetness of doo-wop. I wondered if there was music my mother longed for, what had it been for her? Glenn Miller? I'd never be able to ask.

I closed my eyes listening to the old harmonies and I remembered one of the few times my father had been kind to me. My mother bought me a Madame Alexander doll for my eighth birthday. She was magnificent in a gorgeous satin ball gown, and my father had made a pen and ink drawing of the doll for me to color. I still have it to this day, in a file drawer with our birth certificates, passports and wills. I clicked off the TV, reached for the phone and called him. I'd barely said hello when he started yelling.

"I left the message hours ago, what the hell took you so long? I suppose you put her up to this!" he snarled. "Bob Dennison received a copy of this will from the lawyer she saw. Some woman named Delores H. James. Was your brother in on it, too? You and David are the beneficiaries. She named the two of you, Trevor, Carl, Cass, Ian and the child."

"Sam."

"What?"

"Sam. Your great-grandson. His name is Sam and I told you I don't know anything about this."

"You better go see this James person and straighten this out. We have community property in this state and my art is part of our joint estate, but you better believe there's no way you're going to make decisions about what to sell!" Then he hung up on me.

Damn him. I hated having to deal with him, but more than that—I felt like an orphan. My mother hadn't told me any of this and now I was trapped, stuck with him until I could get this mess straightened out. What had she been up to? I still couldn't believe my mother had done something on her own. But it was beginning to look like my father had been duped, and she'd used me to do it.

I went to the study where Jack was working at his computer. I know he heard me but he didn't look up. It was too much, Jack's distance on top of my father's hostility and I leaned against the doorjamb, covered my eyes and wept.

"Annie." He got up and put his arms around me.

"I wish you didn't worry..." I said, trying to stop crying. "I just want to paint—"

"I know it's silly." He stroked my hair, "but you're still beautiful."

"It's so late. Won't you come to bed?"

Jack turned off his computer and we both got ready for bed. He climbed in after I did and I shut off the light. He held me and I told him about my conversation with my father.

"She didn't even tell me."

"It's not like her. There's got to be some explanation."

"I've never stood up to him—I don't know what she wanted me to do...." I put my head on his chest. I could feel the steady beat of his heart.

"And I didn't mean birdhouses, Jack."

"I know."

And then we made love...it was our north star, the familiar road map, the way we found ourselves home.

Everything seemed more manageable in the morning as it so often does and I called information and got the number for Delores H. James. I left a message for her and she called me back within an hour, and although she said she had a pretty full schedule, she would be able to fit me in at the end of the day on Wednesday. She was very kind on the phone and expressed her condolences about the death of my mother. I liked the way she sounded, which was reassuring, and I was especially curious about her connection to my mother. But the main thing was that I wanted to get this thing straightened out as soon as I could.

I was both excited and scared to start working with Fred. He'd given me a list of supplies to purchase and without it, I think I might have had a panic attack in the art supply store; the number of choices was so daunting. After I collected everything on the list, I went back and forth, obsessing about a cedar case with a leather handle to hold them. The beautiful box was pricey—was it worth it? I kept wondering. But I ended up buying it, knowing the real question had always been, was I, Annie, worth it?

The day of my first class, I was unloading my car in front of the studio when an ancient Mercedes drove up. It was painted fire engine red and smelled like French fries. It must be one of those diesels that run on vegetable oil, I thought as I watched an elderly woman slowly pull herself out of the car. Could this be the other daytime student?

"Hello there, you must be the new student!" She had a raspy voice and wore a multi-colored smock, which draped over her plump figure and made her look like a beach ball.

"Why yes, hello." I walked over and held out my hand and introduced myself. Unlike her shape, the woman's hand had little flesh. It was like grasping a handful of bird bones.

"Nice to meet you, Annie. You did say Annie?"

"Yes, Anne Duppstadt."

"I'm Martha Jane Morrison. One of my pet peeves is when you're in a group and no one bothers to introduce anyone. People are just supposed to fend for themselves and frankly, I don't like it. Now don't get me wrong, I'm not one of those crotchety old people who say everything in the old days was better. Not me. Just tell me what was better about segregation and women not being able to vote, or own anything in their own names?" She opened the back door of her car and slowly pulled out an easel and a box of supplies. "Now what was I saying—"

"About the good old days." I smiled.

Martha Jane leaned the tottery easel against her car and laughed. Her bright white hair was piled high and fastened at the crown with a tortoise-shell comb. Underneath the hair, like a pale pumpkin under a snowdrift, her face was round and doughy with wide-set blue eyes, which, although faded, still looked to me like they sparkled with life and wit. I was enchanted.

"Can I help you unload anything?"

"Oh, no, dear. Thank you, I'll get it. You go on in and get started. I know how precious our time here is."

I carried in my easel and the new cedar case and took out the palette knives and brushes first, then the tubes of paint. Fred came over as I was setting up. "I see you met Martha Jane."

"How old is she?" I whispered.

"Ninety."

"Amazing."

"Indeed she is," Fred smiled. "And she's always ready to quote Marie Dressler—it's not how old you are...but how you are old. Martha Jane's lived on the island for over thirty years, ever since she retired from teaching elementary school in West Seattle. She has a place over on Hormann Road about ten miles south of here."

"Does she come to the studio every day?"

"Usually does."

Martha Jane shuffled in with her easel and set it up near me next to a long high table. "Shall we share the table? The light is quite good here and my eyes aren't what they used to be." She laughed. "Neither is anything else."

"By all means." I slid my case closer to the edge of the table to make room.

In spite of the fact that her voice was weakened by age and she spoke somewhat slowly with long pauses between words, my impression was that Martha Jane had extraordinary stamina. For a number of years, I'd found myself intensely scrutinizing elderly women (the healthy active ones, living on their own) the way I used to watch high school girls when I was in the sixth grade. Then I practically worshiped two girls who lived down the block: Dana Rose and Catherine Aurbach. They were seniors at Roosevelt High, both cheerleaders, and I found their comparative sophistication utterly fascinating. Now, five decades later, I had that same fascination with hale and hearty women in their eighties or older. Who were they? What was their secret? Maybe if I worked next to Martha Jane every day when I was here, some of her spirit would find its way into my psyche, by osmosis. Perhaps I would discover the secret to her vitality and longevity.

She came back carrying a box of supplies. She put it down on the table, opened it and took out a small card and clipped it to her easel. It was hand lettered; the characters a bit spidery, like bird scratching, but nonetheless legible.

Use the talent you possess,
For the forest would be silent
If no birds sang but the best.

She noticed me watching. "It's like a Bible verse for me. I want to remind myself of this each day before I begin, otherwise, one can lose faith—even at my age. I certainly know I won't be Grandma Moses, but I can't let that stop me, now can I?"

"No, certainly not," I agreed, feeling a rush of affection.

Below the card Martha Jane clipped a photo of two very young deer; their coats still had a trace of fading spots. Earlier in the week, she told me, Fred had helped her transfer a drawing she'd made to the canvas by creating a transfer paper, rubbing pastel chalk over tracing paper. Then he showed her how to rub it down with a paper towel soaked in Bestine, a rubber cement thinner, and trace over the drawing with a hard lead pencil. I watched as she added final touches to the sketch of the deer. Her gnarled hands were covered with age spots sprinkled across her thin skin like raisins.

"They're darling, those two. Did you take the photo yourself?"

"You bet. In my yard." Martha Jane smiled. "I call them Jane Doe and John Deere, I don't know if you could literally call them my pets, because they won't let me pet them. Much as I'd like to, frankly. But, they will eat apples from my hand." She turned to me and whispered conspiratorially, "They come to my door every day." Martha Jane turned back to the easel and continued carefully filling in the sketch. "Fred showed me how to transfer this, I want very much to do a good portrait of them."

I moved closer for a better look. "How did they get so tame? I see deer all over the island, but they seem to get spooked pretty easily if you get too close. There was a big doe and a fawn near the salal by the drive the other day, but they took off as soon as I got out of the car."

"Here's what happened. I think it's an outrage, but hunting is legal on Vashon. They can use several kinds of rifles, even handguns with long barrels, and some kind of guns called muzzleloaders—I'm not really sure what those are, but I got the Washington Big Game Hunting Season and Rules pamphlet so I'd know what was legal. Besides the terrible guns, they allow bows and arrows—and these aren't toys! The bow has to have forty pounds of pull—they're murder weapons! Every year in the fall, I drive on all the back roads looking for the hunters, hoping to harass them. I've shrunk considerably so I peer out just over the top of the steering wheel. It usually terrifies them to see someone my age behind the wheel. But I can still manage. Just on the island, of course. I'd never drive anywhere else, and never at night." Martha Jane paused. "Now what was I telling you?"

"About the deer."

"Oh, yes. I digress, I'm afraid. Start to talk about one thing, then find myself on a completely different subject, wandering off somewhere, but I drive better than I talk. I never get lost. I know the island like the back of my hand."

Martha Jane turned back to her sketch and I decided not to remind her about the deer again. But after a few minutes, she piped up, "I had been telling you about how I got so close with Jane and John, wasn't I?"

"That's right."

"It was very sad. I found the mother of these two in the woods behind my barn on Christmas Day last year. She'd been shot by a bow and arrow and must have run away and died some time later, because I followed a long trail of blood that went deep into the woods. I wanted to strangle whoever did it to her."

She went over to the coffee pot. Although Martha Jane moved slowly and with a shuffling gait, her hand was remarkably steady as she poured the coffee. "I'm convinced it was some impotent old flatus, a Cheney type—thank God we've almost seen the last of him. But you know the sort, the ones that never served in the military but want to feel powerful. I always thought if a few of them could gather somewhere, perhaps like Camp David, and dress up in military clothes—what's that clothing hunters wear to sneak up on animals?" Martha Jane frowned, "What's it called again?"

"Camouflage?"

"Right. Camouflage, that's the word. Thank you. They could dress in these outfits and play shock and awe with paintball. I saw a television show about this game. It's popular with adolescent males, I understand." She finished her coffee and returned to her easel and began touching up the sketch. "If the politicians who never served could blast each other with red, yellow, and green paint perhaps they could get it out of their system." She said, sighing deeply. "It could be quite healthy for the world."

My eyes met Martha Jane's and for a second she really seemed to resemble the fairy godmother in Disney's Cinderella, holding a 2H pencil instead of a wand. I almost expected to hear harp flourishes.

She stepped back and squinted, focusing on the sketch, studying it intently. "I'm afraid I'd better stop before I ruin this. It seems to me that it's more difficult to know when to stop than how to begin." She paused, tilting her head further back. "I'm just not sure about their little faces. The eyes. They have such big and innocent eyes—" her voice trailed off. "Maybe I'll ask Fred if I should work on them some more when he gets over to us."

"Were the fawns nearby when you found the mother?" I asked.

"Yes. They just hung around behind my barn, so naturally I began feeding them."

"Naturally."

"I cut up apples, their little mouths were so small they couldn't really get a good bite. I'd put the apples on the ground and gradually they began to feel safe. It took about a month, but they would finally be so eager when they saw me, they came right over and started to eat out of my hand." Martha Jane laughed. "My neighbors call me the Deer Lady of Hormann Road. I guess there are worse things to be called."

"Without a doubt." I turned my easel a little more toward the west windows of the studio, feeling like I was falling in love.

Ever since I first saw the meadow and the view beyond of Colvos Passage, I knew I wanted to paint it. Today I was roughly working out its essential ideas and design and I was hoping to finish a lot of the underpainting. I tried to be patient, but I had put this off for almost fifty years and I found myself working quickly, as if trying to make up for all the lost time. Fred had suggested using an acrylic layer of underpainting as it had all the advantage of an oil while saving considerable time. I loved using lots of color and had been amazed at how quickly it was drying. I had put in the sky from the warmest area above the trees outward to the cooler areas. The colors moved into muted reds, warm violets and then to cool blues.

Martha Jane stood behind me and peered over my shoulder, watching me work. "What you have already is lovely, the finished piece is going to be splendid."

"You really think so?" I shot her a quick glance, surprised at the encouragement, stated as if it were a fact.

"Yes, don't you think so?"

"I don't know. I've been afraid to do this almost as long as I can remember."

"Fred must have forgotten to tell you about the experiment." She quickly left, and returned moments later with Fred.

"Martha Jane says I forgot to tell you about the creativity experiment." Fred looked at me. "I didn't tell you? It's usually part of my standard spiel."

"Maybe I forgot." We laughed about faulty memories, and I thought perhaps this would be how my journey to cronehood would unfold. Laughing with these two, who would lead the way, modeling the mellow path.

"It was a psychology experiment somewhere. They took two groups of college students and matched them carefully for age, intelligence, socio-economic background, gender. Almost every variable they could. And they were large groups, almost one hundred students per group."

"I thought it was two hundred," Martha Jane interrupted.

"Maybe it was." Fred scowled, touching his hand to his forehead. "Oh, no matter, the point's the same," he said, waving his hand dismissively. "They gave each group the identical standard creativity test and told each group they would be taking a test to measure their creativity. But, you see," Fred paused dramatically, "they falsely told the experimental group that each student in their group had been specifically chosen because of their high degree of creative ability.

"The control group was told no such thing, just that they would be taking the test. After both groups completed the test and the results were scored, guess what?" Fred grinned, gesturing as though he were playing a trumpet. "Ta-da! The group who had been told they were creative scored significantly higher than the group that was told nothing." Fred let his hand drop and laughed. "So, it proved the obvious. That creativity is enhanced by encouragement."

"But Fred, I also do think it's unkind to falsely encourage people, as a regular thing," Martha Jane said.

"This wasn't a regular thing. It was an experiment."

"I know but, I'm just saying you wouldn't want to tell a mediocre young athlete that he could play first base for the Yankees. Although I certainly agree that whatever natural ability a person has can be expanded with encouragement, just as it can be inhibited with discouragement."

"But you wouldn't tell that young person to quit the game if he enjoyed playing just because he might never be a pro," Fred countered.

I went back to my easel leaving Fred and Martha Jane to continue their discussion. Occasionally, I'd glance over at them. Martha Jane was a head shorter than Fred, the top of her snowy hair coming just above his thin shoulder. Both their voices were breathy with age, but they still seemed to have a certain passion, a little muted maybe, but without question it was passion and I was inspired by it. I was sad when it was time to go and I couldn't help wondering what my life would have been like, if I'd had a mother as secure within herself as Martha Jane and a father as kind as Fred Weiss.

When I got home from Vashon, I told Jack about how well things had gone and how much I was looking forward to classes there. I thought he'd gotten over the glitch he'd had, but when I said I wanted to make Cass's old room into a studio he sounded annoyed.

"Cass's room is the guest room," he said, "what about our guest room?"

"What guests? We never have guest—I don't want any guests."

Jack fixed himself a drink and I could feel his guard go up. "What if we get some guests? You never know."

"Jack, there's a patient at Woodside whose son was killed in Iraq—"

"What does that have to do with our guest room?"

"If guests come we can get a couch that converts into a bed or something...let me finish, would you please? This woman, when she talked about her son, it just hit me again that we never know how much time we have left. And I feel it so strongly with Mom gone—and then other things, little things just seem to be hitting me."

"Like what little things?"

"Like *People* magazine. Someone left a copy in the art room and it dawned on me that I don't know who any of the people are in *People* magazine."

"So what? I don't either unless it's a sports person."

"Well, I don't know those."

"Why should you? You don't like sports." He finished his drink and went to the liquor cabinet for a refill. "I don't see what the hell this has to do with us."

"It's just that life is passing me by."

"Because you don't know any of the people in *People* magazine?"

"Do you know how many times at work over the years I've been making stuff like Thanksgiving turkeys out of toilet paper rolls and I've thought, Georgia O'Keeffe wouldn't be caught dead doing this."

"Isn't she dead? Was she in *People* magazine? I thought you said you didn't know any of the people in there?"

"Oh, God. Just forget it, Jack."

"No, tell me. I'm listening."

"What's the point?"

"Annie, tell me."

"All right. I feel like things are passing me by and I wanted to take myself seriously. I promised myself I would—and Mom, too, when I took her to Canada—and I have to do this before it's too late."

"So exactly what does taking yourself seriously mean? You hole up on Vashon Island to paint?"

"No, but I want to go there three days a week. I have to commit to the time. And I want to rearrange my schedule, instead of working four half-days like I do now, I want to work two full days, which will give me some good blocks of time. And realistically, I'll be doing less around here. I thought it would be best if I were really clear about it, right from the start, Jack. I just want to be upfront with you."

"What exactly is that supposed to mean?"

"It means I might not always cook, you might have to fix something for yourself, pick up something at the store if you want—whatever, but just not count on me."

There it was out. I knew he wasn't going to like it, but that was just too bad. Jack and I had a Donna Reed,

Ozzie and Harriet kind of marriage. Unlike a lot of our friends, we seemed stuck in the fifties in some ways. Probably because Jack is older, and I'd tried hard to meet his expectations and make our marriage work, which meant being a pretty traditional wife. True, he was bouncing around now about his career, but Jack is a wonderful man and I appreciated him the way you do when you have a nice husband after the first one turned out to be a big jerk. But I'd been feeding people for most of my life and if I was going to commit to painting the way I wanted, it was time for Jack not to expect me to be there every night to make his dinner.

Surprise. Jack was not thrilled by any of this. End of conversation. He left to watch the news. But I was sure he'd eventually adapt. No one likes change and it might take him awhile, but we each had little tolerance for rough patches that lingered too long, and for over thirty years we'd always gotten through them.

I called Cass to let her know that I'd be moving everything from her old room to the basement and she should come over and pick up anything she might not want stored there. As usual she wasn't home and I just left a message. It was so predictable, the way she called back when we were at work, that I knew she was avoiding us. Cass didn't like me to drop in where she worked, but I had that appointment with Delores James next week and her office was on Broadway near the Starbucks Cass managed. If I didn't talk to her soon, I would stop in—that was all there was to it.

11

CASS

Cass could only remember a couple of times when her mother had popped in at Starbucks and that had been early on, before she told her parents she didn't like it—so she was pretty sure the visit had been prompted by all the phone tag. Being ambushed like this really irked her, but when she saw how worried Annie looked, Cass was afraid she might dissolve into tears. What a capable manager, crumpling into the arms of her mother who hovers over her at her job.

Cass forced a smile. "Hi Mom." She waved and went over to Annie. "Here for coffee?"

"I know you don't like me to visit you at your job, but I have an appointment near here."

"Really?" Cass looked skeptical.

"I really do." Annie sighed, "there's a hassle about Baach's will and I'm meeting with a lawyer whose office is on Broadway. She fit me in at the end of the day—anyway, I won't go into all the details—being in this neighborhood just gave me an excuse to see you." Annie lowered her voice. "Is something wrong, Cass? I know you've been avoiding us."

My life is falling apart, that's all.

"Well, I've had the flu and it keeps hanging on. I've just been sleeping whenever I'm not at work and I turn the phone off. I've called you back and left messages, it's not like I disappeared," she said defensively.

"You should have told us." Annie didn't sound convinced and Cass could tell her mother might not be buying this.

"I didn't want to worry you, Mom."

"It's more of a worry not to know what's going on. Well, anyway, I guess you got the message about my clearing out your old room."

"I did, and it's great it'll be your studio."

"Well, your stuff's in the basement if you want anything."

"Thanks. Listen, I really have to run. I'm meeting Lena and Val for dinner."

"You've got to take care of yourself. Flu can turn into pneumonia if you're not careful."

"Mom, I know. Don't worry." Cass gave her a mother quick hug. "I really have to go."

She didn't feel great about lying to Annie, but she couldn't face having to tell her mother the truth. Although it was true she was having dinner with Lena and Val—just much later. Cass wanted time to shower and have a short nap, to put herself together before Richard came over, so she wouldn't look like some pathetic loser. She wanted to look good.

Please let me look good. So he'll eat his heart out.

The nap didn't do anything for the dark circles under her eyes, and in the shower she let the water run cold, turning her face to the spray, hoping it would get the blood flowing and spark some vitality in her washed-out skin. Make-up helped a little, and she spent a lot of time on her hair, leaving it down the way he liked instead of clipping it up the way she did for work, or the ponytail for softball. But she wasn't sure about her clothes. If she wore her soft-ball stuff, it would look like she still had a life and it was no big thing to see him, whereas, a sexy outfit would look like she cared about what he thought. After too much time thinking about something she knew was this dumb, Cass finally decided on her tightest jeans—he'd always com-mented appreciatively on her long legs. Even though they weren't as tight as they used to be, still she wasn't drowning in them. And she'd wear her Battin' Beans T-shirt. She had a life. She did have a life.

Richard arrived on time and rang the doorbell.

At least he knows to do that much. Not to use his key like he still lives here, coming and going like he pleases.

She waited for a minute until he rang a second time, then fluffed up her hair and walked slowly to the door.

"Hi," he said, impassively, with a half-smile that seemed to be a mixture of pity and guilt. He was wearing khakis and a blue, button-down oxford shirt and loafers. Very preppy. The way she loved him to look, his beautiful thick hair, like midnight against his warm tawny skin, the powder blue shirt making his hair and eyes even darker. The shirt was open at the neck. She wanted to touch him. Brush her fingertips along his collarbone.

"Come on in," she said, pressing her lips together. "Want a glass of wine?" She hoped he did. She didn't want to drink alone and she sure as hell didn't want to go through this without one.

"Sure." Richard stood awkwardly by the door.

"Red or white?" She asked, trying to sound casual.

"Whatever's open." He followed her into the kitchen, watching her carefully while she poured them each a glass of pinot grigio. She had red open, too. A bottle of cabernet sitting on the counter next to the microwave, and she knew he preferred red.

He was looking at the recycle bin when she handed him his glass. He mumbled "thanks," then pointed to the bottles spilling out of the bin. "What's all this?" he asked, unable to hide the accusation in his voice.

"Just a party."

"Oh, Cass."

"All right. I haven't taken it out in awhile. So what?" she said, defiantly.

"You shouldn't be drinking like this."

"You came over here to give me a little health lecture?"

"Look, let's just sit down and talk. Like two civilized people and—"

"There's nothing uncivilized about me," she snapped.

"Can't I even finish a sentence?" he asked, reasonably, which made her even madder. How calm. How sensible.

"Fine. Finish your sentence." She tilted her head, taking a long drink.

"Let's sit down—"

"Like two civilized people," she said, her voice dripping with sarcasm.

"Oh for Christ's sake. I'm trying to say, let's just sit down with a glass of wine and talk. Okay?" he paused, and she could see the muscles of his jaw tightening. "Or maybe we should have coffee."

"Sure. And I'm supposed to make the coffee."

"I'll make the fucking coffee," he said, his exasperation breaking through.

"Well, I don't want coffee." Cass took another long drink.

"Fine. Can we sit down?"

"Sure, be my guest." She went in the living room and sat on the couch. Richard took the chair across from it. They'd bought it together, a leather chair from Restoration Hardware, but it had always been his chair, the place where he read, studied, listened to music. She wished she'd claimed it. But the force of habit was too strong, and she curled her legs under her and huddled in the corner of the couch.

Richard put his glass on the table next to the chair and leaned forward with his hands resting on his knees, poised like a player on the bench anxious to get in the game. "We've gotta make some decisions, Cass."

"Like what?"

"Like this apartment."

"What about it?"

Richard sighed. "You're not making this very easy, Cass."

"Oh, that's great," she snarled. "That's just great. I'm not making it easy. Poor Richard."

He stood up and went to the window and stared out, his back to her. After a minute he returned to the chair and spoke slowly, as if he were talking to a child. One that wasn't too bright. "The lease on this place is up June 1st. That's in ten days, did you know that?"

"Of course," she said, casually.

Fuck. The lease. She'd forgotten about the damn thing. Completely spaced it out. She'd been doing well just to get out of bed in the morning, let alone know what day it was.

"I don't want to pay for an apartment I'm not living in."

"The lease is in both our names."

"You're the one who told me to get out, if you remember," he reminded her.

"Oh, now let's see if I get this," she said with fake cheer. "According to you, I was supposed to live with you here while you spent any night you wanted with that bitch."

"Jesus! Isn't there any way I can talk to you about this?"

Cass picked at the cuticle of her left finger. "Just tell me what you want," she said quietly. She watched as he swallowed, and then stared out the window again, then back to her. Then, not quite looking at her, he said, "the apartment is close to the hospital. I want to keep it."

So that was it. Of course, it was. It had originally been her apartment, he was the one who had moved in with her and now he wanted it. Because it was convenient for him. Just the way she'd been.

"And what about what's-her-name?" she asked, icily. "She'll move in here, too, I suppose. Although there's the husband. I almost forgot. What will happen to the husband?"

"Linda and her husband are separating."

"How convenient for you."

"I'm living by myself, I'm not jumping into anything. I'm not making that mistake again."

"So I'll be filed away as one of the few mistakes in your otherwise perfect life."

"I fell in love with you, Cass, and you damn well know

it, but we rushed into it and that wasn't very smart."
Richard sat back in the chair.

"How do I know you didn't just want my apartment
back then? A place to get laid close to the hospital."

"Oh Cass—"

"I'm serious, Richard."

"Who wouldn't fall in love with you? You're a great
person. You were just back from Thailand, you were interesting, beautiful, that's a given. And you liked adventure,
it didn't seem that you'd make demands and that appealed
to me with all the demands of residency."

"So what happened?"

"The pressure to get married, I guess."

"I never said a goddamn word!"

"You didn't have to. It was there, in the air. All the
time. And I started to feel, well, you know—" he paused.
"I felt trapped."

She wanted to throw something at him. And she still
wanted him. What she did not want was to cry, but the
tears came anyway.

"Cass—" he went to the couch and sat next to her, slipping his arm around her.

She sat up stiffly. "Don't."

"I'm sorry, I feel really guilty." He laid his head back
against the couch, closing his eyes.

"Good. If you didn't, I'd think you were a sociopath."
Cass stood up and walked to the door. "I'll think about the
lease. I need some time to think things through, and I'll let
you know." She held the door open for him. "I've got to
get ready for dinner. I'm going out."

After he left, she stood back from the window, watching
him walk to his car, wondering what would have happened

if she'd stayed next to him on the couch—feeling proud that she hadn't and wishing she had.

It was a relief to be having dinner with Lena and Val. When Cass had the energy to do anything in the evenings, it was usually with them. She didn't want anyone at work to know what was going on, or her parents, and it helped her to be with Lena and Val—she didn't have to try to hide how she felt. And they totally got it.

"What nerve," Lena said, "wanting your apartment."

"It really sucks," Val added.

They had arrived at the Taj Mahal about the same time and after they ordered drinks, and her wine came, she told them the whole sorry saga of Richard's little visit. "But I did forget about the damn lease. So I do have to decide. I just don't know what the hell to do."

"The main thing you have to decide is if you'd be happy living alone staying in that apartment," Lena said.

"Or if you want to make a fresh start somewhere else," Val added.

They looked at the menu and Cass let them figure it out and order for everyone. She needed other people to take charge; her mind was such a mess. She closed the menu. "I just don't feel like I'm ready to make a decision. Not just about where I want to live, but what I want to do. Maybe I'll travel again. I just don't know."

"Why don't you live at your folks' until you know what you're doing," Lena suggested. "They have a lot of room."

"It seems like such a step backwards."

"It would just be temporary," Lena said, "people do it all the time."

Cass wondered how much Lena and Val could understand. A lot of her gay friends often seemed to stay in touch with old lovers and no one appeared to mind, as though doors were never completely shut. Maybe they couldn't entirely relate to her worry that if she left the apartment, it could put nails in the coffin of her life with him. Not that she wanted him back right now. Not at all. But would it kill any outside chance they could ever get through this?

Cass finished her wine and flagged the waiter for another. "I'll just have to think about it, I guess—maybe things will sort themselves out when a little more time goes by."

12

ANNIE

I had to wait only a few minutes before Delores James showed me in. She was an attractive African American woman, maybe in her mid-forties, and her small office had a quiet elegance about it: white walls, a teak desk, Persian rugs, warm, saddle-brown leather chairs. A Jacob Lawrence painting hung over her desk, and it looked like it wasn't a print. How had my mother had found her way here? It was the first thing I asked.

"Your mother was referred by Rose Tibonga," she explained. "Rose and I attend the same church and estate law is actually my specialty. My middle initial "H" stands for "Heavenly," she laughed, "so it was all predetermined that I go into this part of the law." She offered me a seat across from her desk. "And please, call me Dee."

Rose was involved in this? Was she trying to get money? The suspicion stabbed me like a poison dart, but I immediately remembered that the only beneficiaries were family and I felt ashamed. Rose had been wonderful to my mother.

"When did my mother first come to see you?" I asked.

Dee opened a file folder on her desk. "It was the first week in March...March 3rd."

The time when she decided to forgo any more treatment. As long as I could remember, my mother gave in to him...even in the smallest things. I looked around the office, wondering what it took for her to do this.

"Mrs. Gunther's earlier will which had been drawn up by Mr. Dennison left her half of the estate to your father, and her concern was that he would bequeath most of his art to various museums and that their heirs would never benefit from the major value of the estate."

I nodded. No surprise that Mom didn't trust him, only that she did something about it.

"So this new will left her half of the estate to her heirs when she died?" I asked.

"That's right, and as Personal Representative your job would be to have the estate evaluated, determine which assets constitute her half and then make arrangements to distribute them, or the proceeds from them, to her heirs."

"Oh my, God." I was appalled, and couldn't hide it. "This sounds like a nightmare."

"I did advise your mother," Dee continued, "that there could be a problem naming you as Personal Representative because in this state, the surviving spouse has the automatic right to serve as Personal Representative to manage the community property in the estate. Even if the will names someone other than the surviving spouse, which means your father has the legal right to challenge and supersede you. But he can't change the will itself, he can't challenge the beneficiaries. The only way he can do that is by contesting the will and claiming it was procured by undue influence on your mother by some other person."

"You mean he'd have to prove someone forced her to make the new will?" I asked.

"That's right, it means he'd have to prove the will was the result of somebody else's intentions and not your mother's. 'Undue influence' is very hard to prove—and in this case, with absolutely no basis for it, it would be next to impossible."

"But even knowing he could take over the Personal Representative job she wanted to name me anyway?"

"She knew Mr. Gunther couldn't change the will, as I said, her half of their joint estate will go to you and the other family members she named, but she knew you might not be allowed to be the Personal Representative to execute it. She clearly understood her wish to involve you might not stand."

"But she did it anyway—" I was struggling to understand.

Dee learned forward over her desk. "I can only speculate about someone's motives, but I had the feeling she wanted to make a statement, even though she understood your father would most likely change it."

Tears stung my eyes. I felt a flash of anger at being used by my mother, at her not telling me. And I couldn't even talk to her. She was gone and I was overwhelmed again by the loss.

In the days since she died, it occurred to me that grief was comparable in its intensity to the joy when Cass and Ian were born, but it was the other side of the coin. Grief too, had labor pains, a reverse of the great effort to bring forth life when the pains got closer and more intense. This labor of grief had waves of sorrow that became farther apart and softened in their intensity. But this present wave wasn't for my own loss, it was for my mother, the fact that the only way she could tell him what she really thought of him was from the grave.

I took a tissue from my purse. "Look, it's fine with me if he wants to be the Personal Representative. I don't want any part of it. Frankly, I'd like as little as possible to do with my father."

"Then I suggest we draw up a statement that says you concur in his being the Personal Representative, and I'll work with his lawyer, Bob Dennison, to find a way to carry out your mother's wishes, which will also allow your father to decide how to divide the assets."

"Anything that avoids dealing with him would be best for me, and I'm sure my brother would agree, and our kids as well."

"The court may want to appoint an independent curator as executor for the art, and there are tax considerations with precedents in the case of the sculptor David Smith's estate and Georgia O'Keeffe's—these things can get complicated, but we'll cross that bridge when we come to it."

She explained her fees and her billing and I was only too glad to have Delores Heavenly James on my team. If my father continued to hound me about any of this, I could just tell him to talk to my lawyer or his, that they were working it out. The last thing I wanted was some legal hassle. I was eager to put this terrible situation behind me, and I called him as soon as I got home.

"Gunther residence," Rose answered.

"Rose, it's Annie. I'd like to talk to my father, is he there?"

"He's in studio. I get him."

"Oh, wait—do you have a second? I want to ask about Dee James, I met her today."

"She's good person. I know her long time, from church. Your mother asked did I like lawyer I had in my divorce. She was so sick and divorce takes a long time, I was surprised, but she said she wanted lawyer for her will. To put you in charge, Annie."

"Did she ever talk about details, how she wanted things changed?" I asked.

"No, only that she wanted children and grandchildren taken care of. She didn't say anything about Mr. Gunther, but she not have to. Your mother know I understand."

"You know you were the only person I ever heard her call imooto-chan."

"Little sister," Rose said, quietly. "I felt same."

"Thank you, Rose."

I thought about my mother as I waited for my father to come to the phone. It gave me some satisfaction and some pride in my mother to think she had come to this on her own. The fact that Rose had left a marriage, had stood up to a man, perhaps had influenced her. Maybe Rose led by example, but Mom took the step herself and I wanted to hold her hand, just put my arms around her.

"Annie." My father's gravelly deep voice. "Did you see the lawyer?"

"Yes, and I'll be signing papers which relinquish my role as Personal Representative. And you'll be appointed."

"I want you to sign this right away, is that clear?"

"I'll sign it whenever she tells me they're ready."

"Your mother was out of her mind, you know, doing something behind my back, like this. And frankly, I still can't believe you didn't put her up to it."

Screw you, Dad.

"Annie? Are you there?" he snarled.

"Look, if you have any questions, talk to your lawyer; Mom's lawyer is going to work with him on figuring this out."

"Fine," he said coldly, "this better be the end of this damn nonsense." Then he hung up.

After I got off the phone with my father, Jack called to say he'd be home in about an hour. Dr. Phriep had contacted him again. He often stayed late at the lab, and when he was home, he was usually faxing and emailing Cambodia. He was so engaged and happy that I'd stopped worrying about him. But I hadn't stopped worrying about Cass. We'd gone back to trading messages and the distance between us bothered me. I knew if I weren't painting and going to Fred's studio, I'd probably be barging in on her again. But art was consuming me. I was in another world. I savored each moment of solitude in my studio; it was a quiet joy. And now that we were farther into spring, the evenings stayed lighter as the days lengthened and the studio stayed bright, bathed in light reflecting off the white walls. I could work longer.

The first few paintings I'd finished hadn't gone that well. At least, I didn't think so. They were muddy and over-worked, and there was one that could have been a still life of one of Sam's mud pies. It was a good thing Fred had recommended I start with canvas paper, so I wouldn't have any qualms about using the painting to wrap the garbage or line the cage of Sam's pet hamster. My description. Not Fred's. What he'd actually said was, "It's better not to invest in a lot of canvases at first, in case you decide to try something else." He was too kind to say that I might want to throw my early efforts in the trash, but I understood what he meant and the canvas paper had a liberating effect. I'd increasingly become less tentative and cautious and it was getting easier to take risks. Fred seemed to be right about everything, or at least at prescribing exactly what I needed.

I kept trying to get the meadow right, and after quite a few false starts, the underpainting I had finished when I was on the island this week seemed to work. It was dry, and as I mixed the first layer of oil I felt a growing confidence. I mixed the color with a medium that he'd recommended: one-third turpenoid, one-third linseed oil, and one-third Liquin, and felt my hand sure and strong, as if Fred had placed his hand on top of mine and was guiding it.

When I began to paint, it was as if I entered what I could only describe as some new plane of consciousness. The zone I had heard people talk about. An hour went by like a minute; I felt almost disconnected from myself physically, detached from hunger or even thirst, lost in the mystery of the color, the emotions it evoked, and the luminous impasto taking shape before me. I had used deep violet for the underpainting of the meadow itself and was now applying large planes of apple green and a color bordering on chartreuse. Using my palette knife, texturing and pulling, I tried to give the impression of the movement of long windswept grass. I had a small radio in my studio set to 98.1, the classical station, and Handel's Water Music was playing.

There couldn't be a better piece to paint by, I thought, standing back carefully scrutinizing the meadow, thinking of my trips across the water to the island. I decided to deepen the next plane toward the trees and mixed an emerald green which, as I spread it over the deep violet underpainting, seemed to take on an almost surreal glow.

"Annie? I'm home." Jack knocked at the studio door,

then opened it a crack and stuck his head in. "It's almost seven-thirty."

"Hi." I continued to apply the color, not taking my eyes off the easel.

"Aren't we going to eat?"

"Why don't you fix something for yourself." I looked up from the painting. "I'm really into this now."

"Aren't you hungry?" he asked.

"No. I had a salad." I looked back at the painting, studying the layer I had just put on the foreground, and added a little cadmium red on one edge to exaggerate the depth even more.

Jack came in the room a few feet and stood between the door and the easel, watching me. "It looks good."

"It's just the beginning, but thank you."

"Couldn't you just take a break?"

I squeezed my eyes shut, telling myself to relax, trying not to be exasperated, then turned away from the easel to face him. "I really don't want a break. Why don't you just fix something for yourself, like you did before?" I tried to be kind. He really had been trying to get used to my not cooking every night, and hadn't complained that much. He was getting to be a regular at the QFC deli.

"I don't want another sandwich. What do we have?"

"Just go and look. There's pasta, soup, stuff for salad. We have a lot of small jars of marinated artichoke hearts—I'd love to get them used up so I can have the jars to mix in."

"I don't like marinated artichokes that much."

"Fine. Eat peanut butter. Whatever. We have tuna fish, make a different sandwich—just figure it out," I said, unable to stop the edge to my voice.

"Fine." He turned and left the studio, punctuating his exit by solidly closing the door, a few decibels below a slam.

I rolled my eyes, and then went back to my painting. While the layer on the foreground dried, I decided to work next on the sky. As I mixed color for it, I tried to remember what Fred taught me about not over-blending the paint, which would lead to flat color, but to touch the colors into one another, letting the brush stroke reveal the mixture on the canvas. To add vitality to the color I limited the chromatic intensity, so that the upper half of the canvas now had a shimmering, glazed effect.

I was mixing paint for a layer of the sky closer to the trees at the edge of the meadow, when I heard a loud crash from the kitchen. Then swearing. Then the clang of what sounded like pots and pans banging.

I listened for a minute before adding more color to the medium and began mixing again. Then another crash, louder than the first.

Oh, for God's sake. I put down the palette knife, yanked open the studio door and tore down the steps to the kitchen.

"What in the world are you doing down here?" I stood glaring at him, with my hands on my hips.

The kitchen counters were covered with almost every pan, skillet, and pot we owned. A mysterious brownish goo was slopped over the stove and dripped on the floor where pieces of vegetables had fallen from the cutting board.

"I'm cooking!"

"What's all the banging? It sounds like a steel drum band."

"I'm creating something," Jack bellowed.

"You're creating noise!"

"You're the one that told me to make my own dinner," Jack said, accusingly.

"Goddammit, Jack. I have worried about feeding someone other than myself for more than half my life. I would like for once, just once, not to worry about what's going in anyone's stomach but my own!"

"So, don't worry about my stomach. I'll worry about it. I'm making soup, a big pot of it and if you ever get hungry, I'll let you have some," he said with a slightly sheepish, half smile.

"Oh, Jack."

"So, go back to your painting. Go away. Don't bother me while I'm cooking."

I sighed and left the kitchen. He was trying. He really was trying; I had to give him credit. After all, he was of the generation that never saw a father cook except perhaps once a year on Mother's Day, making pancakes or something. I wondered if he might actually like cooking. What a bonus that would be.

In my studio I studied the painting, wondering if I could try to put another layer on the sky, but immediately chided myself on my impatience. The last thing I wanted to do was rush it and make another muddy mess. "The Big Muddy, Annie Duppstadt." I could just see the card. Fred was insistent that everyone have a piece for his students' show. It would be held on the island at the Blue Heron Art Gallery and I was already worrying about it. "It will be triumph enough to put something up," he'd said emphatically. And then added, as if to reassure us, "nothing's for sale, there'll be NFS signs on every piece. We're not introducing the commerce of the marketplace only to end up distorting what truly matters, which is making art."

I reminded myself that: (a) the show wasn't juried and (b) no one who came could buy anything even if they wanted to and (c) it should just be for the experience. But my systematic attempt to relieve my anxiety was something of a flop and I remained apprehensive, just hoping this meadow painting could be good enough, or at least not a total embarrassment. Fred wasn't kidding when he said he wanted to break through the fear barrier by exhibiting our work as soon as possible. The show was in three weeks.

I wanted to work next on the trees while the first layer on the sky dried, but wasn't sure of the color and decided to mix some acrylic washes on a separate sheet of canvas paper to see what might develop. I was beginning to experiment with viridian when I heard the phone ring. It stopped after a couple of rings. Good. Jack must have picked up. After a few minutes I heard his footsteps on the stairs.

"Annie," Jack opened the door. "It's Cass on the phone, she wants to talk to you."

I put my brush down

"She doesn't sound good," he said, quietly.

For weeks I'd done my best to ignore a feeling of foreboding about Cass, fighting the urge to go to her apartment or stop in again at her work. I went to the bedroom and I picked up the phone.

"Mom?" Cass's voice cracked.

"Honey? What is it?" I could hear Cass quietly crying. "Cass? What is it?" I sat on the edge of the bed. "What's wrong?"

"Mom...I wondered...." She hesitated, like she was trying to compose herself.

I immediately stood up. "Why don't I come over?"

"No," Cass laughed a little through her tears, "I wanted to ask if I could come there."

"Of course! You can come over anytime, you know that."

"To stay awhile, Mom." She paused for a minute before the words spilled out. "Richard and I have split up."

"Oh, honey. Oh, Cass, I'm so sorry." I sat back down on the edge of the bed. Finally, there it was. The confirmation of something I'd known for a long time, or at least had been pretty sure was coming.

"So am I."

"Did it just happen?" I asked, knowing the answer.

"No. It's been a few weeks, but I haven't been ready to talk about it."

I rubbed my eyes and pinched the bridge of my nose. "So that's why you'd been avoiding us."

"I guess so," Cass admitted, "but anyway, the lease is up on the apartment and I need to figure out what's next and where I want to live and everything and well, I just wondered if I could stay with you and Dad...just while I sort things out."

"Oh, honey, of course," I said, automatically. "Come home."

I remained on the bed after we hung up, sitting and staring out the window at the back yard. The coral azalea Mom loved was starting to bloom, and as much as I missed my mother I was glad she wasn't around to see these kids break up. Mom had such hopes for Cass and Richard. I was sure it was Richard who wanted out, I knew it had to be, and I absolutely hated the thought of him hurting Cass. The only saving grace was that at least they didn't have children. I supposed that was something.

Jack was huddled over the sink, finishing cleaning up the mess of his maiden culinary voyage, when I came in the kitchen. He looked up and shut off the water. "What's happened?"

"She and Richard are splitting up." I sat at the kitchen table, slumping in the chair. "She wants to stay with us for a while." Absently, I picked at a spot of some unknown sticky substance that he'd missed when he wiped the table.

"She's moving out? Why does she have to be the one to leave?"

"I don't know, Jack. Something about the lease. She was crying—"

"Well, what did you tell her?" He tossed the dishrag in the sink and sat across from me.

"Of course, I told her she could come home."

Jack nodded. We were both quiet. We could hear the ticking of the kitchen clock and a dog barking somewhere down the block. I started in again, picking at the goo that was still stuck to the table.

"You know I never liked him that much," Jack said, after a few moments.

"Well don't say that to Cass." I continued to pick at the goo on the table. "What is this anyway?"

"Never mind. I'll take care of it." Jack went to the sink and came back with the dishrag.

"I think you need something to scrape it with."

Ignoring me, he scrubbed the table with the dishrag. "When is she coming?"

"Tomorrow after she gets off work. Can you help me move her bed back?"

He stopped scrubbing the table. "Annie, why do you have to give up your studio?"

"We have three bedrooms—"

"I noticed that last time I looked."

"You don't have to be sarcastic. This isn't easy."

"Sorry."

"All I'm saying is there's our bedroom, your office is Ian's old room, and Cass's room is the studio. So I move the studio."

"Why can't she just sleep on the couch in the living room?"

"She needs our support and I don't want her to feel like she's crashing in some flop house, that's why."

"Our home is beautiful. It's hardly a flop house."

"I want her to feel comfortable. Besides, she'll have her clothes and everything. It's better she has her old room to spread out in."

"Did she say how long she'd be here?"

"Jack, for God's sake, she's hurting! I don't think coming home was exactly her first choice."

"I suppose you're right." Jack scrubbed a few more minutes, then went to the sink and ran the water, rinsing out the dishrag. "Let's move the bed back and get this over with."

"I need to get that plywood I use for a work space down to the basement and my easel and paints out of there first."

Jack followed me upstairs, and flipped on the overhead light, which reflected off the freshly painted white walls of the studio. He looked around the room for a minute. "It's a shame you have to leave this."

"It won't be forever." I picked up one end of the

plywood. "Come on," I said, sharply. "Help me carry this. I can go back later for my easel and paints."

"Don't bark."

"I'm not barking! I just want to get this over with."

"Fine." He picked up the other end of the plywood. "I'll go down the steps first."

Our basement has windows and is considered a daylight basement, but the boxes blocked most of the natural light, which left the laundry room as the only possible space for me to set up my easel. The laundry room's concrete walls, once painted a sunny yellow, had faded to the color of dog pee. The linoleum tile covering the concrete floor had also seen better days. Originally white with multi-colored speckles, it had aged to a flecked gray, strikingly similar to the color of laundry lint. Lighting the small room was a square, frosted Home Depot fixture in the center of the acoustical tiled ceiling which, like the floor below, was now more gray than white.

We put the plywood slab next to the furnace, and together we carried the bed frame, mattress, and box springs upstairs to Cass's old room. The bed frame didn't take long. But carrying the mattress and then the box springs up two flights of stairs was slow going. There were frequent stops. I would check to see if Jack's knee was all right, which increasingly annoyed him. And much puffing, a lot of puffing. After we set up the bed, Jack returned to the basement for the box of drapes, which we hung together. When the drapes were up, I brought bedding from the linen closet to make up the bed.

"Annie, I saw your point about not having her sleep on the couch, but I really don't see why you have to make the

bed. Just leave the sheets for her, Cass can do it herself."
Jack pushed the bed against the wall. "She's not a guest."

"If she had a broken leg you wouldn't say that."

"That she's not a guest?" Jack rubbed his knee.

"No, that she should do it herself."

"She doesn't have a broken leg."

"I know. I'm just saying that when someone has an
injury you can see, like a broken leg, everyone is very sympathetic and helpful. But not if it's a broken heart. Then
you're supposed to just soldier on, when actually it can be
a hell of a lot worse. I want her to come home and have
the bed made and not have to do it herself, okay? Besides,
I don't know how else to help her when she won't talk to
us. Look, just give me a hand with the bottom sheet, I can
do the rest myself."

"Okay. I don't want to argue, but what did she say
exactly? Do you have any idea why they're splitting up?"

"No. But I'm sure she'll tell us when she's ready."

"I still think they should have gotten married." Jack
lifted the corner of the mattress. "Look at all the time she
wasted."

"Don't you dare say that to her," I warned, as I pulled
the fitted sheet over the corner.

"I won't. I'm not an insensitive blockhead, Annie. I
may not switch gears as easy as you do about the kids. But
I certainly feel bad that things aren't working out for her."

He set the corner of the mattress down. "You know
what I heard Andy Rooney say once?"

"What?" I looked up at him.

Jack tried not to smile, but the corners of his mouth
twitched, something which always gives him away when
he's setting me up for something he thinks is funny.

"He said a lot of women today don't want to get married because they don't want to buy the whole pig just to get a little sausage."

I laughed and put my arms around him. "We'll get through it, won't we?"

"We always seem to," he said, kissing me on the top of my head. "Let me know if you need anything else."

"I will."

In the laundry room, I unfolded my easel and set it up next to the aging washer and dryer. Then I went back to the furnace room where I'd set the cedar case and I brought it in, putting it on the shelf over the washer between a box of detergent and a bottle of bleach. I brought the meadow painting down last and propped it on the easel next to the washer and dryer. The overhead light was weak and the painting was dark and poorly lit.

I sat on the clothes hamper across from the painting, folded my arms across my knees, put my head down and just wept. I thought about my father's studio, the entire carriage house, the space my mother so valiantly guarded for him.

I didn't hear Jack come in.

"Oh honey." He put his arms around me. "Come to bed."

"I'm beginning to think this whole thing is futile," I wiped my eyes with the back of my hand.

"Come on, let's go up and get some sleep." He took my hand.

"There is a glass ceiling for women, Jack," I stared at my painting in the dim light next to the washer and dryer. "And it's made out of the people we love."

13

CASS

"Oh Cass, why didn't you tell us sooner?" Annie's eyes filled with tears. Cass knew she didn't look like she'd just spent a week at a health spa, but she didn't anticipate her parents' shock as she struggled through the door, holding a large garbage bag stuffed with clothes still on hangers. She set it down in the middle of the kitchen floor as Annie wrapped her arms around her, and years of her adult life fell away.

"I couldn't."

Daisy whimpered and rubbed against Cass's legs and she knelt down and put her damp cheek against the top of the dog's head. "Good old girl. Don't worry, I'm okay."

Jack was standing behind Annie, and when her father hugged her, she watched herself for a moment crying in her father's arms like a small child and she pulled away, terrified she'd get stuck in their love.

"Okay guys," Cass picked up the garbage bag. "Now that we've got that out of the way, I'll take this crap upstairs."

"We've got your room cleared out," Annie said, "but let me know if you need anything."

162

"You took all your art stuff out?"

"It'll hardly stop me," Annie said, a little too brightly, "Margaret Mead said there's no force more creative than a post-menopausal woman with zest."

"I didn't know Margaret Mead made a soap commercial," Jack said, earnestly.

"Huh?" Cass looked at her father.

"Zest! Get it?" He grinned.

Cass looked at her mother and rolled her eyes. "Now I know I'm home."

Her old room seemed both familiar and strange. It was bare except for the bed, and the newly painted white walls gave the space a modern minimalist feel, like a slick art gallery before any art was installed. The drapes and bedding were the same, but the room had a faint smell Cass couldn't quite identify at first, it wasn't all that strong, and after a minute she realized it was turpentine.

She was putting her things away in the bathroom when Annie came up. "Just thought I'd see if you needed any help."

"Thanks, Mom, but I've got everything put away."

Annie followed Cass into her room and looked around. "You didn't bring much."

"I'm not planning to stay long."

"Remember your father's favorite W.C. Fields' line, the one about taking the bull by the tail and facing what's there?" Annie sat on the bed.

Cass didn't say anything. She knew what was coming and she wanted to avoid it, although she supposed she probably ought to give her mother a clue about what was going on. About the whole sorry mess.

"Cass, I have to ask. What happened with Richard?"

"I guess you've gathered it's not my favorite subject." She sat down next to her mother. "Okay." Cass took a deep breath, not having the energy to put her off. "You might as well know my whole little drama," she cupped her hand, examining her nails. "It's not very original because it seems he wasn't on call all those times. He had—or I should say is having, an affair. With a woman in his program."

"Another resident?"

Cass nodded. "And she's married, but I guess now she's separated from her husband."

"Men are dogs," Annie said, disgustedly.

"How can that be an insult? You love dogs."

"I think it's an accurate description. Like dogs, men can be loyal, affectionate, playful, territorial, protective—which are fine qualities. But when it comes to sex they're also quite similar. They'll mate with anyone in heat."

"You think Dad's like that, too?"

"He's best of breed. Or best in show, but I think he's as capable of—"

"Mounting some bitch," Cass laughed.

"Exactly. As capable of that as any other male under the right circumstances." Annie sighed. "All I know is I just wouldn't want to hear about it."

"You wouldn't?" Cass was surprised.

"No. I learned a long time ago that I couldn't control anyone's behavior. Just my own—and why find out something that's going to make me feel bad? You see, I think most men are basically loyal but I also think they wouldn't mind straying a bit as long as they can hold on to their family. That's if things are going reasonably well at home. Deep down, I think they all want it both ways."

"I wonder if I could ever be that philosophical. Or at

least not have so many thoughts of killing him—oh, God," she shook her head. "I really, really, hate sounding bitter."

"Why wouldn't you want to kill him? Want an accomplice?" Annie smiled. "But listen, Cass—you'll get through this. I know you will. But you've got to take care of yourself." She put her arm around Cass. "Dad and I are worried, it looks like you've lost a lot of weight."

"I know. My clothes have all started to hang on me. I have this new diet. Peanut butter, M&M's, and red wine."

"You've got to eat, honey. It's so important. Are you sleeping?"

"On weekends I can hardly get out of bed, I just sleep all the time. Then at night I wake up every few hours starting around three A.M. But it's getting better, Lena gave me a prescription for some sleeping pills."

Annie seemed nervous as she stood up. "I'm going to go start dinner." She paused by the door. "And you've got to eat a little—even if you have to force yourself."

When Cass came downstairs she saw that her mother had made one of her favorite dinners, fettuccine with green beans, walnuts and feta cheese. It was from a *Sunset* magazine recipe Annie first made when Cass was in high school. Cass had made it for Richard a few times and he really liked it. She winced at the thought; she'd assumed that once she was out of the apartment, she wouldn't be finding so much to remind her of him.

"Can I help?" Cass asked.

"No, just sit down, honey." Her father pulled out a chair for her. "Mom's got everything ready."

Cass helped herself to the fettuccine. "You remembered how much I loved this—thanks." They were being so polite, trying so hard—it made her feel weird.

"I hope it'll help your appetite." Annie joined them at the table. "I tried to remember what kind of cereal you liked when I went to the store. Didn't you used to love Frosted Flakes? Anyway, I got some, and if you don't— I know Sam likes it. I hope Kelly can bring Sam over. Although they're leaving for Hawaii at the end of the week. Maybe when they get back. Oh, and in case you don't like Frosted Flakes, I got some currant scones and some bagels and there's a half-gallon of fresh orange juice, the pulpy kind. The kind you like. And for lunch there's greens for a salad, some red grapes, and little cherry tomatoes and I got some sliced smoked turkey, roast beef, cheddar cheese and havarti from the deli counter."

Annie babbled on about the food while Cass picked at the fettuccine. They were working hard to engage her (asking about her work, her friends, her softball team, restaurants, movies, sports, music, theatre, politics, and even the weather) all the while carefully avoiding any mention of Richard. These cheery attempts seemed more awkward and desperate the harder they tried, and Cass couldn't manage answering with more than a yes, no, maybe, or I guess so, as if she were some sullen teenager. She couldn't help it—shutting down was the only way she could keep from crying.

Cass pushed her plate away; she'd only eaten about a fourth of the fettuccine and Annie looked hurt.

"I'm sorry. This is the best I can do." Cass mumbled "thanks" and started to clear the table, but her parents wouldn't let her help and she retreated to her room—her old room—hoping to God it wasn't to her old life.

14

ANNIE

"She looks awful," I whispered, after Cass had gone upstairs. When I hugged her, Cass's body was so thin it reminded me of my mother's toward the end. She was pale and gaunt and her eyes were inconsolable wells of pain. They were bloodshot and puffy, with blue circles underneath so dark they looked bruised. Even her hair, usually shiny and thick, seemed thinner and lifeless.

"How much weight do you think she's lost?" Jack went to the refrigerator and put the leftover fettuccine away. "We've got to get food in her." He closed the refrigerator and helped me clear off the dishes. "Did she tell you what happened?"

"He's having an affair with some woman in his program, another doctor. The woman is married, but Cass says she's separated now."

"Cass is fantastic! Didn't he know how lucky he was to have her?" Jack sat down at the table, as if he'd received a physical blow. He stared out the window, then sat back, folding his arms over his chest. "I never knew what she saw in that dick anyway."

"His name is Richard." I began rinsing the dishes.

"He's Dick to me, a complete dick."

"Jack, please don't talk that way around her."

"I won't, you don't have to tell me that." He got up from the table and began loading the dishwasher. "She hardly ate a thing. Only drank."

"She'll get better." I turned off the water. "This is just her first night."

"And she hardly talked—'yes, no, maybe'...what kind of a conversation is that? And we didn't dare mention him. He was the big Dick in the middle of the room." Jack reached under the sink for the soap. "And why didn't he get *his* sorry ass out of the apartment, I'd like to know."

"Jack, she just got here! She's running on empty." I put my hand on his arm. "I think getting some good sleep will help and her appetite will come back." I lowered my voice. "She told me Lena prescribed some sleeping pills and—"

"Is that a good idea?" Jack interrupted.

"Shhhh."

"She's upstairs, she can't hear us."

I whispered anyway. "It might help, although I admit I am worried about her having a bunch of pills. When she told me, I immediately thought of Kathy Sato's daughter. The one who tried to kill herself because some guy broke up with her. Although Cass isn't like that girl. I think the Sato girl was always kind of unstable, she was the one in the scout troop who ate all the cookies instead of selling them."

Jack put the soap in the dishwasher and turned it on. "I wouldn't want to sell cookies either, why is that strange?"

"Fifteen boxes, Jack. The Sato girl ate fifteen boxes."

"Cass didn't do stuff like that."

"I know, I'm not saying she did. But if she's still this depressed by the end of next week, we've got to get her to see somebody." I wet a sponge and wiped down the counters. "There's a wonderful psychiatrist who comes to Woodside once a week, a young woman. I think Cass might like her."

"Well, I'm going to watch the news." He turned and left the kitchen; our conversation was over, it was too much for him. I went upstairs to read in bed. At the top of the stairs, I hesitated in the hall outside the door to Cass's room. There was no light from under the door and it was quiet. I was tempted to go in and cover her up, touch her cheek, see if she was breathing.

We saw her only briefly, the next morning. Jack and I were coming downstairs as she was leaving for work; she had a bagel and I saw a glass in the sink, so it looked like she'd had some juice.

"Did you have a good sleep?" I asked.

"I did, thanks, Mom. I've got to run."

"Are you sure you don't want any coffee? It'll just take me a minute."

"I get it at work, thanks. See you later."

And she was off. She reminded me of the Energizer bunny with a faulty battery wearing down, but I did think she looked better. I put coffee on and Jack went out for the paper. Through the kitchen window I saw him wave as her Prius left the drive.

"I thought she looked better this morning? Didn't you?" Jack came in with the paper and took out the sports page.

"I did. Cass is pretty resilient, and she's also young— people bounce back faster at her age." I poured us each a cup of coffee and joined him at the table. "What are you up to today?"

"I'm expecting a fax from Dr. Phriep. I got an email from him and he said there'd be a fax today." Jack smiled, he seemed almost secretive. "I'll pick it up when I go to the lab."

After I finished breakfast, I brought my easel and my paints up from the basement and carried them out to the car, then came back in to make my lunch.

"Are you really going to try to go over there every day?" Jack closed the paper.

"Fred opens the studio at eleven, if I take the 10:20 boat I can get to his place a little after eleven and if I leave by two forty-five, I can get the 3:25 boat and be home to start dinner." I went to the refrigerator and got some roast beef and cheddar cheese to make a sandwich for my lunch. "When I count the time setting up and then cleaning up, with some time to eat lunch, I figure I'll have two hours of actual painting time. It's worth it to me. It's better than nothing."

"I just don't see why you can't paint here."

"The light's terrible!" I snapped.

"I didn't mean the basement. Why not bring your stuff up here and then take it back at dinner."

"It's too disruptive. Back and forth, and in and out of the basement. Besides, I feel like I need to be around Fred and Martha Jane to stay focused. If I stay here, I'll just start worrying about Cass."

Martha Jane was carefully working on the underpainting for her deer. "Did you have a nice weekend?" she asked.

"It was okay, I guess." I gave her a weak smile, set up my easel and went back to the car.

It was tempting to dump all my family stuff on this dear soul, just spill the whole story: Richard's affair, Cass coming home, giving up my studio, Jack trying to figure out the next chapter of his life, the hassle with my father and my mother's will—although that finally seemed off the table since I gave up that Personal Representative business, thank goodness. But as close as I felt to Martha Jane, I hardly wanted to be a burden, talking her ear off and keeping her from her work—or for that matter, avoiding my own.

I came back with my paints. Martha Jane and I shared a long rectangular table, a little narrower than a library table. Fred had found it at Granny's Attic, the island's thrift shop. I set out tubes of viridian, titanium white, ivory black, yellow ochre and cobalt blue, then frantically pawed through my case.

"Oh no...." I took out every tube, then all the brushes and palette knives.

"What's wrong?" Martha Jane peered over her glasses from across table.

"I don't have any medium. I poured some linseed oil, turpenoid and Linquin into three small jars and I guess I got distracted and forgot to put them in my case." I looked through my case again, but the jars weren't there. "Besides, the light was terrible in the basement."

"I thought you had your own studio, a beautiful sunny room. You talked glowingly about it, I'm sure you did." Martha Jane hesitated, "Although perhaps I've gotten it all mixed up. That's always a possibility."

"You didn't get it mixed up. I did have a studio at

home, and I still do," I said, as looked in my case again, just to make sure. "We needed to use the space for something else, but I'll get it back," I said with conviction...then muttered under my breath, "at least I hope so."

"Use my medium. I have lots of jars, too. I save Wax Orchards jelly jars. Wax Orchards was on the island you know." Martha Jane pushed her box across the table. "Help yourself."

"Thank you. You're sure you don't mind?"

"Of course not." She turned back to her painting, dabbed her brush in the paint on her palette and began outlining the legs of the smaller deer, then suddenly put the brush down. "What's wrong, Annie? You're not yourself this morning."

That's all it took. In spite of my earlier intention not to burden her, the caring Martha Jane conveyed was irresistible. Within minutes, leaning against the table we shared, it all tumbled out: a landslide of frustration at having to put my needs on the back burner. It felt like the story of my life—of most women I knew, for that matter.

"...and besides Cass moving back home, Jack's having a hard time with retirement. He'd been pretty depressed until he got involved with helping this Cambodian researcher. It seems to have distracted him for the moment, but I worry that he can't face his career winding down. And there are times I know he resents my involvement here."

Martha Jane moved her box of paints to one side and folded her arms, resting them on the table. "You know, Annie, a lot of couples fight like the dickens when they retire. I remember more than a few women whose husbands made them a little cuckoo. When a woman is used to having the house to herself, and suddenly there's a man there all the time, she can feel invaded." She leaned on her elbows, closer to me. "And a lot of the men get upset not having their work, it's as if they don't know who they are."

"What about women with careers? Do you think we have a hard time when we retire? The ones who always worked outside the home?" I kept my voice down, not wanting to disturb Fred, who was working at the other end of the studio. I had to smile. Martha Jane and I could be two neighbor ladies chatting over the table as if it were the back fence.

"Women are more adaptable. We always have been, as a rule. There are exceptions of course. But women make wonderful friendships, and that always helps them adjust."

"I don't want to give the wrong impression, Martha Jane," I was quick to add. "I'm not saying I wish I didn't have a family. And they come first, that's a given. It's just that there never seems to be enough time. Like today," I looked at my watch, "I have to leave in less than two hours."

"When I was in school, in the last century," Martha Jane winked, "the humanity professors, and all of Western culture to be precise, maybe more than that—it was probably universal," she paused, "now I don't want to get off on one of my little word journeys. What I'm trying to say is that they said there were no great women artists because women's creative needs were satisfied by bearing children, whereas men would channel their creativity into making great works of art, architecture, music, literature and so on. It was utter nonsense of course, women weren't allowed to be serious about doing anything creative, but another great obstacle had to do with time. Women were trapped in the myriad demands of domesticity. We simply never had the luxury of time," she gave me a knowing look and turned back to her painting. "There was never enough time."

We had developed a routine of eating lunch together. Never at an appointed time, but it seemed to work out that when one of us was ready, so was the other. Sometimes Fred joined us, although today he was working on his own painting. He'd only nodded when I arrived this morning and was still deeply engrossed at his station in the back corner.

There were two weathered Adirondack chairs overlooking the meadow and Colvos Passage where we always sat. Sometimes I almost forgot about Martha Jane's age, her mind was so sharp, until I watched her moving from one position to another. Hampered by arthritis, it took her quite a while to lower herself into the chair. She never complained, but I knew her joints had to hurt.

It was the warmest day of the year so far, almost seventy degrees with hardly any wind. The view of the deep green trees against the cloudless sky, with the slice of dark blue water shining beyond, was so bright and sharp it could almost have been stained glass.

"I'm starting to think of this as Annie's meadow." Martha Jane opened her lunch box, a child's metal box she'd told me had been a gift from her great-grandson who had outgrown it. The lunch box had Nemo and other Disney fish on it. Martha Jane called it a hand-me-up, as her grandson now preferred a more sophisticated lunch box, one decorated with Ichiro of the Mariners.

I stared at the meadow, and then took a bite of my sandwich, chewing slowly. I wiped my mouth, "I'm not sure Fred would want the meadow called that."

"Well, in my mind it's Annie's meadow and that's that. Your painting is truly stunning."

"But I'm not done," I protested. I always felt awkward when I received a compliment. Having believed for so long that my work was mediocre and inconsequential, it made me nervous to really believe it could be more.

"When you are, it will be even more so. You have real talent, Annie. Does it run in your family?" Martha Jane asked casually.

"Funny you should ask," I mumbled. Out of the corner of my eye I could see Fred working in the studio. It was obvious he hadn't mentioned my father to Martha Jane, and it made me appreciate him even more. I stretched and turned my face toward the sun. I didn't want to be identified with my father, or have anyone even remotely connect me to him. No Jamie Wyeth ambition for me. But what difference did it make if Martha Jane knew? Was there any reason not to tell her? I'd already spilled everything that was going on with my immediate family to Martha Jane. What did it matter?

I closed my eyes for a minute, cherishing the heat of this beautiful spring day, before I turned to Martha Jane. "My father is Alexander Gunther."

"Oh, my. My daughter and son-in-law took me to his retrospective just last weekend." Martha Jane leaned closer to me. "I had no idea."

"It's not something I broadcast."

"You must have learned so much from him, been so inspired. To think of having a talent like that under your own roof. Like gold in your backyard."

Gold? More like dog shit. Or a toxic landfill that makes you sick. It took me a while to know how to answer her. I didn't know what to say, I could only think of how destructive he'd been. Literally. The time I showed him my pastel. I could see it, the way he'd slashed paint over it, and then not long after that, one of his finer tantrums around the time he returned from Paris right after I'd been diagnosed with ulcerative colitis.

"The bathroom is close, Annie. You stay here." In my parents' bedroom, my mother motioned to the bed and folded back the covers, carefully spreading a thick towel over the sheet. Her love always shown with few words. I lay down and Mom sat beside me. After many frantic trips to the bathroom, the attacks began to subside. I lay in my mother's arms while she stroked my forehead.

Mom heard him first. His footsteps on the stairs. Her body became rigid. The unmistakable uneven gait in the hallway. The door flung open.

"What the hell is she doing in here?"

My mother froze, then whispered, "It's closer to the—"

"God—you stink!" He charged across the room, stumbling as he reached the windows. In his fury he knocked over a plant on the windowsill. He kicked it across the floor, then yanked open first one, then the other window. He stumbled in the bathroom and returned red-faced, teeth clenched, clutching a bottle of cologne. He threw it, splattering both of us, then moved closer to me and doused me, up and down my body, frenzied like an arsonist spreading gasoline. Then hurled the bottle against the wall.

"Annie?" Martha Jane tapped my arm.

"Yes?" I turned to her.

"So I gather he wasn't helpful to you?" she asked.

"Just the opposite, I'm afraid." I would have almost laughed if the memory of his cruelty that day hadn't been so intense. But in spite of the little hum of anxiety, which always accompanied any mention of him, I proceeded to tell Martha Jane what it had really been like to be Alexander Gunther's daughter. My response felt reflexive, the way a hungry person eats without restraint when presented with food; and I revealed the things I'd only told Jack and my therapist. It was like visiting a familiar river, my words moving over what had once been sharp stones of pain, worn down and worked through over the years so that even though they continued to exist, the shards that pierced the heart had disappeared.

"These days they say ulcerative colitis isn't only stress related, but in my heart I know being so afraid of him was a big part of it."

"Is it better now?" Martha Jane asked.

"A lot better. In high school I took Balsalazide to control it and it went into remission when I went to college and only briefly flared up after the break-up of my first marriage. Then years ago I saw a naturopath who prescribed this concoction of fish oil, antioxidants and soluble fiber which I take regularly and I haven't had any recurrence."

"Thank goodness for that, dear." Martha Jane patted my arm. "I suppose we're like animals, some are just born more aggressive than others. But I wonder sometimes why some people can be so much nastier than others."

"The way my father rejected me became more clear to me just recently. When my mother was first hospitalized, she wanted me to get her living will so she could review it. When I went through her papers I found my parents' marriage certificate. I had never known them to celebrate a wedding anniversary—my mother had been vague about it. That was her nature, really, to be vague about a lot of things. Especially anything that made her uncomfortable."

Martha Jane listened attentively as I related what I'd been able to piece together of my parents' backgrounds. During World War II, my mother's family had been sent with many of the Seattle area Japanese Americans to an internment camp in Minidoka, Idaho. Many of the college-age students were allowed to go to school in the Midwest and my mother had gone to Berea College in Kentucky, and returned to Seattle to finish her education at the University of Washington. In addition to attending classes, she held a part-time job as a file clerk in the Art Department where she met Alexander Gunther when he hung around the artists on his vacations from Princeton.

"I was born in late December and was probably conceived in the spring that year, most likely when he was here on spring break. The wedding certificate said they were married August 26, when my mother would have been five months pregnant with me."

"There were many, many fuzzy wedding dates then, well, not only then, since the beginning of time," Martha Jane said, reassuringly, "and in wartime young women in love especially wanted a child in case their young men didn't come back."

"My father wasn't in the war. He had a deferment, he had polio when he was a child."

"I see. Do you know much about his family?"

"A little. My father's mother was from a wealthy east coast family. She was the daughter of a banker from Connecticut and married beneath her status, at least economically. Her husband, my grandfather, was the son of an

Episcopal vicar from upstate New York; he attended Princeton on a scholarship and met her at a social when she was at Mt. Holyoke. There was a considerable trust fund and my grandmother controlled it. I'm sure that's how she controlled my father. I suspect that word must have gotten to her that he had all but abandoned us in Yonkers, when he was hanging out at the Cedar Street Tavern with that bunch in New York, and I think my grandmother probably threatened to cut him off if he didn't come back to us and behave like the family man he was, but wished he wasn't."

"What about your mother's family?"

"Her father was one of the first Asian American physicians, he graduated from the University of California Medical School. They were a prominent family in the Japanese American community, but they disowned my mother when she married my father. It was such a disgrace, I guess. I never knew them, they settled in California after the war."

Martha Jane didn't say anything for a minute; she rested her chin on her hand and looked out over the meadow, then closed her eyes. "What a loss for them not to have known you."

"It must have been awful for my mother, and perhaps why she couldn't leave my father. I honestly think on some level my father hates women. Or at least wants power over them, some reaction to his having such a powerful mother, and a weak father by comparison. He treated my mother terribly. And she wasn't able to stand up to him."

"I see." Martha Jane leaned over the side of the chair and set her lunch box on the grass. "Fred spoke so kindly of your mother, he told me she knew his wife. How is your father doing since your mother died?"

"He seems to be thriving, he has a full-time house-keeper, Mrs. Tibonga. She's originally from the Philippines. Honestly, I don't think he can tell much difference between Mrs. Tibonga and my mother except that Mrs. Tibonga goes home at night. But I doubt he's lonely, there's always some woman around who's enchanted by him. At the reception for his retrospective, it was a beautiful collector, a woman in her seventies. She was wealthy and elegant, but the same species as all the rest. An art groupie—they'll always be there for him."

I watched Daisy and Pablo at the edge of the meadow for a minute, and then laid my head back against the chair. "I used to idealize him, you know. And I wanted everyone to know I was his daughter, but as I got older, I found it hard to make sense of the contrast between his charming public persona, the esteem in which he was held, and how he behaved toward me at home."

I turned my head toward Martha Jane. "He was different with my brother. David was athletic and our father took a keen, vicarious interest in all the sports David played and it gave them something to talk about. My father traveled a lot, but he was nice to David when he was home. We weren't much of a family, but we were one that operated as two distinct teams: my mother and I on one, David and my father on the other."

We sat in the warm sun in the quiet of the meadow, hearing only birdsong and the faint rustling of trees at the meadow's edge as the wind picked up. I looked down at my lap and brushed off some crumbs. "My father showed his contempt for me either by occasional hostile outbursts or for the most part by almost completely ignoring me," I continued after a few minutes. "I thought he was treating me like I didn't have any value, because I wasn't worth much. That it was my fault, that somehow I deserved it."

"Children always think it's their fault when they don't get what they need. It never occurs to them that there's something very wrong with the parent who can't give."

"Years later I finally understood that." I smiled, although I felt sad. "With a couple years of help."

"You know, Annie, your father had great talent, but it reminds me of something the outstanding composer and master teacher Nadia Boulanger said. She was the first woman to conduct major symphonies, New York, Boston and Philadelphia, I think. She was French of course, but they say there was no one with more influence on American music in the twentieth century. Unlike most women at the time, she had extraordinary encouragement and family support. Her grandmother was a celebrated singer, and her grandfather, father, and mother all studied at the Paris Conservatoire, and she had a sister—she died young. Her sister was really her first composition student and became the first woman to receive the Prix de Rome." Martha Jane looked over the meadow, slowly moving her head from left to right, breathing deeply. "What a gift, this day." She rested her head on the back of the chair and closed her eyes, basking in the sun.

"And what did she say?" I asked.

"Who, dear?"

"Nadia Boulanger. You were talking about—"

"Oh yes, of course. About your father's talent," Martha Jane sat up. "Why she said, 'It is one thing to be gifted and quite another to be worthy of one's gift.'"

15

CASS

In the apple tree next to the garage, birds began chirping as the sun came up. It was four-thirty in the morning and although Cass was ordinarily a bird-lover, she wished they'd shut the hell up. It was only the third time in weeks that she hadn't woken up intermittently throughout the night and she was grateful that the pills Lena had prescribed were finally doing their job. She put the pillow over her head, trying to muffle the irritating birdsong, and actually had some success, sleeping another two hours until the alarm went off.

Cass opened the drapes to see the noisy culprits: a flock of starlings. Her least favorite bird. When you looked closely they were actually quite beautiful, the long yellow bill against the dark, glossy plumage with its handsome iridescent emerald and deep purple sheen. But they had shitty personalities and made her think of Richard: great to look at, but aggressive. Starlings were known to have pushed out the Purple Martins and the Western Bluebird, who'd been unable to defend their nests against them. It was exactly how she felt when she caved on the apartment.

She still didn't know if she'd made the right decision, and wasn't even all that sure of her motives. Maybe if he lived there without her he'd miss her. Maybe he'd appreciate her generosity in letting him have the apartment. Right. Maybe the Pope isn't Catholic. Maybe Richard could go to hell. The only reason to keep it was to spite him and in the end, that didn't seem reason enough. Deep down, Cass knew she needed a fresh start, somewhere that didn't remind her of him, once she could figure out where she wanted to live. But she wanted to make damn well sure she could take her own sweet time getting her stuff out. They could figure out about their jointly owned furniture when she was good and ready. In the meantime he signed the new lease and she left with a bag of clothes.

As she showered, Cass noticed that the bathroom had changed the least. The familiarity of the tile and fixtures made her feel nostalgic, although being back home was a little like trying to fit into a favorite sweater that had shrunk in the wash. She couldn't wear it no matter how much she'd loved it.

But at least she'd been able to sleep. Thank God for that, and each day she was home, she felt better and more energetic. Her old bed was like a cocoon, a sweet space she'd never shared with anyone (at least on a regular basis). Daisy had been a frequent cohabitant and there had been a few times in high school when her parents were out and she'd snuck in Jeff, her boyfriend at the time. But the bed was all hers, not too soft, not too hard, and especially now—just right. There was no memory of Richard here, not a trace or so much as a whiff, so that being back home was restorative in a way she hadn't anticipated.

Her parents had been wonderful, kind and undemanding,

and hanging out with them each evening after work was giving Cass the respite she needed. Space and time...to just breathe. By the end of her first week at home, she was beginning to joke again with the regulars at work, and each day there were flashes of feeling like her old self. Friday morning when she went on break, Cass was surprised to realize she hadn't thought of Richard for almost three hours, the longest stretch yet. She felt more in control and it couldn't have come too soon.

Yesterday Cass had gotten a call from her district manager, Lou Reeves, wanting to meet at the end of the day today. "I'll give you the details when we meet," he said, "but I wanted you to know up front that you're being considered for District Manager."

Lou's call had come during the morning rush and the news certainly gave her a lift, but she hadn't thought a lot about it. Ordinarily, she would have tried to psyche it out, imagining all kinds of possible scenarios, but the past few weeks it had taken all her mental strength just to get out of bed in the morning. Brushing her teeth seemed heroic. Cass felt like she was trudging up a mountain, putting one foot in front of the other, trying not to fall, and her mind couldn't begin to handle anything remotely akin to contemplating the scenery or speculating about the journey. She didn't even mention Lou's call to her parents, only telling Annie that she had a meeting at the end of the day and wouldn't be home until after dinner.

Lou arrived at the store around five-thirty. A big, stocky guy with an athletic build, he had blue eyes, sandy hair and a great smile—and what Cass thought of as the quintessential retail personality: warm, friendly, and outgoing; although it hadn't taken her long to discover that underneath his easy exterior was a bit of an anal streak. He was very detail oriented, but Cass hadn't seen him lose sight of the big picture either. She liked the guy. She'd even had a bit of a crush on him when she first met him. Not a big one, just a low level, mini crush. She was attracted to him and got a little charge being around him. Cass had met his wife and kids at the company holiday party and he went up even more in her estimation. He had a darling wife, an African American woman, and two boys, identical twins, ten years old. She always felt positive toward white guys who married black women. Those guys could turn out to be jerks like anybody else, she knew that—but they obviously weren't hung up on color and that always got points with her.

"You've done a great job here, Cass." Lou rested his arms on the corner table and looked appreciatively around the store.

"Thanks," she said, pleased to have his praise. "I can't say it hasn't had its challenges, but we have wonderful partners here. I couldn't ask for a better crew. Everyone— assistant manager, shift supervisor, the baristas."

"Challenges," Lou laughed. "That's a positive way to frame it. Good for you. How many 'challenges' this month?"

"The number of drug zombies passed out in the bathroom was up a bit, the panhandlers harassing customers was down somewhat, and the shoplifting's holding steady."

He laughed again. "We may joke about it, but I don't need to tell you, this is a tough location." He opened his brief case and pulled out her evaluations. "With the number of employees here," he said, looking at the sheet in front of him, "it says twenty-five, is that right?"

"Counting the part-time people, that's right."

"Twenty-five makes it one of our larger stores and all the evaluations mention your ability to handle difficult situations. They say you can calm obnoxious customers and defuse altercations."

"No one's thrown coffee at me, yet," she said, laughing.

"And besides the usual—capable, fair, reliable, pitches in to help the baristas, everyone says you're fun to work with. No one who's ever worked with you has ever wanted to transfer to another location."

Too bad Richard didn't want to stick with me, she thought.

"Let me get to the point. We're impressed with how you handle everything, Cass."

"I had a good teacher." Flattery had never been her style; she was merely stating a fact. Lou truly had been a huge help to her.

"Thank you, but you're also a quick study." Lou leaned forward and lowered his voice. "The opening I mentioned on the phone is District Manager in Bellevue."

"Really?" Cass was surprised. It was a huge job and they already had one of the top district managers. "Isn't Virginia Klemke there?"

"Yes, and she's outstanding. But she's expecting her first child in August and she's decided to get on the mommy track. She wants to be a full-time mom."

"I see."

The envy hit without warning like a pain-filled cloudburst. It pissed her off that her mood was so fragile. So Virginia Klemke is going to have a baby. So what? But in spite of her best efforts to ward them off, tears filled her eyes. Cass fumbled in her pocket for a tissue, then abruptly stood up.

"Excuse me a minute, Lou."

She walked quickly to the women's room in the back of the store and pushed the door open. Good, it was empty. She wouldn't have to worry about trying to put on a good face in front one of the staff, or a customer. Cass grabbed a bunch of toilet paper from the stall and then splashed water on her face and blew her nose. She stayed in the bathroom a few minutes, waiting until she'd regained her composure before she went back to the table, toilet paper in hand.

"You've had a cold?" he asked, sympathetically.

"Allergies. It's the spring thing. They sneak up on me." Cass blew her nose.

Lou waited for one of the baristas, who'd been refilling the cream station, to move back behind the counter out of earshot, before he continued.

"We'd like you to put in for the Bellevue DM." He smiled, enjoying being the one to give her the good news, not only of a possible promotion, but this one. It was one of the best DM jobs in the area. A real prize. DM positions were hard to come by, they didn't open up that often and he was certain Cass would jump at it.

"When do you need to know?" She wadded up the toilet paper in her lap.

"Do you have questions about it?" He looked surprised.

"I'm sorry," Cass mumbled. "I'm not really myself. First, thank you for considering me. I appreciate it very much, I really do—and I'm grateful."

More than you know because I've been feeling like a worthless piece of shit lately.

"And there's no question Starbucks is a great company—"

"You can't beat the benefits and stock options, the

policies for domestic partners, the number of women executives, the—"

She put her hand on his arm. "You don't need to sell me on the company."

"Right." He leaned back in his chair. "There's also a significant salary increase. A first year district manager in this slot would start at sixty-five thousand. You'd be managing fifteen stores, it would be a great opportunity for you, Cass."

"I totally get that, it just really caught me off guard. I've never been one of those people with five-year career plans and stuff like that. In fact, when I came back from Thailand three years ago and started with the company, I just saw it as a fun job. I mean, I liked it and I've enjoyed managing the store, but I hadn't really thought of it as, you know—a long-term career. I'm not sure I've thought about anything as a long term career," she continued, quickly pushing away the thought of Virginia Klemke's new career. "This would mean thinking about the job in sort of a new way and there's some logistics to consider. It would be more of a commute unless I decided to move over there."

Lou pulled his car keys from his pocket. "So, I guess you'll have to think about it a bit."

"I guess I do."

"I'll need to know by the end of next week at the latest, if you'd like to put in for it."

"Sure. Thanks for giving me a little time." She walked with him to the door. "I'll get back to you next week and I want you to know I really do appreciate being considered."

And she did. At least someone thought she had something to offer, even though the whole thing made her face the fact that the future she had wanted wasn't going to happen. And as to what she wanted to do now—she was clueless. How the hell was she supposed to decide in a week? What *did* she want to do? Her cell phone rang as she watched Lou walk down the street. Cass took it out of her pocket and checked the number. Richard. Oh great. What the hell did he want?

16

ANNIE

It was the best day I'd had in weeks. I hadn't heard a peep—or even a growl to be more accurate—from my father and I started to believe that we were on our way to the non-relationship I had hoped for. Not only that, but Cass was doing a lot better and I didn't feel like I had to rush home to fix dinner for her. And then there was my painting; the meadow was coming along well and I was excited about it, and to top it off, at work Lauren Thomas had improved so much that she would be going home soon. The sum total made me think of a quote I always liked, "The thankful receiver bears a plentiful harvest." I don't remember who said it, maybe William Blake or maybe Browning, but what I did know was that it expressed the way I felt. Grateful.

The morning before Lauren was going to be discharged we were in the art room where she was finishing a collage she'd made from tissue paper and scraps of fabric. Earlier that week I'd brought in a book about Paul Horiuchi, a Seattle artist famous for collage, and she'd been inspired by it. She was carefully cutting the scraps and placing them on a canvas board and I loved watching her work.

"I've decided to get a dog," she said. "I hope I can find one like Daisy." She leaned over to pat Daisy, who sat next to her.

"I'm sure you can. Daisy's from a shelter and there are wonderful dogs needing homes." I wrote down the websites for the local shelters and handed it to her. "Checking out the internet is good way to start."

I looked at the bulletin board at the pastel I'd made of Lauren and Daisy. "Would you like to take the sketch of you and Daisy?"

She smiled. "Thanks, I'd love to have it."

While I was taking the sketch down for her, my cell phone rang. I didn't want to answer it while I was with Lauren, but as soon as she left to go to group, I picked up the message. It was Jack saying he wanted to go to Tomiko's for dinner. Usually one of us might suggest going out after we both got home. For him to call to confirm we were going out was odd. Later, I realized why. He wanted to drop his bombshell in a public place to keep me from stomping out, as I might have done at home. The restaurant provided a lid of restraint and Jack judged (quite correctly) that I would be too civilized to cause a scene in at Tomiko's.

We were halfway through dinner when he told me. I suppose it had taken him that long to get up his nerve.

"Annie, I've had a job offer that I seriously want to consider."

I put down my chopsticks and sipped my wine. I didn't know what was coming, but I suddenly felt afraid.

"Dr. Phriep wants me to set up a lab at Phnom Penh Medical School."

"Phnom Penh Medical School?"

"In Cambodia."

"Cambodia?"

"Phnom Penh—in Cambodia. I would need to commit to it for two years. And Annie—" Jack leaned forward, and said softly, "I'd really like to accept."

I was speechless.

"Annie?"

"What?"

"Well, what do you think?"

"What do you mean, 'what do I think?'"

"Just that. We could rent the house, and it could be an adventure. I know how you like animals and just think," Jack laughed, "You could ride an elephant."

Was he crazy?

"That's not funny, Jack."

"Sorry. But seriously, what do you think?"

"What about my job?" It was the first thing that popped into my mind.

"At Woodside? Well, you've already cut back to paint and anyway, it's just a part-time job. I don't see why you couldn't paint in Cambodia as well as anywhere."

Just a part-time job...Like it was nothing! What was he thinking? Obviously not of me. Did he think I was a paper doll? Admittedly, a middle-aged version, sporting crow's feet and a turkey neck, but he really was acting like I was just something he could pick up and move into a space beside him to complete his picture—just the way I had years ago.

We had moved a lot and I always went along without

question, even though deep down I never liked it. I hated living away from Mom and having to start all over in a new place; new faculty wives to try to get to know (most of the doctors were men back then), new neighbors, new pediatricians, new grocery stores, new everything. I'm a total homebody and I love our friendly house. The house where Jack and I had lived all these years was a home. It still felt like a sweet oasis to me. There's no way I wanted to leave it—I've always felt that I'd have to be carried out. And what about Sam? *Two years is an eternity for a little guy like that.* And leaving Cass, and Ian, and Martha Jane and Fred!

"I want to be very clear about this." I took another sip of wine and tried to control my emotions. "I am not going to move to Cambodia."

Better to get craziness over with, straight out.

"Just like that?" He stared at the ceiling, jaw muscles twitching, then snapped, "You won't even *think* about it."

"No, there's nothing to think about. I don't want to leave our grandson, our children, my work, my classes with Fred, our home, our friends, or our dog. I won't go with you, Jack."

He got very quiet and he seemed not only hurt, but a little lost. I see-sawed between being pissed that he actually thought I'd be willing to give up everything and go with him, to feeling sad that he was bouncing around and being so weird. I knew he'd resent what I was about to say, but I felt I really had to spell it out for him. It was long past due.

"Jack, you've had a great career, you've had top faculty appointments and you've made an important contribution to your field, but you have to face not having that last grant funded. It doesn't mean you can't still keep your hand in—teach doctoral candidates, and be a mentor. Just because you never won the Nobel prize or don't have funding for some big project now doesn't mean you can't be useful, and find new things to enjoy. Why not find new challenges outside of work? How about putting your mind to developing some interests other than research, something different—how about something fun? It seems to me that starting a lab in Cambodia, or whatever this thing is, just postpones what you have to face."

"You know there are women who would give their eyeteeth for an adventure like this."

"Oh, really? Well, let them give their eyeteeth and their molars, too. You can go with them." That's it. I'd tried. I pushed my plate away.

Jack had devoured the rest of his dinner while I couldn't finish what was left of my shiyoki salmon.

"Are you going to finish that?" He eyed my plate.

"No. Do you want it?" My voice was icy.

"I'll take it for lunch tomorrow." He caught the waiter's eye. "Unless of course, you want it for *your* lunch." His sneer barely above a whisper.

"I said, I don't want it."

"No, you didn't. You said you weren't going to finish it. So, you might have wanted it later. They're two entirely different things, Annie."

When that tone oozed into his voice, patronizing and just short of a jeer, it really fried me. "So now we're arguing about the food, a food fight."

"A food fight is when you throw it," he said smugly. "We're not there yet."

If we'd been at home, I wondered if I would have taken

that as my cue to clobber him with the shiyoki salmon, decorating his receding hairline with moist chunks of pink fish.

On our way out, we waved to Tommy with a little show of phony cheer, and drove home in silence. I was too tired for any more of it, not even cathartic fantasies of hurling food at him, and the distance between us was thick with anger and hurt. Daisy was excited to see us as soon as we got in the house, and we patted her in turn, extravagantly bestowing on her the affection we withheld from each other. Then Jack fixed himself a drink and settled in the den in front of the TV and I went upstairs with the dog. I went in the bathroom to take an Excedrin PM. I was tired, but I knew I'd lie awake seething about what he'd said unless I took something. Most often, just one pill did the trick and I'd fall sleep easily. With two, I felt drugged, much like how I assumed the patients at work felt a lot of the time with their cocktails of Haldol, Trazodone, Zyprexa, Lithium, and Ativan. Just a part-time job. Is that what he'd thought of my work at Woodside all these years?

I always made Daisy jump down before Jack turned in, because although Jack liked Daisy, he drew the line at letting her stay on the bed all night. "I'm not sleeping with a dog!" He'd been adamant about it, so Daisy slept at the foot of our bed and it became one of a string of little compromises in the weave of the fabric of our long marriage.

After the eleven o'clock news, when Jack came upstairs, he found Daisy's dark, furry body claiming his half of the bed.

17

CASS

Richard's number was programmed into Cass's cell phone. She'd have to change it, make it harder to call him, she thought as she listened to his message.

"There's some mail here for you, and I figured you might want to pick it up." His voice was calm, friendly, not a trace of the exhausted, slightly annoyed tone he'd had for months before they split up. She couldn't read much into it—did he want to see her, or was he just trying to be considerate? Who knew? The only thing Cass was sure of, was that she wasn't in any hurry to return the call.

On her way home she had a craving for Indian food; it was the first time in weeks that she'd wanted it. As soon as she got to her car, Cass called The Taj Mahal and ordered take-out. Yum. Lamb biryani, boondi raita, mint chutney, garlic naan, chicken vindaloo. Without a doubt, Lou Reeves had lifted her spirits. In spite of her little setback when Lou mentioned the mommy track, his news perked up her whole system and she couldn't wait to eat.

When Cass got to the Taj Mahal, her order wasn't

quite ready. It had been a beautiful, warm spring day and the evening had yet to cool off, so she went outside to wait. Cass hung out on the street, looking in the window of the frame shop next to the restaurant, which also sold posters and some original art. Prominently displayed was the poster from her grandfather's retrospective, and she got furious all over again to think that she'd missed it because of letting Richard get to her. That fucker. She didn't seem to be able to think of him without adding that particular phrase as if it were all one name: Richardthatfucker.

As she lingered in front of the window, Cass also thought about all the prints and the beautifully framed temple rubbings from Thailand that she'd left in the apartment. What a contrast with her room at home, so stark now with its bare white walls. Last week when she'd first come home, she was too wasted to care; but the more she looked in the frame shop window, the more she wanted her stuff back. Not to actually hang it in her old room. For sure she didn't want to start nest-building at her parents' house. (How backasswards would that be?) But just to put them on the floor around the room. Propped against the wall so she could look at them, like old friends.

And music. She was ready to get that, too. She wanted her CD player back. Cass admitted she might be clueless about what she wanted to do with her life, but this much she knew: it was time to reclaim her art and music. And as far as the rest of the stuff went, as soon as she figured out where she'd be living, Cass would take back everything that had been hers before Richard moved in.

It was the decisions about their so-called community property that weighed her down: the dishes, their few appliances (actually it was just the coffee pot and the microwave) and their furniture and all the things they'd gotten at Ikea. She couldn't deal with it. Not yet anyway, and now having to make a decision within the next week about the DM job—it was too much.

Her take-out was ready when Cass went back in the restaurant, but she changed her mind and decided to stay and eat there. Sanjeev Gilani, the owner, was always good to the regulars and showed Cass to her favorite table in the corner. She ordered a Tikka Gold beer and dug into the lamb biryani. Cass sighed. Enjoying food again, how great was that? She tore off a piece of garlic naan, her favorite bread, and chewed slowly. Then a swig of the Tikka Gold. Then she pulled her cell phone out of her purse to call Richard.

One advantage of giving him the apartment, Cass realized, was that along with whatever guilt he was feeling, it also made him somewhat obligated to her. It had let her call a few shots, like keeping her key and setting the timetable for getting her stuff out. Even Richard wasn't slimy enough to make demands about that. Cass decided there was a tiny bit of power in being the dumpee, as opposed to being the dumper. She didn't relish the victim position, but there was also the added bonus that no one felt much sympathy for the dumper.

"Richard?"

"Hi, Cass."

"I'm coming over to get my mail and also some of my stuff. Just thought I'd let you know." Not asking permission, you shit. Just a heads-up in case you have company and don't want a smarmy little drama.

"Thanks. I'll be here."

"No need."

"I'm catching up on a bunch of journals. I'll be at it awhile."

"Okay. Whatever."

Cass went to the women's room and combed her hair and put on lip-gloss. Damn. She looked like a raccoon. She wished she could do something about the dark circles. She wet a paper towel with cold water and pressed it to her eyes. After a few seconds she brought her face up close to the mirror. Still a raccoon. Oh the hell with it. Why should she care?

When Cass arrived at the apartment, she turned off the engine then pulled down the mirror on the visor, took a quick look, then quickly snapped it back. She hesitated a minute, staring at the building. Cass had loved that apartment. She remembered being hit with culture shock when she came back from Thailand, and her parents and Lena had helped her move in. All the ethnic restaurants on Capitol Hill, the mix of faces and accents, had made the re-entry easier. It was hard to imagine living anywhere else in the city, to say nothing of a suburb on the eastside if she took that job. It took her an amazing five or ten minutes to get to work now, and if she stayed on Capitol Hill and the traffic were bad it could take almost ten times as long to get to Bellevue. A lot of the eastside reminded her of southern California and it was hard to see herself there. She wished she knew what to do.

Cass walked briskly to the building and used her key to get in the outer door. At the apartment she rang the buzzer, then immediately unlocked the door and let herself in.

Richard sat in their leather chair with a pile of journals on the floor next to it. He'd want the chair when they split up their stuff, just the way he appropriated the apartment.

Of course he would, she thought, watching him get up to greet her.

How polite.

"Can I get you anything?"

Polite and solicitous. When she lived here, he'd hardly look up or even acknowledge she'd come home.

"No. I've just got a few minutes." Might as well keep up the impression she had a life. Cass went to the bookcase and began to unhook the speakers of her CD player.

"Need a hand?" Richard stood awkwardly in the middle of the room.

"I can get it."

"Here, I'll get the other one."

He went to the end of the bookcase and unhooked the speaker while Cass unplugged the CD player from the outlet under the desk. As she wrapped the cord, she was drawn to the photo next to the phone. She glanced at it, then couldn't wrest her eyes away, fixated, like staring at an accident on the freeway. Last summer. Their bike trip in the San Juan Islands. The pure delight on her face, her head leaning against his shoulder, his eyes so dark and flirtatious, his dazzling smile. She thought they were home free. She thought they'd make it. She thought she'd be on the mommy track by now. Fuck. There it was again. Blindsided, like she'd been in her meeting with Lou, although this time the trigger was literally the two of them, radiant like the sun had been that hot summer day and she shut her eyes against all she'd lost.

"Cass," he took her in his arms.

"Don't." The tears spilled down her cheeks and he put his hand on the back of her head, stroking her hair, pulling her to him until her face rested against his chest, his T-shirt blotting her tears. Her arms reached around him automatically and he lifted her chin, his lips so gentle she responded without thinking as waves of sadness were swept with desire. It was like a riderless horse they couldn't control. He slipped his arm under her shirt, caressing her back, then her sides, moving his hands along her ribs to her breasts, then he lifted her shirt and pulled her to the floor.

The curtains were open and the room was brightly lit; he glanced at the window and whispered, "Cass, come in the bedroom."

And she followed him, stumbling and leaning against him as if she were drunk. In bed, they were feverish, teeming with passion and grief, and a ferocity so consuming it frightened her, and then afterwards, they clung together, holding on in the debris of their love, as they lay in each other's arms and wept.

She cradled his head against her breast and felt his breathing deepen as he fell off to sleep. Usually after they'd made love, she was the first to fall asleep, while he seemed energized and would often get up to get a drink or something to eat. This time it was the opposite. She felt him slip from her and watched him sleep for a long time before his weight made her uncomfortable and she moved, freeing herself, and soon she, too, drifted off to sleep.

Hours later as Cass shifted, her hand felt something under the pillow, a small object of some kind. She pulled it out. A shiny oval hair clip, possibly sterling silver.

She was dead inside with something barren and unyielding that made her feel sick. Desolate and no longer capable of tears, she placed the hair clip prominently on the pillow, dressed quietly, got her CD player and left.

18

ANNIE

We were all avoiding the subject of Richard. Jack had put it crudely when he said there was a big dick in the living room, but now there was another elephant: Cambodia. And I still couldn't believe Jack had said, "I could ride an elephant," as if he were bribing a child. It was astonishing. How could our versions of reality have been so different?

But nothing perplexed me about my decision. Not only was I not going, but it was clear to me that Jack had only a few options: he could go without me, he could not go, or he could try to go for less time. I was pretty sure he wouldn't go without me; it would be hard to imagine our relationship surviving a two-year separation at our age. But it caused me to think about marriages ending. I knew something about that, and Jack and I certainly weren't there yet. Far, far from it—at least from my perspective. And in spite of Jack's self-involvement with this Cambodia idea, he was so different from my first husband, it was as if they were a different species. I hadn't thought about my first marriage in ages; it had only lasted a little over two years and was as if it had happened to another person. But what Cass was going through with Richard had brought it back. It produced a reaction as if I'd been poisoned by toxic seafood and felt nauseated all these years later.

I met Bill McIntyre at a party the spring of my freshman year in college. He was a senior, a musician, and he looked like James Dean. The chemistry was irresistible; something had happened at first sight, most likely lust. When I was alone with him, he had the quiet demeanor of my mother, and in a group displayed my father's capacity for charm, a magnet that drew people to him while obscuring his self-absorption. It was a lethal combination and it attracted me like a moth to a flame (or, as I later observed in therapy, like a fly to manure). The attraction was mutual. I think there was just enough of a Japanese flavor to me that I evoked a fantasy of some geisha-like creature, who would worship-fully meet his every need, leaving him free to develop his considerable (in his opinion) talent. He pursued me relent-lessly and after a few weeks we were inseparable.

He flattered my father, who lapped it up. And if my mother had reservations, she never expressed them, taking the position that as long as I was happy that was all that mattered to her. Besides, her marriage to my father had caused an irreparable rift with her own family, and the last thing she wanted for her daughter was a repetition of that painful history.

When we got married after my junior year, I quit college to work as a receptionist in a brokerage firm so my husband would only have to work part-time and could pursue his career. Bill worked a few days a week, clerking in a music store and playing with his band on the weekends; while

I, indistinguishable from a growing number of groupies, beamed adoringly from every audience. After a year, I got a raise and a promotion to administrative assistant to the firm's operations manager, enabling Bill to work even less at his day job, ostensibly to concentrate on writing music.

Less than six weeks into the marriage, I discovered Bill had a terrible temper. His tantrums, which took the form of swearing, yelling, and throwing things, rivaled any two-year-old's and were a regular part of a repertoire that I'd only glimpsed before we were married, and probably denied because he'd been romantic and charming and I was swept away by how much he wanted me. After he'd blown up and calmed down, he justified his infantile explosions as little outbursts that were supposed to be a natural by-product of his artistic temperament. This line of reasoning (of crap, I later observed in therapy) was a familiar refrain. I had been raised on a diet of the same feeble explanation for my father's rages and at first I didn't question it. That destructive dynamic was my childhood reality and it didn't occur to me until years later that it was a corrupt myth that enabled my father to treat everyone like shit and my mother to put up with it.

Looking back, I could say I married such an asshole because my father was one. (A brilliant deduction.) I'd embarked on the classic and doomed dance, hooking up with someone who psychologically resembles the parent with whom there is painful conflict in the hope that the story will turn out differently. And of course, it's never repaired because you've hooked up with the same kind of asshole.

Bill's band got better gigs and went on the road, and between the late nights and the days spent sleeping, the music he was going to write never materialized. It wasn't long, not more than seven months, before the marriage began to lose its appeal for him and he would return feeling tied down and resentful—and, I suppose, somewhat guilty from taking advantage of the many opportunities he had to cheat on me on the road.

To justify his resentment, he looked for things I did "wrong" so he could blame me. Each time he came home, the house wasn't clean enough, I didn't iron his shirts right, the food wasn't cooked enough or was cooked too much. And in running the household, I spent too much money (it didn't seem to register that I earned the lion's share of it. Or if it did, it didn't matter).

At first I took it to heart. I tried harder to please him. It was a bad case of what I once heard Jane Fonda on a talk show describe as the "disease to please." I tried patiently to endure his tantrums, a lesson I'd learned from my mother.

But I wasn't my mother. The times and the culture were different. I had a different history, a different temperament, and as time wore on, I became increasingly unable to put up with his crap. "It doesn't do any good to please him so why bother?" was the thought I couldn't shake.

I got another promotion at work, and with it came the recognition that I did have value and a realization, like the slow emergence of landscape into first light, that it would be better to be alone in this world and face the shame of a failed marriage, than be treated with such hostility.

When he began to travel, with gigs now in northern California, I went to the Seattle Humane Society and got Max, a black, mostly lab puppy. The idea was that with Bill gone so much of the time, I needed a watchdog. It turned out Max wasn't really watchdog material, but he fulfilled his real mission: he gave me something to love, and he loved me back. But there was a terrible downside. On the rare occasions when Bill was home, Max became the focus of most of his tantrums.

Now when Bill screamed and my dog was the victim—I began to stand up to him. He started to stay out all night, even after gigs in town. Once, on one of his infrequent evenings at home, he became enraged at what he said was the "filthy" kitchen, and sat down and drank two six-packs of beer and proceeded to flip lit cigarette butts on the linoleum floor, shouting that if he had to live in a pig pen then he'd treat it like a pig pen.

I despised Bill McIntyre and when I was honest with myself, I knew I was staying married to him only to postpone the humiliation of divorce.

I'm not sure if it was because of Cass and Richard, or if Jack actually expecting me to move to Cambodia had stirred things up, or perhaps learning about my mother's separate will, her final statement to my father—but the memory of the day my first marriage ended was in front of me, as sharp and clear as if it happened five minutes ago.

It was late in the afternoon on a cold Saturday in June. The ironing board was set up in the kitchen where Bill stood ironing between taking long swigs from a can of beer he had set on the wide end of the ironing board. It had been over a month since I stopped taking care of him, leaving him to cook for himself and take care of his own clothes and he was still incredulous that he was actually forced to do these things for himself.

"God dammit, I can't see why the hell you can't get off your fat ass and do something around here."

I ignored him. "I'm taking Max for a walk." I'd found that ignoring him and leaving was about my only defense.

Hearing his name and the word "walk," Max bounded toward the door.

"What the hell good are you!" Barely in control, Bill fumed and swore, slamming the iron, pressing the cloth into the board with a frenzied rage. Max got under foot, knocking into the legs of the ironing board, and the beer spilled.

"You fucking piece of shit!" Bill lunged at Max and shoved the iron on his back.

"NO!" I screamed. "No! Stop it! Stop it!" I ran to Max as Bill kicked the dog across the room spewing obscenities, kicking repeatedly. I reached for Max and Bill kicked me while Max howled—then he hurled him outside and I ran to Max, who lay whimpering on the ground. Bill left the house, glaring at us lying there like we were a pile of garbage, and he drove away, wheels screeching as he sped around the corner.

After I rushed Max to the vet, I came back, packed my bags, loaded my car, and left. On the following Monday, I saw a lawyer. All I took with me that day were my clothes, my books and records, Max's leash, and his dog dish. I didn't want anything to remind me of Bill McIntyre and that marriage. My friends thought I was crazy. I walked out on the wedding presents, furniture, dishes, posters, plants—all the things we'd been given or bought together. But I came out of it knowing something I hadn't known going in: that the absolute minimum requirement for a relationship is respect.

When I met Jack, it was six months after my divorce was final and despite plenty of opportunity, I hadn't been going out much. I was gun-shy around any man who seemed artistic or creative, and found the young stockbrokers I worked with shallow and boring. One of the secretaries at work was a friend of Jack's sister Lib and wanted to fix me up with Jack. He was new to Seattle, doing research at the University. I can't say it was love at first sight, even though I was attracted to him—but I liked him immediately, and we began seeing each other. At first I didn't take him too seriously, but he began to grow on me, and what really surprised me was Max's reaction.

Max's back had healed from where it had been burned, but he'd been branded with a deep fear of men. Most guys who tried to approach Max were met with a low growl, before he slunk away, cowering with his tail between his legs. But whenever Jack came to see me, he took to stopping at the Leschi Market near my house where the butcher would give him beef bones. When I first opened the door and Jack came in, he never tried to pet Max; instead, he just unwrapped the present from the meat counter and put it on the floor in the kitchen and gave Max his space. Gradually Max would greet Jack by wagging his tail, with the fragile trust and growing expectation that something good was about to happen. After two months of this steadfast seduction, Jack was petting Max and throwing balls for him when we took him to the park.

I found that Jack was even-tempered and reliable, a "what you see is what you get" kind of person. He was unpretentious and fun, and even his Norman Rockwell, boyish look had more and more appeal. Like Max, I began to trust him and although I still wasn't falling madly in love with him, my capacity to trust spoke as much to my resilience as to his trustworthiness. I warmed to his optimism and good will as if they were compounded in a healing balm. And when we first went to bed, he was so gentle that I looked at him with quiet astonishment and wept at the safety of it.

Thinking back on our early days together, and the contrast to the awful years of my first marriage, made me worry that I'd been taking Jack for granted. Maybe I'd been a little too blunt when we had that Cambodia conversation last night. Not that I was about to change my mind, but maybe I should have tried to be more tactful. We'd hardly said a word since. We were distant, both last night and this morning, and when he came home from the lab— the minute he walked in the door, I could tell he was still upset.

I was roasting a chicken, trying to cook him a nice dinner, I suppose either a peace offering or a penance for upsetting him by not agreeing to drop my life for two years. What a terrible wife.

"Hi honey, it's just the two of us, tonight. Cass had a meeting after work." I tried to be pleasant.

"Good, maybe you can relax so you won't have to watch how much she's eating." His tone wasn't very friendly, but not exactly hostile either. He took his briefcase to his office, then came back and fixed himself a drink.

"Or drinking," I added.

"What?" He seemed defensive.

"That I won't have to watch how much she's drinking." I opened the oven door to check on the chicken. The table was set and all I had left to do was sauté the spinach, but even if there had been something for him to do, it was obvious he was in no mood to offer to help the way he'd been doing lately.

I cooked the spinach, then put the chicken on a platter and surrounded it with the new potatoes I'd roasted with it. "You can sit down if you'd like." I carried the food to the table. "But her drinking's gotten better, have you noticed?"

"I guess so."

"No, seriously, Jack. I'm sure she didn't have any wine at all last night." I brought his favorite salad to the table from the refrigerator, sliced tomatoes and fresh mozzarella with basil. Ordinarily he would notice and say something nice about it, but he concentrated on carving the chicken and kept talking about Cass.

"Good. Because I was beginning to think we should say something." He helped himself to the chicken. "I'll be glad when you stop worrying about her."

"You worry, too."

"I know, but it's not the same way you do."

We sat and ate in silence, and I realized there would have been a time when I would have taken it on as my job to try to cheer him up, help him feel better, as if my equilibrium depended on making sure he was happy. But I'd already said my piece, and this was just something he would have to work out for himself.

After we were through eating, I put decaf coffee on, but Jack said he didn't want any. He went to the liquor cabinet and took down his bottle of Laphroaig, single malt scotch, a Christmas present from Ian and Kelly. He filled a glass with ice cubes and poured in the Scotch, took a long drink and then looked over at me as I was clearing the dishes.

"So, I suppose you want us to take up golf." This time

his tone was rather hostile. "I could just see us. A couple of old duffers hacking away."

"I didn't say anything about golf, Jack. I don't like golf."

"How do you know if you've never tried it? I don't remember you ever trying it."

"I didn't. But I just know, that's all. But if you're interested, I think it would be wonderful if you played with some other men. Hal next door plays all the time. Maybe you could play with him?"

"He's got a two handicap."

"He's bald and fat, but I'd hardly call those handicaps," I bristled, finding his comment somewhat offensive.

"A two handicap—that's about his golf game. It means he's very good, and I wasn't serious anyway."

"Could've fooled me."

Jack went upstairs to his office and I went to the basement to paint. The light was terrible down there, but this afternoon I brought a lamp down from the living room to see if it would help, hoping I could get a little work done. I was worried about the show. It was getting closer every day. I worried that I shouldn't have attempted such a large painting. The area in the landscape where the trees divided the meadow from the sky was a pivotal focal point and I was beginning to think I'd gotten it all wrong. Too intense. Maybe garish even. My use of color was odd. I knew that, but it was how I experienced things, although maybe this had just gone over the top and it was all turning dreadful. I'd been working about a half hour when I had to stop to answer the phone.

"Hello Annie." My father's gravelly deep voice. His tone couldn't be called pleasant, but there was an absence of malice in contrast to the last time I'd talked with him. "I thought I should let you know I'm leaving for Palm Springs and I've told Rose to call you if anything comes up about the house."

"Fine."

"And Bob Dennison is getting everything ready for probate, it will take months as he's recommending another representative I can work with around the art...the tax consequences could be significant if this isn't handled properly."

"I see."

"Annie, I don't want my legacy to be a legal battle with my children. I want you to know that. I only want control of the decisions about my own work and if your mother hadn't been so sick, and not been herself, I'm sure she wouldn't have gone to this James woman."

Oh, she was herself all right. You just didn't get it. She wanted one unprecedented final gesture. Her curtain speech. Just one line: Screw you, Alexander Gunther.

But I wasn't going to take the bait. "Where will you be in Palm Springs?" I just wanted to make him say it.

"I'll be staying with Mrs. Meldon."

"Mrs.? Oh, so there's a mister Meldon?"

"She's divorced."

"I see."

"No, I don't think you do see. Your mother would have wanted me to get on with my life. Akiko only wanted my happiness, she always put other people first."

Right. And she just loved putting you first when you were screwing your students and every collector who came your way. What happiness that must have given her.

"Annie?"

"Yes."

"I'll call when I get back from Palm Springs."

"And how long will you be gone?" Like I cared. He could stay forever and it would be fine with me. I'd just have to help Rose find a new job.

"I'm not sure. I'll let you know when I'm back."

He certainly didn't waste any time, not that it was much of a surprise, but it made me feel sad for my mother. If she thought this separate will business was sending him a message about how little she trusted him, the only message he'd gotten was that she must not have been herself, slightly off her rocker.

By the time I came up from the basement Cass still hadn't gotten home and I thought it was a good sign. Instead of collapsing here after work the way she'd been doing, she probably met up with some friends after her meeting.

As usual, Jack was sound asleep when I came to bed. He usually fell asleep practically the second his head hit the pillow. I lay awake for a while, obsessing about my painting. I finally dropped off, but awakened again with my mind spinning. It was always the same anxiety: Am I any good? Always fueled by the same echo, the pronouncement from the great Alexander Gunther, replaying, like a broken record. It's representational, decorative crap. You'll never be a serious painter, you don't have it.

I looked at the clock on the bedside table. Three A.M. My thrashing about hadn't affected Jack at all. He was out, dead to the world. I envied his ability to sleep no matter what worries he might be having. I finally decided to go down to the basement and just look at the damn thing. Maybe carry it up to the kitchen where the light was better.

I put on my bathrobe and tiptoed out of the bedroom. At the top of the stairs I noticed the light coming from under the door in Cass's room. Perhaps she couldn't sleep either. I tapped on the door and slowly opened it. It took a minute for me to digest the sight of the empty bed. I went to the adjoining bathroom Cass used. Also empty. Then I looked in the bedroom again, as if somehow I'd been mistaken. Why was the light on? Did she leave it on when she left for work in the morning? The bed hasn't been touched. She hasn't even been here. She hasn't come home! Frantic, as it finally sank in, I ran back to the bedroom and woke Jack.

"Annie, I'm sure there's some explanation," he said, reluctantly sitting up. "Did she say where she was going?"

"Just that she wouldn't be home for dinner. She had some kind of a meeting at the end of the day. When we went to bed and she hadn't come home, I just figured she probably met up with some friends."

"Do you know who?"

"I have no idea, and I'm not even sure that's what she did." I immediately thought the worst. My mind often ran away in downward spirals whirling to the extremes, and although I always tried to rein in my fears, most of my life I hadn't met with much success.

"The bars close at two," Jack looked at the clock next to the bed. It was 3:35. "But there are all-night restaurants."

"That's a long dinner! I'm sure she would have called."

"Maybe she and her friends met some guys," Jack tried to sound reasonable.

"Oh, my God. Like Mr. Goodbar."

"Annie, Cass isn't that stupid."

"What if she had an accident? We better call the police."

"They won't file a missing person report for thirty-six hours."

"Oh, right. I remember that from when Ian was in high school."

Jack pushed back the covers and swung his legs over the side of the bed. "I guess I could call the hospitals."

"Would you?"

"Sure." He patted my hand, then pulled open the drawer of the nightstand and took out the phone book. Placing it on the bed, he opened it and was looking for the hospital listings when we heard the door closing downstairs. Daisy ran from the room wagging her tail.

Jack and I rushed from the bedroom and flipped on the hall light. We stood at the top of the stairs looking down at Cass. Flooded with relief, I tore down the stairs and hugged her.

"Oh, honey. Thank God you're all right."

I held Cass for a minute, gripping her tightly before I finally pulled back. Relief quickly gave way, knee-jerking to parental authority: an age-old stance, so easily reconstituted.

"Cass, do you know what time it is? Where have you been?" I raised my voice.

"Out. I was out," she said, coldly.

"I can't believe you didn't call us. Your mother's been worried sick waiting up for you," Jack bellowed.

"I never asked you to wait up for me!"

"Where were you all night? Don't lie to us, Cass." I demanded.

"Fine," she said, defiantly, "I was at Richard's."

"Richard!" Jack exploded, "what were you doing with that dick!"

"I can't believe this—all I heard was how he lied. How he hurt you, how he cheated on you and now you just go back there and sleep with him!" I was outraged.

"You have no right to tell me who I can sleep with!" Cass yelled.

"Then you have to be home by midnight. It's almost four o'clock in the morning." Jack glared at her from the top of the stairs.

"A curfew! How weird is that? I'm thirty-two years old. Just who are you kidding?" Cass was indignant. "That totally sucks. It's ridiculous!"

"At least call us when you're not coming home." I said, trying to back off.

"I'm supposed to call and report my every move?"

"Your father and I call each other when we're going to be late. That's just common courtesy."

"Listen young lady," Jack shouted, "as long as you live here you're going to live by our rules and one of them is that you tell us when you're not coming home and the other is that when you do come home, for God's sake be quiet and don't wake us up!"

19

CASS

In the morning Annie, Jack, and Cass all made a concentrated effort to be civil to each other. There didn't
seem to be any reason to re-hash what happened the
night before. Cass knew she should call them when she
was going to be late, and she was sorry they'd been worried. Whatever they thought about her relationship with
Richard, her parents at least had the good sense not to say
anything else about it. If they had, Cass knew the peace
they were all trying to restore would have gone down the
toilet.

After work she was going to meet Lena at Allegria, a
small Italian restaurant in the University District with a
cozy bar they both liked. The drizzle that had been steady
all day had increased, and by the time they arrived within
a few minutes of each other, it was raining hard. They were
early enough to get a table by the fire and ordered their
usual drink for dreary days: coffee nudges.

"My Dad actually called me 'young lady.' How weird is
that? I couldn't believe it." Cass said, giving Lena the play-
by-play of the dust-up with her parents.

"Young lady?"

Cass nodded. "I've got to get out of there, Lena. They've been great, except for last night, which was hideous. My Dad even said I should have a curfew!"

"That sucks. He really said that?"

"He did, seriously. But Mom backed off pretty quick. And things were better this morning. Of course, they were right about phoning them. That's no problem. And they didn't say anything about Richard, but I know what they think. They think I should get rid of him. And I should." She sighed. "I don't know what happened."

"Valerie and I vote with your parents." Lena picked up the bar menu. "I'm going to order some food. Want anything?"

"Sure, might as well."

The bar had filled up; it was a favorite with the University faculty, although it couldn't be categorized as a college hangout; the drinks were too pricey. Lena looked around the crowded room before she spotted their server and motioned to him.

"Have you decided yet about taking the job in Bellevue?" she asked.

"I'm leaning toward it, but I have such a great commute now, all of five minutes—it's hard to give that up, and I'm pretty sure I don't want to live over there."

"Would you like to house-sit for a while? I didn't think of you until just now, but there's a woman at work, Audrey Pardington—her house-sitter fell through and she's been asking around to find someone. It's a cool house near the university; Audrey will be working at a clinic in Guatemala for three months. She has a nice dog, Elvis. Actually he's a great dog."

"I would love to talk with her!"

"I'll give her your number. I'll call her when I get home and tell her about you."

"That is so great, I hope she hasn't found anybody." Cass was afraid to get too excited, it seemed like such a perfect solution.

"I don't think she has, she just mentioned it to me this morning. And I've got some good news on the wedding front." Lena said, with a smile. "My brother came through. Val and I couldn't believe it. He's always been the prince and I never figured he'd stand up to Mom and risk his favored nation, preferred customer status. His style has mostly been to just go along on the surface, but quietly do whatever the hell he wants.

"Anyway, Doug actually found some backbone." Lena continued after the server had taken their order. "He told Mom that if Val and I weren't in the wedding party and treated like any other couple, that he and Sandra would get married at the courthouse and she wouldn't be invited. Neither family would. Actually, I think that's his dream wedding anyway. I think he was disappointed when she caved. But he did it, he stood up for me and Val and it actually got me a little choked up."

"Let's drink to Doug." Cass said, raising her mug. "Who'd have thought?"

"I know. Maybe there's hope for a few men. I don't know about Richard, though."

"He called me at work this morning and said that now that I'm not there anymore, he realizes that he loves us both. He says he feels like Dr. Zhivago, torn between the two women he loves."

"Tell him that if he wants to be in a Russian novel, he

can be Anna Karenina," Lena smiled sweetly, "and throw himself in front of a train."

When Cass got home, Daisy was thrilled to see her, jumping around the way she met all the family when they opened the door. Daisy was one of the bonuses of living with her parents, she thought. Dogs love you no matter what. She hoped it would work out for her to house-sit for Audrey Pardington; it would be fun to take care of a dog.

Cass was in the kitchen when Annie came up from the basement. "I'm just making coffee. Want some?"

"Sure, thanks."

"Where's Dad?"

"He stayed late at the lab. I think he picked up something to eat on the campus."

It seemed to Cass that her mother wanted to tell her something, but then Annie turned and got coffee mugs down from the cupboard.

They sat across from each other, each with her own thoughts. It was dusk and in the yard Cass could still see the beautiful rhododendrons, the huge deep purple blossoms still wet from the rain. This was a beautiful house, but she didn't want to be here. She decided to wait to mention the house-sitting possibility until she knew for sure. It could be a Godsend because Cass was afraid if she stayed longer, in spite of last night—she could see it getting comfortable here. The longer she stayed, the harder it could be to move out. One thing was clear though; she would never go back to that apartment. And not to him. Ever. Dr. Zhivago, my ass.

"Cass, this thing with you and Richard—"

"Mom, I really don't want to go there."

"Just hear me out. I know I've never said much about my first marriage, but this thing with you and Richard has stirred it up, I guess. And I just need to say a few things. I'm not prying into your life; I just want you to know more about mine. Okay?"

"Fair enough."

"When that marriage broke up, I wasn't in any hurry to find someone else. Back then people thought you were very odd if you weren't Mrs. Somebody. But after Bill—to say nothing of my parents' dreadful marriage, I had some pretty serious doubts if loving marriages existed. There was a TV show I used to watch, the *Dick Van Dyke Show*, and the couple—their names were Laura and Rob; they were very kind to each other. It made me feel good to see them living together so happily in TV land. But I thought it was a fairy tale."

"Wasn't it?" Cass couldn't figure out what she was getting at.

"Yes and no. Life is never as smooth as it was on that show. But there's one thing that has to be non-negotiable, and that's to insist on respect. The real power is knowing that you can always leave, that you never have to put up with being treated with contempt." Mom put down her cup. "Cass, why didn't you tell us sooner?"

"Tell you what?"

"About you and Richard."

"Do you really want to know?"

"Of course. That's why I'm asking."

Cass refilled her cup, added milk and stirred it slowly. "Because it's a failure and I wasn't allowed to fail."

"You what?"

"I wasn't allowed to fail."

"I have no idea what you're talking about."

"Fine. Forget it, then." Cass got up to leave.

"Don't walk out. That's what your father always does—just tell me what you mean."

Cass leaned on the table, still standing. "Ian was allowed to fail. He bashed up the car two weeks after he got his license, he could stay out all night and no one asked any questions and he just got bailed out. His crap was laughed off. You and Dad both cut him all kinds of slack, but oh no—not me...I was supposed to be perfect."

"We never said you had to be perfect." Annie said, raising her voice. "Not once!"

"Oh sure, not in those exact words, but it was there. Always listing the opportunities that I had that you didn't have. Like I was supposed to do everything you wanted to do—have a great career, travel, and somehow fit in a marriage and of course, kids."

"I don't see what's wrong with my wanting you to do more with your life than I've done with mine," Annie said, defensively.

Cass's eyes filled with tears. "What's wrong with your life?" she said, her voice breaking, "I'd give anything to have some nice guy like Dad take care of me while I play with the dog at my little part-time job!"

20

ANNIE

I've never been one to believe in the geographical cure. A change of scenery might take one's mind off a problem for a while, but the issue still would rear its head at some point if it weren't really dealt with. Distance by itself, in my experience, never changed a thing. But when my father went to Palm Springs, the distance from him brought me quite a lot of peace. I'd hardly thought about him since he'd gone to stay with Mrs. Meldon. And this morning I also wanted a geographical cure in terms of my daughter. I wanted to get away from the house. I hate conflict and if I was running away from it, I didn't much care. I woke before Cass or Jack, got my stuff from the basement, fed Daisy, dashed off a quick note for Jack and left to catch the ferry for Vashon. As I was backing down the drive, I saw the newspapers on the front porch. It might be nice to take the *New York Times* to read on the boat, but Jack wouldn't be too pleased. That's all I'd need. Not getting along with either one of them. Although things with Jack had thawed a bit since the night we'd been so worried about Cass. And he hadn't said any more about the Cambodia thing, which led me to believe he was trying to figure out some kind of long-distance consultation with the medical school there. At least I hoped that was what was going on. I kept my mouth shut about him needing to develop interests, but he said a curious thing the other day. It seemed to come out of the blue. He said one thing he was very interested in was food.

The streets were almost deserted and I loved the quiet. First light is my favorite time. I almost worship the unspoiled peace and freshness of another day. When I came to the top of Beacon Hill, I caught sight of the Olympic Mountains and the view of the violet peaks lifted my heart. It was a gorgeous spring morning, crisp and cloudless. Maybe I'd have time for a sketch before the boat arrived. I'd taken to carrying canvas paper and oil pastels with me everywhere now in case I wanted to make a quick drawing.

In West Seattle I stopped at the Starbucks, ordered a latte and started to pick up a paper but thought better of it. Why not let the bad news stay out of my head for a while? Sketching the mountains while I waited for the ferry had far greater appeal than keeping abreast of the latest disaster, political or natural.

The young woman who was making my latte seemed about Cass's age. I couldn't be in this place without thinking about her. And it stung. Is that how she saw my work at Woodside all these years? Playing with the dog at my little part-time job? Did she really mean that? Jack had used a variation on that theme when he wanted me to go to Cambodia, "just a part-time job." Is that where Cass got it? And did she really think that Jack just took care of me, as if I were a little girl? What bullshit. It made me furious.

As if I didn't pull my own oar in the marriage with Jack getting something in the bargain.

I really couldn't let this one go. It would eat away if I didn't talk to Cass about it, although there was no way I was up to it now. I hadn't even wanted to see her this morning and was just glad I had Fred's studio to go to. It felt like a sanctuary.

I called Ian on my cell phone while I waited for the ferry, maybe Sam could make Cass feel better—since I obviously couldn't. Ian answered and I brought him up to speed on all that had gone on while they were in Hawaii.

"How come she's the one to move?" Ian was indignant. "Why didn't she throw him out?"

"I honestly don't know. You'd have to ask her." I put the window down so Daisy could stick her nose out. "Anyway, I really think it would help if she could see Sam pretty soon. I know you just got back, but do you think you and Kelly could bring him over to see her? Maybe she could take him to the zoo or something?"

"I don't see why not. I'll talk to Kelly and call you back."

"Call Dad at home and talk to Cass. I'll be on Vashon most of the day."

"Okay."

"They're loading the boat, let me call you back in a minute so I can talk to Sam. Is he up?"

"He's watching a Barney DVD, I'll get him."

I was directed to the far right lane on the lower deck. From there I could see Blake Island and behind it the peaks of the Olympics. I had an impulse to sketch, but wanted to hear Sam's voice first.

"Hi Gran."

"Oh, Sam, I'm so glad you're home. I missed you." If

225

there were any sweeter sound than that little voice, I didn't know what it was.

"I missed you, too, Gran. I can swim."

"That's wonderful. Your Mom says there are a lot of pictures of you in the water. I can't wait to see them." I paused, and then took on a serious tone. "Sam, I'd like to ask you a favor."

"Okay."

"Would you draw me a picture of the water in Hawaii?"

"Sure, Gran. I can do that."

"And have it ready for when I see you?"

"Okay."

"I'd really like that."

"I'll do that for you, Gran." Sam said, earnestly.

"Thanks, honey. I appreciate it. See you soon."

"Bye Gran."

The minute I drove off the ferry, I could feel the tightness in my shoulders begin to ease. I put the window down and the scent of the salt air and the sight of the tall firs on the hills worked their magic like an instant formula for stress relief. The drive to the west side of the island this sparkling morning was pure bliss. Tension washed away like it was going out with the tide.

The studio was empty when I arrived, but as I unpacked my car, Fred emerged from the yurt with Pablo, much to Daisy's delight. Fred waved, and then strolled toward his daughter's house, while Pablo took off with Daisy on their usual jaunt.

After carrying in my painting and supplies, I stepped outside to study the firs that lined the meadow. They were the darkest green; looking at them evoked a feeling of depth and mystery that felt almost primordial. I hadn't been satisfied with what I'd done on that section of the painting up to this point, and wanted to begin experimenting with the palette, mixing shades of dark purple, greens, and blues, hoping to produce colors that would capture it. I wanted something that gave off a sense of the secretive. Something deep and unyielding.

Fred came in after I'd been painting for about a half hour. "I put coffee on, if you want some," I said, pleased to see him. I continued working, mixing colors on my palette.

"Thanks. I had my quota at Melissa's house. On weekends I usually have breakfast with her and Mike. But not during the week. It's too hectic, they both leave early for work."

He stood a few feet behind me, quietly looking at my painting. Fred had never critiqued my work. It wasn't his style to critique anyone's unless he was asked; he enjoyed being a resource. When I'd asked about technique, he'd showed me a range of brushwork—scumbling and impasto, and a variety of ways to use the palette knife. His knowledge of color theory had been far reaching and I found it invaluable. Everything Fred taught me, I'd gobbled up. But as important as his knowledge was his attitude. Early on he said, "I have great faith in the capacity of the human spirit to flourish if it has the right conditions, and I think basically leaving an artist alone to experiment is the best condition."

He was silent for such a long time that I could only conclude he must be wrestling with himself, searching for words that wouldn't crush me. Trying to be gentle and tactful, because he was so kind. The silence grew and the longer he went without speaking the more my heart sank.

"Annie," he began quietly, and I bit my lip, bracing myself as my stomach twisted with a long-ago ache. "I don't know quite how to say this, because we each of us want to be unique. And we are. No two people paint or sing or write or dance exactly alike, it's the same miracle as snowflakes. But nevertheless, comparisons are still made and quite a few art critics and teachers make their living doing it. And I'm hesitating because I'm afraid it might be too early in your development for me to say this, but neither of us is young—we never know how much time we have and I don't want this left unsaid."

Fred paused, and then stroked his jaw. "This painting is extraordinary. It reminds me of several landscape painters. Neil Welliver, who died recently, used to paint en plein air, then translated those studies to charcoal drawings, and then from those he created monumental oil paintings. He used to say that he looked very hard, and then made it up as he went along. Welliver said he never painted the color he saw.

"But even more than Welliver," he continued, "your work reminds me of Tom Thomson's, the great Canadian painter from the early 1900's. His paintings vibrate with color. You think of water and sky and blue comes to mind, but in his work there's pink, violet, green—all kinds of color and he does his underpainting in rich color, then often allows spots of color like red from the underpainting to show through.

"And the fascinating thing about the Impressionists was the way they were influenced by Japanese wood block prints. The ukiyo-e or floating life pictures. Your work has that juxtaposition of contrasting colors found in ukiyo-e prints and it's absolutely remarkable."

It took awhile before I could speak. I sensed my mother's presence; I could feel her with me and I drew in my breath and looked out toward the meadow. The dark firs stood guard circling the soft grass, their tall loden branches were woodcut sharp, deep and clear against the sky. Green pastures. Beside still waters. My dear sweet mother.

"Do you know them? Ukiyo-e?"

I nodded, still looking at the meadow. "My mother loved ukiyo-e art and we went to an exhibit at the Asian Art Museum. I think it was work by Kobayashi Kiyochika, but I'm not quite sure. It was a long time ago. We also saw the work of the Group of Seven at the National Gallery of Canada."

"I'm sure Thomson's work is there, although he wasn't technically one of the Group of Seven; he drowned in a canoeing accident around 1917, I think, so he pre-dated the Group of Seven, although he was still a major figure in early Twentieth Century Canadian art." Fred coughed, a little self-conscious. "I did a lecture series on the Group of Seven when I was at Gonzaga. There was always a waiting list to get in it." He seemed happy, remembering, then looked again at my painting. "It's our northern light with the edge of wildness that I think you feel so strongly from this. I get the same feeling from Thomson's Northern River. The edges of the lights are modeled into the half tones of the shadows but the colors remain bright and clear. It gives that true north feeling with the warm highlights playing against the cool shadows."

Fred stood back from my painting. "Artists are born—

then made, is what I believe. I hope I'm around long enough to see much of what you'll do with your gift."

He put his arm around me, squeezing my shoulder in a fatherly hug, and I smiled with tears and a joy that almost hurt. No words could come. Only love and gratitude, and it was awhile before I could look at him.

21

CASS

Her father was reading the paper when she came downstairs. "Where's Mom?" Cass leafed through the *New York Times*, pulling out the travel section.

"She went to the studio on Vashon," Jack said, not looking up from the paper.

"Does she usually go over there on Sunday?"

"This is the first time. She left before I was awake."

"Probably didn't want to see me." Cass got a banana and peeled it, then took a bite. "I was mean to her, and I feel bad about it."

"What happened?" Jack put down the paper.

"Well, basically, I told her I'd give anything to have her life. Only I didn't say it in a very nice way, and I know I hurt her feelings."

When Cass was in high school, most of the sparks that erupted were between her and Annie, and Jack often found himself in the middle, the person they'd each confide in. Cass remembered he was also usually the one to bring them together. She finished the banana and put a bagel in the toaster. This all felt too familiar, déjà vu all over again.

It was too teen-agey and all she could think was that she really, really had to move on with her life.

"What did you say about her life?"

"Just that I think she's lucky to have you and only work part-time."

"Cass, she may only work part-time, but her job is important to her. It's a big thing for your mother, I admit maybe I didn't truly get how important until recently. She loves it and she helps people. And as far as I'm concerned, she certainly put you kids first, and me, too. And she didn't do that halfway."

"Don't you think I've wanted that!"

"Cass, you can do much better than this guy. I know you don't want my advice—"

"Listen, it's over with him. And I'm pretty sure I won't be here much longer. Lena found me a house-sitting job and I'm meeting with the woman this afternoon. Unless her dog knew me in another life and despises me on sight, I'll be moving out soon."

"I hope you're not feeling forced out." Her father sounded worried. "We don't want you to feel like you can't stay here, honey."

"It's for the best, and I might be taking a new job, too. I haven't quite made up my mind." Cass got her bagel and sat next to him. It was easier with her Dad, she never felt like she'd let him down the way she did with her mother. At least not the same way. It was less intense somehow. Cass spread cream cheese on her bagel. "I've been offered a District Manager's position. Managing fifteen stores, only it's on the east side."

"Great!" Jack grinned. "Take it."

"But I'm not sure that's what I really want for a career.

I started working there when I got back from Thailand, just for something temporary."

"It's an outstanding company and getting experience like that can translate into all kinds of things. I think the change will do you good—new stomping grounds, new faces and it will be a challenge."

"You really think I should take it?"

"Absolutely. And if it doesn't work out, I know you'll figure something else out. Something better. Maybe even make your own job somewhere, the way Mom did."

"The way Mom did?"

"Sure. The way she got funding for the pet therapy program, when she brings dogs from the shelter to Woodside. Look, here's the best advice I can give you. Have fun. I don't mean turn your life into a party. Just because things are hard doesn't mean they can't be fun." Jack folded the paper and got up from the table.

"So that's it, Cass. Do things that are fun, and don't worry about Mom. If you feel bad about what you said, just tell her you're sorry and she'll forget it in a second." He patted her hand. "You have so much ahead of you kiddo, I'm so proud of you that Starbucks has the good sense to know talent when they see it."

After talking to her father, Cass felt her spirits perking up. And Kelly and Ian had asked her over, which also made her feel she might be turning the corner. It was great to be actually looking forward to something—she couldn't wait to see Sam. She wished she could just hang out with the little guy and not have to say anything to Ian and Kelly about Richard, but it would've been weird to pretend everything was fine. Besides, she figured they probably knew anyway.

When she finally got around to it at dinner, trying to sound matter-of-fact, Kelly was so smarmy and sympathetic, Cass wanted to dump the pasta primavera on her head. She felt like she had a big zero on her forehead or a red "L" on her chest, for Loser.

"Oh Cass, I'm so sorry," she gushed. "What a cad!"

Cad? Where did she get that? Kelly was so out of it. Richard was an asshole and a shithead. But cad? Please. (She liked Lena's reaction best when she'd first told her, "There are two sides to every break-up—yours and the shithead's.") Ian had been a little better. He said he'd like to beat the crap out of Richard, which Cass thought was an appropriate response. Except for right after Baach died, she hadn't been as close to Ian since he'd married Kelly, but she still had the feeling that even though they were in very different places in their lives, she could count on him to come through if she ever needed him.

After dinner Cass helped Sam get ready for bed. Quite a big production with lots of stalling between the major events: getting in pajamas, brushing teeth, going potty. When everything had been accomplished, Sam got under the covers and snuggled against her as Cass read to him. His latest favorite was *How Do Dinosaurs Say Good Night?* The book had illustrations of ten different kinds of dinosaurs, and what totally amazed her was that Sam knew them all, ones she had never heard of like Apatosaurus and Dimetrodon. She was convinced he was a genius (with the brains coming from her side of the family). After he named the last one, he'd go back to the top and start all over again. Repetition was a big thing with Sam.

While he was cuddled next to her, Cass thought about the district manager job. She was leaning toward taking it;

the experience would be terrific and the salary certainly had a lot of appeal. And working in the Bellevue area had a big bonus she hadn't thought of at first: Sam. It would be easy to pop in and see him after work or maybe during a lunch break because the stores she'd be managing were all nearby. Cass kissed the top of his head. Sam, the three-year-old deal clincher, had put it over the top.

She noticed his eyes beginning to droop as he stared at the page without naming any more dinosaurs. His little body grew heavier against her, and she kissed the top of his head again, then slowly closed the book.

"Time to sleep, Sam," she whispered. He snuggled under the covers and she tucked him in.

"Cass...."

"What is it, honey?" she asked, leaning over the bed.

"Have Mommy come in."

"Sure, Sam. Shall I turn out the light?"

"Mommy'll do it when she comes."

"Okay. 'Night, Sam. I love you."

"'Night, Cass. I love you, too."

Cass went downstairs to get Kelly, wondering what it would be like to be the one a child wanted like that. To come first in a child's heart.

22

ANNIE

The caller ID said "A. Gunther" above my father's number; he'd gotten a cell phone a few days after Mom died. I glanced at the clock. It was seven-thirty and I'd just put a bagel in the toaster. Too early for a considerate person to be calling, although it was my father and that never applied to him.

"Annie, I'm coming home a day early," he said, never one to waste any words. "I want you to call Rose and have her get the house ready."

"What do you want her to do?" I asked. "No one's been there to mess it up since you left."

Uncharacteristically, he didn't say anything and I wondered if Mrs. Meldon was throwing him out. Maybe the Great Alexander Gunther didn't wear so well up close and personal.

"Why don't I give you Rose's number and you can call her yourself," I suggested.

"Did I ask you for her number?" he snarled. "Just call her and tell her I'll be coming on the twenty-second. She knows what I want. Why the hell can't you just do what I ask?"

I'm not your secretary. I was trying to get up the nerve to actually state that fact, when he hung up.

My father probably wanted Rose to air out the house, dust everything, and get food in for him. He was fastidious, probably obsessive compulsive in the degree of cleanliness and order he required. As an adult, I had come to understand there was so much chaos inside him that he needed everything around him in place and structured just to maintain some kind of equilibrium. But as a child, I never knew what would set him off.

I remember days when sometimes I would be in the living room, playing with my toys on the floor and he'd come through and barely notice. But at other times, the identical amount of clutter would evoke his rage. One morning when I was about eight, Mom went to take a shower and left me at the kitchen table where I was cutting out clothes for my paper dolls. I had blunt scissors and tried to be careful, but scraps of paper covered the table, some floating to the floor.

"Akiko!" my father shouted from his studio. "Where's my coffee?"

After a few minutes he burst in the kitchen. "Where's your mother?"

"Upstairs."

"What the hell is this?"

He kicked at the scraps of paper on the floor.

"You wreck everything around here. What a goddam mess!"

Then he swept up my paper dolls, charged to the sink,

flung open the cupboard under the sink and stuffed them in the garbage.

Maybe Mrs. Meldon wasn't a neat freak and decided not to put up with him. Well, it wasn't my problem. I'd call Rose after breakfast and she could deal with him. At least she was getting paid, although I had my doubts about how long she'd stay now that my mother was gone.

I was finishing breakfast when Cass came down. We'd hardly spoken since our flare-up and I didn't feel very welcoming, especially after starting the day with my father. I continued to drink my coffee and look at the paper, although I did manage to say "hi."

"Mom, I just want you to know I'm sorry about the other day." Cass studied the nails of her left hand, pushing back the cuticles. It was something she did when she was nervous.

I went to the sink, rinsed out my coffee cup and put it in the dishwasher before turning to face her. "What you said was mean, Cass. But I'm afraid if I point that out you'll just take it to imply that you have to be perfect. So I feel like I'm in a bind with you."

"I'm sorry. Sometimes I think I'm like a wounded animal that lashes out when someone's just trying to help me."

"I have to say it bothers me that you think I laid some kind of trip on you to be perfect. And as far as my job goes—"

"Look, I'm sorry...what else can I say!"

"Can't I say anything?"

"Fine. Tell me I'm a bitch."

"Oh, Cass...don't you think I know what you're going through? When I was married to Bill McIntyre, he treated me like dirt. There were always other women and even though it was years ago, I haven't forgotten how worthless it can make you feel."

"But you got over it," she said, coolly. Cass got the orange juice from the refrigerator. I was afraid she'd withdraw and get gloomy the way she had in high school when our spats seemed to drag on for days, but then her voice lost its edge. "How long after you were divorced did you meet Dad?"

"It was about six months after my divorce was final, I can't remember exactly how long it took from the time I filed. Maybe three months. But I was pretty gun-shy about men and hadn't been going out much."

"I get that." Cass smiled.

"Coffee? Guess I'll have another cup, want one?" She nodded and I poured us each a cup and we sat together at the breakfast table, clearly both wanting to leave the flare-up behind; a barometer, it seemed to me of the fact that we weren't back in teenage land.

"Did Dad tell you about the new possibility with my job?"

"He did tell me and I think it's just great."

"I made up my mind last night—I'm going for it. I'm calling my district manager this morning to tell him. You know, another advantage of working there is that it'd be easy for me to drop in to see Sam," she paused, "if they end up choosing me."

"I'd be surprised if they didn't."

"And Lena has a friend who needs a house-sitter and I'm going over there after work, and I think it's going to work out. I'll know more when I meet with her, but Lena said she wants someone right away." Cass smiled, "I think it could be the best thing for all of us."

"I'm for whatever helps you feel like your old self." I hadn't known quite what to say. I didn't want her to feel unwanted, but there was no question it would be a big relief to have my studio back.

After Cass left, I called Rose. As much as I didn't want to be involved with doing things for my father, I figured I could withstand these small hassles. Not that they were a walk in the park, but I could do it. I certainly preferred not having anything to do with him, but I was sure contact with him would be pretty sparse, and most likely, I could look forward to months without ever hearing from him. The real damage, the way I'd bought into his deprecating attitude toward me, had been done. All these years, I had stopped myself, thinking it was his voice, when it had been mine. But it was damage that could be repaired, and little by little, I was beginning to believe in myself.

But the best antidote to even a minor hassle with my father was Sam, and on my way back from Vashon that afternoon, even before going home, I went over to Ian and Kelly's. It had only been a few days since they'd returned from Hawaii, but I couldn't wait any longer to see Sam.

He ran to me the minute he heard my voice and jumped in my arms. He was brown in spite of the gallons of sunscreen I was sure Kelly had slathered on him and seemed to have grown in just the short time they'd been gone. I vowed not to ever let a week go by without seeing him, at least if I could help it. There was so much change, so fast, I'd blink and he'd be gone, grown up with a family of his own. It was the thought I had every time I saw him and I always wondered if I'd live to see it. I'd become so aware of time since Mom died—I didn't want to waste a second by doing things I didn't want to do, or miss a second of doing what I did.

Sam showed me the picture he made for me of Hawaii. "This is the water."

Blue scribbles.

"How lovely. Was it warm?"

"Kind of. This is the swimming pool. It was more warm."

Blue blob in the right hand corner.

"So you swam in the pool?"

"Uh-huh."

"And what's this?"

Green pointy scribbles next to the blue blob.

"Trees."

"Oh, of course. Palm trees. Beautiful." I hugged him. "Thank you for such a beautiful picture. May I take it home?"

Sam nodded. "It's for you, Gran," he said, earnestly, "like you asked me."

"Thank you, Sam. Maybe we can make more Hawaii pictures the next time I see you."

"I'll put a boat in the next one."

"That's a very good idea."

When I got back from seeing Sam, Cass was home and happier than she'd been in weeks. She'd be house sitting for Lena's friend...the dog was great...the house was great...it was in Montlake, not far from the bridge across Lake Washington she'd take if she got the Bellevue job. It was wonderful to see her energy and upbeat mood, which seemed genuine—not an attempt to soldier on the way she had when she first moved back. "And I'm going to have a new look." Cass pulled a box from her purse. "It's a perm—Revlon from the drugstore 'cause I didn't want to spend an arm and a leg at a salon, in case I don't like it."

About two hours later, I was in the kitchen fixing dinner when Jack came home. The minute he shut the door, he set down his briefcase, scowled, and began sniffing the air.

"What stinks?"

"Cass is giving herself a permanent."

"A what?"

"For her hair."

"You mean she's deliberately making her head stink?"

"What you smell is a permanent. Her friend at work advised her to make a change. Something to make her feel better."

"It changes the way she smells—it makes her stink!"

"She washed it out, Jack, it doesn't end up smelling like that. And she has some news—"

"What news?"

"She's going to live at a house in Montlake, house-sitting for a few months. The woman needs her right away."

Jack took a glass from the cupboard, filling it from the bottle of cabernet we had open. "What a relief. It's bad enough that we've had to listen to that singer she plays all the time who sounds constipated, but now this place smells like we have plumbing problems."

"I don't think Nora Jones sounds constipated."

"Well I do. And she plays it over and over. I can't believe you don't mind."

I finished setting the table and began tossing the salad. "You never said anything about it before."

"I didn't want to upset her. But now that she's leaving,

I can tell you that it really got on my nerves. And now this smell." Jack waved the air, fanning it. "I can't believe people actually choose to put that on their heads."

"Jack, the hair thing is a good sign. They always say that one of the first signs a woman in the hospital is getting better is when she asks for a mirror to fix herself up."

"So, we've gone from running a hospital to a hair salon," he grumbled.

I laughed. "Soon to be art studio. Right? You can smell turpentine again, isn't that great?"

"Yeah, great," he said. "Oh well, at least you don't play constipated music."

"No, I'll be putting the radio back in the studio, tuned to the classical station. I've lost some time, but I really think I can get the painting ready for the show. Ever since Fred was so encouraging, I've been more confident and I feel pretty good about how it's coming."

"I'm happy for you, Annie," he paused, "I really am."

I put my arms around him. Jack hadn't said anything more about Cambodia and with him, actions were often the way he communicated. I noticed he'd been trying to do more to help around the house, and he seemed to want to spend more time with Sam. Jack spent a lot of time emailing Dr. Phriep and faxing articles and papers to him. But what surprised me the other day was coming home to find him watching the food channel on TV. He said he thought he might want to learn to make Vietnamese food and Thai food. As far as I was concerned, he could make tofu with chocolate sauce and I'd try to eat it. I just wanted him to be happy.

23

CASS

"Hi, Cass." Richard's voice was rich and deep, the caramel voice that used to make her melt. "I'd really like to talk to you. Give me a call if you can. If you can't get me at home, try me on my cell."

So, now what did he want? She let him have the apartment, what else could he want from her? Well, one thing was for sure: she wasn't in any hurry to call him back. She'd take her own sweet time and he could just see what it felt like to wait. Cass didn't want to play games, and she didn't want to be bitter, but she couldn't help thinking about all the nights she waited for him to come home, only to have him call hours later to say something had come up at the hospital and he'd be late. Or wouldn't be coming home at all.

Screw him. She'd call him when she damn well felt like it, or maybe it would slip her mind and she'd just forget to return the call. If it was so fucking important he'd call again.

"Did you get my message?" he'd ask.

"Oh yeah. Sorry, I guess I forgot," she'd say, and he'd

learn what it was like to get blown off. Cass liked that little scenario, liked it very much and decided maybe she really would just "forget" he'd called.

It was wonderful being in Audrey's house. It had been completely remodeled and the place was awesome; just being in a new environment seemed to be helping Cass look at things in a new way. It reminded her of a proverb Baach once told her. A frog in a well thinks it sees the whole sky. She felt like she'd been seeing Richard and her life from the perspective of living with her parents, stuck in a well where her vision had been limited to either being back with him, or staying where she was. She hadn't been able to imagine other possibilities, and now she could.

She was standing in front of the mirror in the master bath. Cass had never been that much of a girly girl. Her ideal of female beauty was Mia Hamm or Hope Solo, the goalie for the women's national soccer team; but she had to admit, the wavy hair was kind of cool. More than cool, she thought it was kind of sexy and liked the change. Cass was brushing it and fooling around with different ways of styling it when she had an impulse to return Richard's call. Why wait? What the hell, she needed to talk to him anyway about their furniture. A while back when she'd talked to Lena and Val about it, they'd had a good idea about how to handle it, although she hadn't been ready to deal with it at the time. Now that she was at Audrey's, she was motivated to get it over with. Cass decided to call at the apartment and leave a message if he wasn't there, and not try his cell. She wasn't eager enough to talk to him to track him down.

"Richard?"

"Hi Cass. I guess you got my message."

"About wanting to talk or something."

"Yes."

A long silence. She had never been good at tolerating silence and Richard counted on her to make most of the conversation happen, to figure out what he wanted to say and almost say it for him. Not this time. It was awkward, but Cass waited, holding back, controlling her habit of jumping in to fill the space and make a connection.

"Cass?"

He blinked. It made her feel rather smug. "What?"

"Could we meet somewhere?"

"Like where?"

"I don't know, do you want to come over here?"

No way in hell would she play that scene again. Maybe there'd come a day where she could trust herself to be alone with him, but her heart, soul, and mind didn't always seem to be in sync with her body. Cass admitted she was frankly beginning to feel a bit lusty and juicy, as if she was waking up from some numb frozen state—and she was not about to let chemistry take over.

"No, Richard. I don't want to come over there."

Silence. He was undoubtedly waiting for her to suggest a place. For her to figure it out, make it happen, take the initiative and he could just go along, as if he wasn't really responsible for any part of the relationship. Things just happened with Richard, and that way it made it quite easy for him to change direction or avoid a direction he didn't like. Because after all, he hadn't willfully decided anything in the first place. It had all just happened.

Again, she held back, not willing to play her old role and make it easy for him. He'd have to initiate. Poor thing.

"Is there somewhere you'd like to meet?"

Good. He blinked again. And of course, he wanted her to suggest where. "Not really."

Another silence, but this one not as long. He seemed to be getting the idea.

"I suppose you've had dinner..." his voice trailed off.

"Yes."

"I was thinking about the Taj Mahal."

Would wonders ever cease? He actually remembered her favorite place. Give that boy a hand. High fives all around.

"The Taj Mahal?" she repeated.

"They have a bar, don't they? Would you like to meet there?"

"All right," Cass sighed, "what time?"

"Can you meet tonight?"

She looked at her watch. Might as well get it over with. Besides, she wanted her stuff. "I'll be there at eight," she said flatly, not asking if that time worked for him.

"Thanks, Cass. See you soon."

It was a beautiful night. Another warm spring evening. If she'd still been living on Capitol Hill, she could walk to the Taj Mahal; it was only a few blocks from their old apartment. Although now she wouldn't walk anywhere to meet Richard—even if she could. Cass was aware she needed to be able to retreat and lock herself in the fortress of her car, safe from Richard and safe from betrayal by the lust of her lesser self.

Richard was in the bar when she arrived. Great. He had to wait for her. He was sitting at a table against the wall near the kitchen, drinking a beer, and stood when Cass got to the table.

"Thanks for coming."

"Sure." She quickly sat down and took off her jacket.

"What would you like?" He looked around for the server.

"Diet Coke."

"Really? You don't want a drink?" He looked surprised.

"I'm not a total lush, Richard."

"That's not what I meant, I was just surprised, that's all."

The server came over and Cass ordered. She actually had wanted a beer until she saw Richard. The chemistry was as strong as ever. Shit. Would his looks, the sound of his voice always affect her so much? Even the scent of his aftershave—for crissake. At least she'd had the good sense not to meet him at the apartment, or walk here, and she most definitely did not want to drink and risk messing up her head.

"How've you been, Cass?" Richard looked at her warmly.

"Fine."

"You look different."

"Do I?"

"I can't tell what it is, but something's different. Your hair, maybe?"

"A little."

"I like it."

"Thanks." The waiter brought her Coke and she took a sip. There was a long silence. Richard didn't seem to know how to get out of the old pattern, where he would just sit back and react. But as she had on the phone, Cass refused to make it easy for him and after a few minutes he seemed to grasp that it was going to be up to him.

"I've been thinking a lot lately," he paused, searching for words, "and things seemed to have just, well—gotten out of hand, I guess."

"I'm not sure what you mean, but I needed to talk to you because Lena and Val had a great suggestion about how to divide the furniture and stuff we bought together." She looked away, and then down at her Coke, still not meeting his eyes. "They suggested we put everything on Craig's List. You don't commit to selling it the way you do on eBay. But when we get offers, that's how we'll determine the price." She barreled ahead, all business, steamrolling him with her efficiency. "I'm house-sitting for a few months, but then I'll be getting a place and I'd like the couch, the kitchen table and chairs," Cass ticked them off. "I had the coffee table, and the end tables and lamps when you moved in, so I'll be taking those. I want to get everything out by the end of the week and we can sort out the finances when we get the prices from Craig's List," she finally paused, "or if you want the money right away, we can ballpark it and then adjust it after we get the Craig's List bids."

He took a long swig of beer. "I didn't want to meet to talk about our stuff." He looked sad; his dark eyes met hers before he looked away.

"So what did you want?"

"Everything ended so fast, the way it all came down. I feel really shitty about it."

"You should."

"Well, I do," he paused, "I'd do things a lot differently if I could."

"And what would be different? Not getting caught?" She couldn't look at him.

"Cass, please."

"Please what?"

"I wish none of it happened." He looked away again. "With Linda. I wish it hadn't happened."

"Well, that makes two of us," she said, staring intently at him. This time her voice was calm. Being able to hold her own, she felt his looks, his voice, his very physical presence losing some of their initial power, so that the intense sexual attraction she always felt with him became a little muted. Or at least manageable, maybe replaced with a kind of Richard fatigue.

"What I want to know is—if you'd ever consider trying again, giving us another chance."

"So it didn't work out with her, I guess." Cass almost laughed; it was so pathetic and predictable.

"No, but that's not why I want us to try again."

"Why then?"

"Because I've missed you. There's no one like you, Cass. And I realized I still love you."

His eyes were shiny and he reached for her hand. She didn't draw away because she felt something totally unexpected. She actually felt sorry for him.

"Richard, there isn't enough in the bank."

He looked puzzled, so she continued. "You can weather a lot with a person when there's enough good things to be a strong reserve. A hedge against the bad times—but we don't have that. We had a fantastic six months in the beginning, and then you began to take me for granted so that by our third year together—you basically related to me with a bunch of lies. It wasn't a small blip in an otherwise strong relationship. It was almost a year of distance and lies and not being there for things that really mattered to me. Like Sam's birthday. If you felt trapped, you should have talked to me about it. Maybe back then we would have had a chance, but not now. Those first incredible months weren't enough. There wasn't enough love built up, I'm not talking about sex and that was great—but love. Not enough to withstand the shit that happened."

"There's nothing I can say to make you change your mind?"

"No." She stood up. Cass thought of saying she was sorry, because that seemed kind, or at least polite. But she wasn't, so she didn't. "I'll get the stuff out of the apartment at the end of the week and leave the key. And if you can wait for the money—"

"I can wait," he interrupted, signaling the waiter for the check.

"Then I'll send you a check for your half as soon as I get bids from Craig's List."

Cass put on her jacket and smiled at him. "You won't be alone long, Richard. Men with good jobs who look like you never are."

Walking to her car as she left the Taj Mahal, Cass felt sad, but she also felt stronger than she had in years.

24

ANNIE

Sunlight slowly filled the empty room. It was Sunday morning and I stood in the doorway, soaking up the silence as the early light streamed through the bare windows. The apple tree outside Cass's old room had a few lingering blossoms, creamy white tinged with pink, glorious against a robin's egg sky. I could paint it. Right here in my own studio. All I had to do was open the window and look out. What bliss.

I had four days to finish the meadow painting; Fred wanted everyone to come to the Blue Heron gallery on Thursday night to help hang the show. The past week I'd gone to Vashon every day and the foreground was finally coming together. Thank goodness. It seemed strange that it was the last thing, but it had just turned out that way and Fred reassured me that almost every piece had its own trouble spots or challenges, and you could never predict where in the work they'd be.

"Annie, occasionally, something will just sing. And you'll sail ahead as though an angel's guiding your hand.

But you can't count on it and when you start a painting you'll never know if it will be the one."

"I can't say I've had that experience." I laughed.

"You will someday. But I always rather like the challenge, when the thing isn't working and you keep at it, and keep at it, until you either figure out what it needs, or stumble on the solution. It's like you've won a battle."

I'd brought the radio up from the basement after Cass left and it was still tuned to my favorite classical station. As I started mixing paint, Vivaldi's Sonata in C Minor was playing. After it was over the announcer gave a little biography of Vivaldi.

"His father was a professional violinist who taught the young Antonio to play at an early age."

Her father was a professional artist who taught his daughter to paint at an early age. What would that have been like, if he'd encouraged me? It was impossible to imagine, and it didn't matter. It really didn't matter. Martha Jane had the right attitude about not looking back.

"Vivaldi had a relationship with Anna Giraud, which caused the city of Ferrara to reject one of his operas."

I laughed. If he'd been painting in the eighteenth century, my father would've had one rejection after another. I hadn't heard a thing from Alexander the Great since he called about Rose, which was fine with me. Let sleeping dogs lie. He never cared about anyone but himself, why should I worry about him? But I had to admit to a fleeting image of him coming to my show, a thought quickly discarded because I recognized it for what it was: a ludicrous fantasy. It only meant the wish for his approval had never been completely extinguished. It was like a small, pathetic eternal flame, sputtering at a grave that held his cold indifference to me. Maybe it would always be there, but I'd never let it stop me.

I was putting highlights in the foreground when I heard the phone. Jack was out, so I let it ring, continuing to work another few minutes until I came to a good place to stop. I went to the bedroom to pick up the message. It was from Kelly. She didn't phone that often, so I called her right back.

"Hi, Kelly."

"That was sure quick. I thought you must be out."

"I couldn't get to the phone right away."

"Annie, I hate to ask at the last minute, but I just heard from our nanny and she's come down with the flu. I have a doctor's appointment tomorrow and I wondered if you could baby-sit for Sam, if I could drop him off with you?"

"Of course, we'd love to have him."

"Ordinarily, I'd just cancel, it's just a check-up—but these appointments take months to get."

"Don't worry about it. Just bring him over anytime."

"I'll be there about 9:15 if that's okay."

"It's just fine. See you then."

I was thrilled that Sam was coming over. It had been hard for me to disguise my disappointment when Kelly had hired a nanny as soon as Sam was born. I had looked forward to doing a whole lot of babysitting, but the way it turned out, Kelly only asked me when the nanny had her days off or was on vacation. I was the second string, at least that's how I felt sometimes.

I went back to the studio and studied my painting. Maybe a few more shadows near the trees and that would about do it. I could put them in first thing in the morning before Sam came and if it were just the thinnest film, it would have almost two days to dry before we hung the show.

The house was deliciously quiet. I moved my easel closer to the window and stood back, looking at the painting in the stronger light. Fred, that dear man, had proved to be right again. At first the idea of a show seemed like pushing a child off a dock to teach her to swim; sometimes all that came of it was a lifelong fear of the water. But he'd made plunging in with a show as comforting as possible. Nothing was for sale; there were no critics, no reviews. The work was there, displayed, to be seen. Here's where we've been... this is what we've accomplished. And I was excited. Still a little anxious, but in truth, I could hardly wait for the show. How many years had I dreamed of committing myself to the work, only to be trapped by my own fear? This was a little student show, at a small gallery, on a small island. But to me it was monumental.

In the morning Kelly arrived with a huge bag of toys and books for Sam, enough stuff, it seemed to Jack and me, to fill several preschool playrooms. "He loves to throw this around," Kelly showed us a soft rubber softball. "But we don't let him do it in the house." She held up a DVD. "And this is his latest favorite. He's gotten more sophisticated lately and sometimes wants more than Barney has to offer. It's *Toy Story*. He loves Buzz—"

"And Woody." Sam added.

"Buzz and Woody, okay. Well, we might have to check those guys out, buddy." Jack tousled his hair.

"He had cereal for breakfast and if he wants something more, I usually give him an apple cut up, or a banana."

"Sure. Will do," I said, holding Sam's hand. "Do you know when you might be back?"

"Hopefully by eleven, but they often run late. I'll call

if it's going to be after that and if it gets close to noon, he can have some soup or a sandwich."

"Peanut butter and jelly, Gran."

"Okay, Sam."

"What kind of soup do you like, Sam?" Jack asked.

"Chicky noodle."

I looked in the pantry after Kelly left and realized that we didn't have any peanut butter or chicken noodle soup. We also didn't have any apples or bananas. Yes, we have no bananas. As far as meeting the requirements of Sam's menu preferences, we had bread and jelly. That was it.

"Jack, I'm going to run to the store for a minute to get stuff for his snack, or for lunch if Kelly's late. Can you watch him?" The store was ten minutes away. It wouldn't take more than another ten minutes to do the shopping and then ten minutes back. A half hour at the most, Jack could handle that without getting too antsy. He loved kids, but enjoyed them the older they got. Even though lately he seemed to want to spend more time with Sam, he usually reached his limit after about an hour.

"Sure." Jack picked up the bag Kelly had left. "What'll it be, Sam? Shall we read a book, or how 'bout this?" He pulled out a plastic cell phone with musical buttons. "We could play telephone."

"Let's see Buzz and Woody."

"You got it." Jack carried the bag and took Sam's hand and went to the den where the DVD player was set up.

It was raining when I left for the store and the wind had picked up. The rain blew in huge sheets as I trotted across the Safeway parking lot, dodging puddles. Once inside, I pulled off the hood of my parka, grabbed a small basket and walked quickly to the produce, weaving around grocery carts like a running back. Apples, bananas, that was easy. Now on to the soup aisle. Chicky noodle. Might as well get a few cans to have on hand. I scooted around to the next aisle for the peanut butter. Chunky or smooth? I couldn't remember which one Sam liked. Can't go wrong with smooth, I decided, and picked out a small jar, then headed for the fast lane checkout. Jack always went to the self-checkout, but I liked a person; the machine made me nervous.

The rain still hadn't let up when I got home, and it was pouring when I brought the groceries in from the car. The house was quiet, except for the rain drumming against the windows and the sound of Sam's movie. A good day to be huddled inside, that's for sure. Maybe I'd read to him when the movie ended. I put the groceries away and went to the den to see how they were doing.

No Sam.

And no Jack. Only Buzz and Woody. Sam probably got sleepy and Jack took him upstairs to our bed for a morning nap. As I mounted the stairs, I heard the low murmur of Jack's voice coming from his office.

The door to my studio was open.

"Gran, look! I made a wahee picture."

Palette knives and brushes were scattered over the floor. Clutching a tube of paint like it was toothpaste, Sam was squishing it over the canvas, gauging the meadow painting with the edge of the tube opening. Dark blue paint was spread over the lower third of the canvas as high as he could reach. The foreground, the lower part of the meadow I had struggled with day after day, week after week, had been destroyed, obliterated with ugly smears of thick paint.

"Oh no!" I ran to him and grabbed the tube of paint. "STOP IT, SAM!"

He stared at me, and then burst into tears. I squeezed my eyes shut, trying to control my anger. Where the hell was Jack for God's sake? I scooped up Sam, who was now sobbing and rushed to the kitchen, plopping him down on the counter next to the sink.

"Put out your hands," I commanded.

"Gran—" he sobbed.

I reached under the sink for a bottle of liquid dishwashing soap. "Sam, put out your hands."

Reluctantly, he stuck his hands out over the sink, tears rolling down his cheeks.

"Other way. Turn them over."

Sam put his palms up and I poured the soap on each hand. "Now rub them together."

His sobbing had quieted, settling into quivering sniffs as he rubbed his hands. I turned on the water. "Now we'll rinse and do it again."

We repeated the whole procedure three more times, until the only trace of paint was a little blue on the knuckles of his right hand. By some miracle he hadn't gotten paint on his clothes. There were only a few spots on his shoes, which came off easily when I scrubbed them.

"Sam, those aren't your paints. They belong to Gran. You are never, ever to do that again. Do you understand?"

"Okay."

I hugged him and lifted him down from the counter. I'd talk to Jack when we were alone, I didn't want to let Sam out of my sight and I didn't want him to witness my confronting Jack. It might scare him to death, scar him for life. Years later he'd recall the trauma to some shrink, the time his grandmother went insane and attacked his grand-father with a palette knife.

I cut up an apple for him, got the dinosaur book from his bag and took him to the den to read to him while he had his snack.

Sam was going down the list of the dinosaurs for the fifth time when Jack came in. Clearly, he'd been so engrossed in whatever he was doing upstairs that he hadn't heard a thing. He looked at the dark TV screen. "Guess you had enough of Buzz and Woody, huh buddy?"

"Look in my studio, Jack." I spat out the words, glaring at him. Then I heard Kelly's car in the drive, as Jack went up to the studio. A few minutes later as Kelly was coming in the door, from upstairs I heard Jack bellow, "Oh, shit!"

"Mommy!" Sam ran to Kelly.

"Sam Man," she picked him up. "I didn't have to wait long at all," she said to me.

Either she was ignoring Jack's outburst from upstairs or she hadn't heard it, I wasn't sure.

"Everything okay?" Kelly smiled sweetly.

Sam's head was nuzzled against his mother's shoulder. He turned his head slightly and peeked at me.

"Fine. Except for one little problem. Sam got into paints, but you know about that now, don't you, Sam?"

Sam looked away, resting his head again on Kelly's shoulder.

I went to the den and got the DVD from the machine and the dinosaur book, then put them in his bag and handed it to Kelly.

"Thanks again, for taking him on such short notice."

I kissed Sam, who was still clinging to Kelly. "Bye, Sam."

"Bye, Gran," he squeaked.

I knew Jack had to have heard Kelly arrive, but he hadn't come downstairs to say good-bye, the coward. I went up and found him staring at my studio, as though he were studying the situation (with all the intelligence of a turnip).

"Goddammit, Jack. You'd think I could trust you to watch him for a half-hour!" I exploded, "what the hell were you thinking?"

"Look, Annie," he said defensively, "I'm sorry. I got a phone call and he was all set up in front of that movie. I didn't hear a peep."

"He's a three-year-old! You have to check on him!"

"Listen, I said I was sorry. You know I feel terrible, now what can I do to help with the mess?"

"Nothing. Not a damn thing. I can't believe you didn't check on him! How could you let this happen? You couldn't stay with him for fifteen minutes! What's wrong with you!"

Jack looked miserable, but I didn't care. I gathered my supplies and got ready to leave for Vashon. I didn't want to touch the painting until Fred saw it. He might be able to show me how to go about salvaging it, if it could be at all.

I left Daisy at home, the weather was just too nasty and I didn't want to have to worry about a wet, muddy dog on top of a painting that was now a total mess. It wasn't until I was on the ferry that tears came. I felt like I'd been in a ring, knocked down on the canvas and had struggled to pull myself up on the ropes. I was finally standing, reclaiming my studio with Cass gone, only to be knocked down again. And my precious Sam. I felt bad that I'd scared him, but damn Jack anyway. What the hell was he thinking, getting involved in a phone call? Men just didn't have the right wiring for children, that was all there was to it! There were exceptions, I knew, but I still thought they were too easily distracted, which was hardly an attribute that made for a great recommendation when it came to looking after children.

When I carried the painting in the studio, I didn't bother to cover it to keep it out of the rain. I was pretty sure it was hopeless, or at least there wouldn't be much I could do to fix it. Certainly not in time to hang for the show. That was over. Nice try, I thought, feeling totally depressed.

"Oh, Annie," Martha Jane came over as I was putting the canvas on the easel. "What happened?"

"My grandson. Jack was watching him."

"Oh, I see." Martha Jane nodded, not needing any more explanation. "Let's get Fred over here and see what he thinks."

I waited by the painting; it almost hurt to look at it. I unpacked my supplies and laid them out on the table while Martha Jane went to find Fred. I wanted to have them ready in case he had some miraculous solution, although I had little hope of that, mostly I felt like I should just give up. I was sick of feeling like Sisyphus.

"Your grandson's quite the artist, I see." Fred came over with Martha Jane.

I wanted to laugh, but I couldn't. "Is it worth saving? I don't know what to do."

"Of course, it is. The first thing is to carefully scrape off every bit of paint he put on. Don't use turpentine, just very cautiously scrape. Then, where it's still wet, you'll want to take a rag and very lightly dab as much color as you can. There'll still be his color, but you'll want to let that dry. It shouldn't take too long to dry because I assume your little artist didn't use medium, just used pure color."

"He did, right from the tube."

"Good." Fred laughed, "well, you know what I mean. 'Good' that there wasn't any medium involved. Then Annie, I'd take gesso. I can get you going with some—then you'll work it over the whole area that's been damaged. The entire foreground there." Fred pointed to the lower part of the painting. "It will be like laying on a new layer of canvas. Then when it's dry, you can start with your underpainting, beginning the composition of the foreground again. Your instincts will take over and I think you'll find it will be quite similar to your original. It will be different, of course, but I'm very sure you'll recapture the basic feel."

I gave Fred a hug. He was so confident, he made it sound almost possible to salvage it, and even though I was still frustrated and pretty discouraged, my spirits had lifted a little. Maybe I'd be ready to start pushing that rock again. I'd stay as long as it took to fix it, and then start in again when it was dry. And while it was drying, if I wasn't too tired, I'd start another piece.

"I'll get the gesso," he said, patting my shoulder.

The rest of the afternoon I worked carefully to remove the paint. Scraping meticulously, I wondered if this was what it was like to work in art restoration. After an hour, Fred thought it was ready to apply the gesso. He mixed it and was demonstrating its application when my cell phone rang. "Here Comes the Sun," the Beatles song Ian had programmed on my phone for Jack's calls. My chest tightened, he never called me here. I pulled the phone from my purse,

which I kept on the floor under the table I shared with
Martha Jane.

"Annie."

"Is something wrong?"

"Mrs. Tibonga just called and your father's had either
a heart attack or a stroke...."

The cramp in my stomach was sudden and painful,
and for a minute I couldn't breathe.

"Annie? Are you there?"

"I'm here." I put my hand over my stomach.

"He collapsed right after he got home from the airport.
She called 911 and the medics are taking him to Swedish
Hospital. She called a minute ago—they just left the house
in the ambulance."

"I'll get the next ferry."

"Shall I meet you at the hospital?"

"Yes...please," I paused, "hang on a minute." I got the
ferry schedule from my purse; my hands were shaking as I
opened it. "I won't be able to make the next boat which is
at 3:05 and then it's almost an hour until the next one at
4:00. I'll catch that and hopefully, I can get to the hospital
by 5:00. Can you call my brother? There are parts of the
island where my cell doesn't work, and on the ferry."

"I'll take care of it. Should I call the kids?"

"Let's wait until we get to the hospital. And thanks.
Jack?"

"What, honey?"

"I guess, just...thanks...."

While I was on the phone, Martha Jane and Fred had
gone to the other side of the studio and were sitting by the
wood stove. I put the phone back in my purse and went to
tell them. My head felt disconnected from the rest of me. I

was very factual, strangely calm, carefully repeating Jack's words.

"I'm so sorry," Fred held out his arms and hugged me. "I'll help you load everything in the car."

"I'm going with you." Martha Jane got her purse. "Just 'til the ferry comes. I'll follow you in my car and park on the road by the landing and stay with you in your car until the boat arrives."

"You don't need to do that."

"Yes, I do."

"You can't argue with her, Annie," Fred said. "I've rarely known anyone so stubborn."

"I take that as a compliment. As they say, 'well-behaved women rarely make history.'"

I could see Martha Jane's ancient car, her fire engine red Mercedes, in my rear view mirror as I drove along the West Side Highway. What a spirit she had, that line about well-behaved women, and here she was still driving. At ninety. I wasn't sure it was such a great idea, but then letting sixteen-year-olds drive wasn't the greatest idea either. And my father still drove at eighty-four. Oh, God, if only he'd gone first. If he'd died first instead of Mom.

The 3:05 was leaving just as I got to the dock and I watched the seagulls sitting on the pilings like statues, oblivious to the rain. Mine was the second car in the lane for Fauntleroy, so I'd be among the first to get on the 4:00. I felt yanked away—torn from the safety of the studio just as Fred was showing me how to get back on my feet, and I waited on the dock, remembering the last teacher who'd told me I had talent when my father had destroyed my work for my own good.

Was this for my own good? I wasn't one to easily

succumb to paranoia, but it felt like he was deliberately trying to destroy my dream all over again. It couldn't actually be deliberate, no one shot themselves in the foot to spite someone else, at least not usually, but the result was the same. I was trapped. The way my mother must have felt her whole life. God damn him. I hit the steering wheel with my fist, then lay my head down on it and wept.

After a few minutes I heard a tap on the window and looked up to see Martha Jane. I opened the passenger door and she got in beside me, staying with me until the boat arrived, an amulet against my demons.

25

ANNIE

I scanned the weary faces in the emergency room. An emaciated elderly African American man was snoring with his head resting on his chest; a mother with blonde, stringy hair held a fussy baby; a teenager sat with his arm in a sling—he was either Asian or Hispanic, I couldn't quite tell—maybe a creature of uncertain race, like me. Illness and injury was the common denominator of this disconnected assembly: a potent leveler, even for my father, I thought, as I saw Jack walking quickly toward me from across the room.

"He's in intensive care and the intake person wants to get some information."

I followed him to an office at the back of the room. "Did you get David?"

"Yes, they're eight hours later than we are, so it was about ten-thirty their time when I called. He was up, he wants you to call after you've talked to the doctor."

"No matter how late?" I looked at my watch. "It's two in the morning there now."

"That's what he said."

266

In the intake office, a young woman with streaked hair and a small stud in her nose asked me to verify that my father's address and phone were current and that I was his next-of-kin. My father's Medicare and insurance cards were in his wallet; they'd been able to process his admission and just needed me to sign the forms.

"Will they let us see him?" I asked.

"Yes, since you're next of kin, you can go on up to intensive care."

"And my husband?"

"I'm not sure if he can go in the room, but he can go to the floor with you. There's a family waiting area and they'll let you know at the nurses' station."

I walked to the door. "When can we talk to the doctor?"

"They'll let you know at the nurses' station," she answered, not looking up from the computer.

"Well, he must still be alive," I whispered as we got on the elevator, "or I guess they would have told me."

"I'm not so sure. While I was waiting for you, the place got slammed with a bunch of people from an accident and it looked pretty chaotic."

"This is surreal, I feel like we could be discussing the weather."

Jack reached for my hand as we got off the elevator. "I know better."

At the nurses' station, we waited for the head nurse to return from break while a young man looked for my father's chart. "Carol should be back any minute, but if you'd like, there's a waiting room at the end of the hall. Or you can wait here."

"How is he?"

He looked at the chart, "I think he's stable, but she

can fill you in and you'll know more when you meet with the doctor."

"When does he come?" Jack asked.

"The neurologist on call tonight is Dr. Sturgis, Lynne Sturgis. She should be here about six."

I looked at Jack and raised my eyebrows. "Let's go to the waiting room."

"Don't say it," Jack whispered as we walked down the hall.

"Why would I say anything?" I smiled. "Just because you assume that all doctors are men."

"See, you said it." He put his arm around me. "I knew you couldn't resist. But hey, give me a little credit, I knew that guy was a nurse."

"Very astute. It said 'R.N.' right on his name badge."

"Mrs. Duppstadt?" A woman caught up with us at the door to the waiting room. She was tall, with short dark hair. I thought she looked about forty, and it occurred to me that the whole place was run by people who could be my children, they looked that young. "You're here for Mr. Gunther?"

"Yes, I'm his daughter, and this is my husband, Jack."

"I'm Carol Cummings, I'll be here the rest of the evening. You can go in and see your father if you'd like. Room 231."

"How is he?"

"We won't know for a while, but he seems to be stabilizing. Dr. Sturgis will fill you in."

"Can my husband go in with me?"

"Yes, that's fine."

It was a large room with two chairs next to the window. At first all I could see were the machines, then the hospital bracelet on his thin wrist, and the IV and the bottle of fluid. Then his face. He lay with the bed raised at a forty-five degree angle, with his hair, his usually glorious mane, in wild disarray against the pillow. He was pale, breathing with his mouth open, taking shallow breaths that were measured but even. His eyes were closed.

I stared at him. He looked so helpless and pathetic, I was at a loss to make a connection between this sick old man and the person I'd last seen, the magnificent Alexander Gunther, descending the Grand Staircase at the Seattle Art Museum like a monarch greeting his subjects. I stood a few feet from the bed, fixated on the bottle of fluid, watching it drip.

"Annie, come sit down." Jack whispered, motioning to the chairs. "I'll sit here, next to you."

"Okay." I crossed the room, going around the foot of the bed to the chair closest to my father. Did he know I was there? If he did, did he care? I wanted to feel something. Anything would be better than the emptiness, so numb and desolate that my emotions felt as lifeless as his body appeared to be. I pulled the chair closer to the bed and before I sat down, I touched his hand. "It's Annie, Dad. I'm here."

There was no response so I sat with Jack, waiting for the doctor while my mind tried to grasp the point of the vigil, one that I seemed to be programmed to do, just as much as I'd been compelled to touch his hand.

When I waited for the ferry I'd confided in Martha Jane, telling her that I knew what would lie ahead if he lived, because I'd done it for my mother: arranging for caregivers, visiting nurses, paying bills, checking with doctors, hassling with insurance companies. I didn't know if I could stand it.

"To be involved with him on a regular basis, for God knows how long," I'd told her, "I don't see how I can do it, unless I can bring myself to feel differently about him, and I can't imagine that."

"I don't know how to explain this exactly. But sometimes you do things to meet your own standards. It's not like it's for the other person, really. More like for your own sense of integrity." Martha Jane paused, stroking her chin. "That's it, I've got it. That's what it is."

"What is?"

"It's so you don't betray your humanity."

"Are you saying I have to forgive him? That seems like a pretty tall order."

"Oh, not really. I'll tell you what I think about that. I don't think you can genuinely forgive someone unless they genuinely have remorse. They've got to own up to what they've done, feel truly terrible about it and let you know that."

"In my wildest dreams, I can't envision my father being capable of that." And then I confessed, "It feels like once again he seems able to wreck what I'm doing. Take me away from art."

"Annie," she said gently, "you're the only one who can take you away from art."

I slumped in the chair, staring at my father's ashen face. Please let me remember what she said. I'm the only one that can take it away.

I was thinking about the show, trying to tell myself that hopefully someday there'd be another one, when Dr. Sturgis came in. We shook hands as she introduced herself and suggested we talk in the family waiting room. I wondered how someone who looked so young could be a neurologist. She had an intelligent face, with wide-set blue eyes and curly blond hair. Despite her youth and the fluffy hair, she conveyed an air of quiet authority.

Following her down the corridor, I remembered being at the hospital with Mom after her last surgery. It seemed like it might have been this same floor although it was all pretty much of a blur. But one incident was clear in my mind, more potent for its omission. The thing that didn't happen. My father never showed up.

Another couple, who looked like they could be close to our age, sat in one end of the waiting room in front of the television. The similarity ended with my take on their age. The TV was turned to Fox News. They were interviewing Dick Cheney and I felt a surge of rage that I'd have to be subjected to the sound of that jerk's voice. The woman didn't seem to be watching, just absently leafing through a magazine. But the man seemed to be.

"Can't we ask him to turn that off?" I whispered to Jack, as we went toward some empty chairs at the opposite end of the room.

"I'll try," Jack said, turning to Dr. Sturgis. "I'm going to see if we can have the room quiet." He motioned toward the TV.

"That's fine. We usually let families watch when they're the only ones in here, but if it's a problem for anyone, we ask people to turn it off. Would you like me to ask him?"

"Thanks, that's okay." He walked to the end of the room. I watched him as he spoke with the people. In a minute the TV was shut off.

I sat across from Dr. Sturgis. "Jack's good at things like that. I'm afraid I'm not." Besides despising the way Cheney thought about the world, there was something about him that reminded me of my father. Not his opinions, but the smugness, the appalling arrogance. Of course, my father also knew how to be charming, whereas Cheney had all the charm of a flea-infested rodent.

"Your father has had an ischemic stroke," Dr. Sturgis began, when Jack came back and sat next to me. "This is the most common type. It just means that a thrombus, or blood clot, has formed and it's blocked the blood flow in an artery, which brings blood to part of the brain. He got to the hospital early enough that we could treat it with tPA, a tissue plasminogen activator; it's a drug that dissolves the clot and restores the blood flow to the brain."

"So he'll recover?" I asked.

"There's every indication that he'll survive this, but we won't know about damage. His stroke was on the left side of his brain, which may weaken his right side and he may have aphasia, which can affect his speech. It can also impair his ability to listen, read, and write. And there may be problems with dysphagia, problems with chewing and swallowing."

I listened intently. I heard every word, but my brain was muddled by the task of trying to grasp the degree of impairment that could be my father's fate. I couldn't shake the image of having just seen and heard Dick Cheney and my mind wandered from my father's possible prognosis. Isn't a hospital hopefully a healing place, where people can be made better? And to have a person so toxic, polluting the airwaves, spewing war like so much pus... contaminating....

I'm losing it, I thought, as I folded my hands in my lap and looked intently at Dr. Sturgis, trying to focus.

"...we'll know more tomorrow and there's an excellent rehabilitation program which we'll start as soon as we can. There's often spontaneous recovery within about thirty days of a stroke and there can be good gains in a person's ability to function."

"Should I wait here tonight?" I asked, tracking again. It was a question that had never come up when it had been Mom. Then it was "Can I stay?" which I did. All night. Every night that Mom had been in the hospital.

"Only if you want to, there's really nothing you can do. And it's usually better for the family if they can get some rest. But of course, it's your choice, sometimes family members feel they want to stay and we're quite used to that."

I looked at Jack. "I think we should go." I turned back to Dr. Sturgis, "When should we come back tomorrow?"

"I'd suggest early evening." She looked at the chart. "It will be over twenty-four hours then and he should be alert, or at least we'll have a better idea of the prognosis."

As soon as we got home I called my brother, then Cass and Ian, letting them all know what had happened, and telling them that I'd call tomorrow after I met with the doctor. I also called Martha Jane, leaving a message when there was no answer.

"Martha Jane, it's Annie. My father is in intensive care, and he's had a stroke. It looks like he'll pull through, but it might be a while until we know how it's affected him. I just wanted to thank you for staying with me while I waited for the ferry. And for reminding me that I'm the only one who can take away my art. I'm going to try to remember that. And good luck with the show. Maybe I'll make the next one. I'm sure everyone will love John Deere and Jane Doe. I'll check in with you in a few days when I know more, and I want to hear all about how the show went."

26

CASS

Elvis lightened the night. She loved that dog. He helped her sleep, too; his snoring was like a lullaby. No wonder Audrey had a hard time saying good-bye to him. Cass had never been partial to male dogs; she was wary of all that leg humping business. But Elvis was a perfect gentleman: a noble beast and he expanded her world in a surprising way. The dog park. A new horizon. There were men there, nice men with dogs and it was a comfortable way to start up a conversation. Everyone who came to the dog park knew the names of the dogs, but not the people, and Cass found herself beginning to casually notice if Tanner's owner, or Lucy's, or Griffin's was wearing a wedding ring. At work, Sherrie was trying to get her to go on Match.com, but there was no way she was ready for that. The dog park, however, was a whole other thing. It was a safe way to talk to guys, and every day after work, Cass found herself looking forward to taking Elvis there for a romp.

Today, as usual, Elvis sat on the front seat, staring straight ahead at the road. His head was level with Cass's and he seemed almost human the way he sat next to her in the passenger seat. But a few blocks from the dog park, he was all dog: whimpering, whining, wiggling, panting and even drooling with excitement. Cass was parking the car across from the park when her cell phone rang. It was her father, unusual for him to call, especially on her cell phone.

"Elvis, shhh," she reached over and patted him. It was hard to hear with all Elvis's whining.

"Cass," her father's voice was tense and he seemed to be in a hurry. "They think Grandpa's had a stroke...."

"Oh, no...."

"...and I'm meeting Mom at the hospital."

"Which hospital? I can come as soon as I take the dog home."

"Swedish, but Mom wanted you to wait until we get there and we find out what the story is. We'll call you from the hospital—will you be around?"

"Of course, I'll wait to hear from you. I can bring dinner over for you guys, anything. Just let me know what you need."

"We will. Thanks. Ian's in New York and Kelly was out, so I just left a message, but I'll call Ian when we know more."

"Poor Mom. First Baach and now this—although it's got to be different with him. I thought he was in Palm Springs—"

"He'd just gotten back. Listen, Cass—I've got to go. I'll call you from the hospital."

Cass was incredibly relieved when she got off the phone. Thank God it wasn't her mom or dad. Ever since Baach died, she'd realized that someday she'd have to face

276

losing her parents; that if life took its natural course, they'd be next. Not that she didn't feel sad about her grandfather, about seeing anyone suffer, but the person she really felt bad for was her mother.

It was close to ten when Cass heard from Annie. She called to tell Cass that her grandfather had definitely had a stroke, but they wouldn't know the extent of the damage for at least another twenty-four hours. Cass was surprised when her mother said she'd be going to see him when she got off work the next day.

"Can't you take the day off, Mom?"

"When Baach got sick, being with patients let me feel I could still function in spite of what I might be going through. I guess it takes me out of myself in a good way."

"What can I do to help? Can I bring dinner tomorrow?"

"Thanks, but I don't have much appetite. Maybe Grandpa's stroke is good for something—I might lose a few pounds."

Even though her mother laughed, Cass thought she sounded really down.

"Actually, I'll have some time to kill after work before I go to the hospital, I'll probably take Daisy for a walk at Seward Park and if you want to meet me there, that'd be great. Dad has meetings—he offered to cancel them, but I don't want him to—I'd love your company, Cass."

"I'll leave work a little early so I can get Elvis. Is it okay if I bring him?"

"Sure. Daisy gets along with all creatures, great and small."

Cass hadn't been to Seward Park since she and Richard used to bike there. It was a beautiful peninsula on Lake

Washington with a path around the perimeter and trails winding through the lush forest inland. Going with Elvis was a marked improvement. Much better company. A superior male being, she thought, as she parked near the art building on the north side and waited for her mother. Cass got Elvis out of the car and stayed in the parking lot waiting for Annie. It wasn't long before she saw her mother's Volvo with Daisy in the back drive into the lot.

Cass watched her mother get out of the car and was struck with how much older, almost fragile she looked. When Cass hugged her, Annie became tearful. "Sorry, I guess it's catching up with me."

"Why wouldn't it, Mom?'

She wiped her eyes. "I know. You're right."

They let Daisy and Elvis sniff and circle for a few minutes before they began walking along the path by the lakeshore. It was still warm and the asphalt path was filled with people on bicycles, joggers, and people walking, both with and without dogs. They didn't say anything for quite a while. Cass had slowed her usual pace to stay abreast with Annie, and seeing everyone pass them was like watching a tape on fast forward.

"I'm sorry you're going through this, Mom."

"Thanks, honey."

"It's different with Grandpa isn't it?"

"Yes, I'm afraid so. I was so close to Baach, but—you know, not to him. He was horrible to her. And to me, for that matter. And frankly, Cass, I just don't know if I have it in me to help him." Annie stopped to let Daisy sniff one of the trees at the edge of the path. "And then something I saw at work today has been hounding me."

"A patient?"

"No, actually, it was on TV. They had the news on in the day room. A murderer was being sentenced and the victim's family was in the courtroom. They got to speak directly to the guy. You see this all the time now, I guess it's part of the healing for the families."

"And you want to speak like that to Grandpa?"

"I guess that's it. I'm not sure I have the courage, though. And I don't know if it would do any good."

"Look, I know this isn't the same at all, but it makes me glad I didn't let Richard get away with treating me like shit."

Annie put her arm around Cass, "I'm glad, too."

They came to a bench nestled by the trees across from the water. "I know you like to walk fast, I think I'll just sit here and rest for a little while." Annie looked at her watch. "Why don't you and Elvis go ahead and come back for me in about twenty minutes?"

"Are you sure you'll be okay?"

"I'm sure."

"Okay. Come on, Elvis."

Cass walked on ahead, but hesitated right before the path would curve out of view and looked back at the bench. It was empty. Then she caught sight of her mother, standing at the edge of the water, staring out at the lake.

27

ANNIE

I watched Cass and Elvis move briskly between the people on the path. I know I'm prejudiced, but she stands out, she's so lovely and thank God she's doing so much better. The house-sitting job has been great for her. I stroked Daisy's head and looked out at the lake, wishing I could turn back the clock so none of this had ever happened. Alexander the Great would be bopping around, basking in all the limelight from his retrospective and I could go back to my life. Working with patients, and working with Fred Weiss the rest of the time. Hours and hours to paint. Peace, that's what I wanted, and freedom, too. Freedom from responsibility.

The fresh air helped. My stomach had started to cramp as soon as I left Woodside and it made me furious. This old response, my body acting out my fear the way it had so long ago. Been there, done that, thank you very much. I rubbed my stomach for a minute, then walked to the edge of the lake. Its glittering surface in the late afternoon sun reminded me of the island. Near the shore I saw a family of ducks in the weeds. Mack, Lack, Quack...I couldn't remember all their names, but all "ack" sounds and Mom's soft voice as she turned the page of *Make Way for Ducklings*. I watched the fuzzy babies following their mother, swimming behind her in a line, telling myself not to idealize nature. There were creatures that ate their young.

In the distance I heard the sound of a siren, a reminder that this oasis was still in the city, and I thought again of the news I'd seen: the segment of the sentencing I'd described to Cass. The judge letting the victim's family have their say.

Had I ever had my say? I'd gone my whole life intimidated by my father, never once standing up to him and letting him know what I really felt. Not once. Just the idea of it triggered another cramp in my stomach, but I couldn't get rid of the picture of having my say, telling my truth whether he understood or not. Before he died. Or even if he lived. I thought about what it takes to go on, like the Truth and Reconciliation Commission in South Africa. Sometimes there isn't always justice, but there can be a reckoning. Would I be able to do it? I didn't know, but the idea seemed to be gaining strength, even if I wasn't. There could at least be a reckoning. And it occurred to me it might be more painful not to do it. I thought about my mother's attempt with her separate will. It was so like her to make a non-verbal statement, a gesture that for her was loaded with meaning. Well, if there was to be a reckoning, I'd have to do better than that for both of us. With words. Explicit, unequivocal, so there could be no mistaking how I felt.

Cass and Elvis came back and we headed to the parking lot; it had been so good to be with her. She told me she was thinking about renting a little house, maybe on the eastside so she could be closer to Sam—a house with a yard, so she could have a dog. This Elvis seemed to be doing a lot for her and when we reached our cars, I bent down to pat him. Then Cass hugged me again, holding me tight, giving me the kind of mothering only a daughter can give.

When I got home, for a minute I almost thought I'd landed in the wrong house. The whole kitchen looked like a small Asian grocery store that was having a fire sale. The counters were covered with bottles: fish sauce, hoisin sauce, two kinds of soy sauce, chili sauce, bean sauce, shrimp sauce, sesame oil and jars of tamarind and lychee. Next to the stove there were piles of tofu, and sheets of rice paper were strewn among packages of rice noodles, egg noodles, saifun noodles, and rice vermicelli. Vegetable peelings were piled in the sink and scattered over the floor, and sauces, mostly various shades of red and brown, were slopped on the stove.

"I'm making dinner. We're having four dishes and an appetizer. All authentic," Jack announced triumphantly. "I bought a cookbook."

"Wonderful. Do you need any help?" It was wonderful that he was excited about something. A total mess, but still wonderful.

"I've got it covered."

"Looks that way," I agreed. Goo was everywhere. I tried not to laugh.

"Fix yourself a drink and read the paper. Whatever you want. I invited Cass and she'll be coming after she takes the dog back. Oh, and Rose Tibonga called." Jack handed me a slip of paper with some phone numbers.

282

"Did she want me to call her back?" I looked at the paper. "What's this?"

"It's a number for a gallery in London. Rose didn't think there was any hurry, she just wanted to give you all the messages. The other number's a call from a museum in San Francisco. She wasn't sure what to do about them."

I sat down at the kitchen table and looked out at the yard. So it had begun. I was in it, so it seemed, whether I liked it or not. "I'll call Rose when I get back from the hospital."

"I'll get my jacket. I can finish cooking when we get back."

"Jack, I'm going by myself."

"I don't mind going with you, I'd planned on it. I've prepped everything as they say, and I just have to put it together."

"It's not that, I need to talk to him alone. It has this now-or-never feel to it, like if I don't I'll be stuck in a big black hole. I have to tell him how I really feel about him. What I think of how he treated Mom and what it's truly been like for me—because if I don't I'm afraid I'll be harboring so much resentment that I'll literally make myself sick."

"Annie, what if he's out of it and has no clue what you're saying?"

"I'll say it anyway, it'll be a dress rehearsal for later on if he improves."

Jack looked baffled, so I tried again. "I know it's hard to understand, but the things I say to him are for me. For my self-respect, and my health, too. If he hears me and understands, fine, I'd like that. But the main thing is that I say it, that I speak my truth."

Jack followed me out to the car. His hair was tousled and he had some kind of goo splattered on his shirt, it made me think of Ian when he was about five, and it made me smile. Jack looked so dear to my tired eyes.

"I could wait for you," he said. "I don't have to go in the room."

"It's better if I go by myself. Maybe it's a rite of passage. Oh, God, at my age, how pathetic is that? Do you think I'm terrible?"

"Of course not. He's lucky to have you."

"If Mom had gotten senile and nasty and abusive the way some people do, it would have been hard to hang in there, but I could have done it. Because it wouldn't have been her, I could have understood it was her illness, that her brain was screwed up. And I'd have a lifetime of good memories to draw on. But if he gets obnoxious with me, yelling and throwing stuff, it will be the same-old, same-old, and Jack, I just won't put up with it."

"Good. Don't."

"Don't what?"

"Don't put up with any crap."

"Right." I gave him a quick kiss. "Nothing to it—just a day at the park."

I waited at the stoplight at the end of the block, watching the cars pass in front of me. I felt disconnected from the everyday rhythms: the UPS guy getting out of the truck in the drive of the house with the blue shutters, the plump, red-haired woman two houses down watering her lawn, the teenage girl in the car in front of me fiddling with her hair in the rearview mirror. The world was different than it had been just a little over twenty-four hours ago. I felt alienated from everything around me, cut off by my own intensity, set apart, as people moved through their lives oblivious to me, as though I was sitting there with my car on fire and no one noticed.

I drove down the ramp of the Swedish Hospital garage and stopped at the ticket machine. I put down the window and grabbed the ticket, holding it until I found an empty space two levels down. I carefully put the ticket in my wallet, slowly, deliberately, afraid I'd misplace it somewhere if I didn't concentrate. Walking quickly through the garage to the elevators, I wondered if I'd been stupid not to come with Jack. It would have been good to hold his hand.

When I got to intensive care, the head nurse, the same one who'd been on the shift yesterday, was at the desk on the phone. What was her name? Karen? Carrie? I used to be good with names, but the older I got the harder it got and yesterday was a blur. I waited by the desk. Carol Cummings, I read on her nametag. Well, I'd been close.

"You're here for?" She turned to me as she hung up the phone.

"Alexander Gunther. I'm his daughter, Annie Duppstadt."

"Oh yes, of course. I met you yesterday."

I nodded. "How is he?"

"A little better I think, but Dr. Sturgis will fill you in. She'll be here soon."

"I'd like to talk with her before I see my father. I'll be in the family waiting room."

"I'll send her in as soon as she gets here."

"Thanks."

It was quiet in the waiting room; the TV was turned off and the room was empty. I took a seat, picked up a magazine and absently leafed through it. There were some watercolors on the wall that I hadn't noticed when we were here yesterday. Yesterday? Was it only yesterday? It felt like a month. The paintings were all of Northwest ocean beaches, misty and silvery—quite lovely. I thought about painting, wondering how long it would be before I could get back to it, when Dr. Sturgis came in.

She smiled and took a seat next to me. "I have some good news," she said. "It's still early, but your father is doing remarkably well. He's lucky he got here as soon as he did, because there seems to be only mild aphasia which has affected his speech. His ability to chew and swallow are normal. His right arm is weak, but his left is fine and I think we should see good improvement. As long as he continues to progress, he can start in the rehab program at the end of the week."

"Does he know what's going on?" I asked. "Or understand what's happened to him."

"There's every sign that he does. He can write a little with his left hand, although the speech pathologist won't want him to rely on that. He'll need to work on his speech, but the spontaneous recovery just in the past twenty-four hours is a good indicator that he'll see a lot of improvement each day."

I looked at the watercolors on the wall next to the television. "How long would he be in the rehab program?"

"It's hard to tell. It all depends on his progress, of course, but it could be three or four weeks."

"I suppose I'll need to arrange for transferring him."

"The social worker on staff can help you. At the nurses' station they'll give you an information sheet about contacting that office." Dr. Sturgis stood up. "In spite of the degeneration from the polio, your father's in pretty good shape for his age. I'd say you're all lucky."

I thanked her and walked to the end of the corridor. I stood outside my father's room wondering what I was going to say, wondering if I'd end up disintegrating and not say anything at all.

Give me strength, Mom.

After a few moments, I opened the heavy door. The room was bright, silent except for the beeping of one of the monitors next to his bed. The first thing I noticed was his hair. It was far from being elegantly groomed, the hallmark of his vanity, but it was no longer in such wild disarray. It looked somewhat smoothed out, as if someone had tried to comb it and his face did seem to have more color than it did yesterday, and his eyes were open. When he saw me, he immediately tried to speak. It was very hard to understand, he had trouble with consonants and I couldn't make out what he was saying. It sounded like "aw essie."

"I'm sorry, Dad. I can't understand." I went the foot of his bed.

He said it again, this time louder and the inarticulate sounds in his deep, gravelly booming voice made me cringe.

I shook my head and shrugged. "I don't know what—"

He grabbed a pad of paper and pen and wrote with his left hand, gripping the pen and stabbing the paper with a frenzy, like it was a knife. I moved closer and looked at the paper. It said, "Leslie M" in large childlike letters.

I stared at for a few minutes and he got more and more agitated. Finally I said, "You want me to call Mrs. Meldon? Is that right?"

He nodded ferociously and then grabbed the notepad

with his left hand and threw it at me. It grazed my arm and then I watched it skitter across the floor.

I stared at him for a few minutes, then I slowly crossed the room and picked it up.

"Not this time, Dad," I said. "Not this time."

I walked back to the edge of his bed. I looked at him directly. I clutched the notepad, my palms were sweaty and my throat felt tight. I stood there for an eternity, but the words finally came, like rain that couldn't be stopped.

"You've had a stroke, Dad," I began. "Your doctor thinks you'll get better, but we won't know for a while—so right now, I don't know what you're up against. I can't tell you what to expect."

I thought of my mother again and knew if I didn't do this now, at the very beginning, no matter what lay ahead, it would only get harder. Harder, put off maybe, but not impossible I suddenly realized. Not any more. Because the train had left the station.

"Whatever happens, I can't be involved unless I tell you something." I paused, gathering resolve. "Just now you ordered me to call Mrs. Meldon and it's likely that you'll expect my help with a lot of things," I continued, "but I have to say it's not something I'm eager to do. Not like with Mom, anyway, because you and I hardly have a relationship. You've treated me with contempt my whole life. In fact, you wished I'd never been born. But you were even worse to Mom—you were hostile and cruel to her."

I swallowed, pausing again, staying in control. "I don't think you're evil, or a monster, I just think you're selfish and self-centered. And you have a mean, sadistic streak. And for some reason you've allowed yourself to give in to tantrums, throwing things, and yelling. But that doesn't imply I think what's happened to you now is justice or retribution. I think it's just bad luck. But I also need you to know, that in spite of everything, I'm thankful you were my father. We're born with genes that are just a roll of the dice. And I've come to believe, am starting to believe, that I actually do have a gift. And I know that came from you. And I want to be worthy of it, which is why I won't abandon you.

"But you have to know this. I won't tolerate your abuse." I put the notepad on the table next to his bed. "I just won't put up with it, Dad. Not ever again. You'll have the care of strangers, but I won't be there if you can't treat me with respect." I drew in my breath, and moved away from the bed rail.

My father raised his hand slightly and his eyes filled with tears. I'm quite sure they were tears of self-pity.

I left his room and walked down the corridor to the elevator. The door opened and I stepped on. I'd call Mrs. Meldon and let her know what had happened to him. It would be wonderful if she flew out to take care of him, but I knew better. It would be my job, and as unwelcome as it was, as reluctant as I was, I knew I could take it on. It had taken me sixty-four years, but I'd finally drawn the proverbial line in the sand.

28

ANNIE

When I got home from the hospital, Cass was setting the table. The kitchen looked like it had been in the path of a hurricane, but Jack seemed oblivious, whistling and humming while he stirred something on the stove. He turned down the burner, held out his arms and hugged me.

"How did it go?"

"Basically I told him I'd help him, but I wouldn't put up with any of his crap."

"Good," Cass and Jack both said.

"Right. Just a day at the beach. A walk in the park, whatever. Easy as pie...I wonder where that came from— it's hard to make good pie." I sighed, and took off my coat. "I think I was still shaking all the way home, although now I'm honestly feeling sort of calm. It's strange. Sad, but actually a weird sort of calm." I looked at my watch. "He might move to rehab at the end of the week—the doctor's pretty optimistic, I'll give you the details later—but I better call David, first."

I'd left his number on the pad by the phone in the

living room when I'd called last night. A hundred years ago. I looked at David's number, then called, trying to concentrate, slowly putting in the country code and all those digits, saying each number aloud and then checking it, not trusting my brain so heavy with fatigue. David picked up after one ring. He must have been waiting by the phone, I thought, reassured by the sound of his voice.

"How is he, Annie?"

"I just got back from the hospital and he's more alert today and he's eating. The doctor said his speech has been affected and there are clear signs of aphasia, but she thinks it's mild. They want to continue to observe him and then the plan is to transfer him to the rehabilitation unit where he'll start treatment. She actually thinks he's doing well and said it was lucky he got to the hospital so quickly."

"Annie, I want to help you with all this. Although I don't know what I can do from here."

"Just come in September to spell me, I think Jack and I will want to take a trip then."

"I'll be there. I was planning to visit him anyway, so I'll make it work then. How're you holding up?"

"The thing that keeps me going is that I'm painting, finally. Classes at a studio on Vashon Island."

"You were always so good, Annie. I never knew why you stopped."

"It doesn't matter now, but thanks."

"Can you give me another update tomorrow? I don't really care when you call, just leave a message if I'm out, or email me."

"Sure. I'll be meeting with the social worker about getting him into rehab and I'll know more after that."

After I talked with David, I called Ian and left a message

at his hotel, then joined Cass and Jack in the kitchen. The table in the breakfast room was covered with four platters and a smattering of little sauce dishes. In front of each place setting was a pair of shiny, black enameled chopsticks. "I wanted to be traditional," Jack said, pointing to the chopsticks.

I'd often eaten with chopsticks as a child. Usually when my father, who insisted on having a fork, wasn't around. But Mom had a supply of the small wooden ones in the paper wrappers. I wasn't sure if the ones Jack bought actually were Vietnamese, but they were quite elegant (in contrast to the mess on the platters).

"This is Gà xào nâm," he said proudly pointing to the first platter.

A mushy looking pile of vegetables and some mysterious meat.

"I'm trying to learn the correct names. This one is phó gà."

A pile of gluey noodles swimming in a thick, brownish broth with chunks of rubbery tofu.

"And this is bún suông."

An equally unappetizing mound that looked identical to the first.

"And here's the appetizer," he said, proudly. "Fresh spring rolls. I forget the Vietnamese name, it's goi something, I think. Anyway, we'll start with these."

Cass and I sat down and picked up our chopsticks. "I think I'll get some water," I said. "Would you each like a glass?"

"Oh, I forgot. I got some Vietnamese beer. It's called Bai Hoi, which means 'fresh beer.'" Jack rushed to the refrigerator. "You can have wine if you want, but I thought I'd try this."

I followed him to the refrigerator. "I think I'll just have water. Cass?"

"Me too."

I filled glasses with water for each of us and returned to the table.

"Some people eat the spring rolls with chopsticks, but it's fine to just pick them up if that's easier," Jack said.

The rice paper wrapper was slimy, like tracing paper that had been dipped in hand lotion. It must have been left in the water too long, but unlike the slippery covering, the rice vermicelli stuffed inside had hardened to the consistency of dental floss, while gritty vegetables stuck out the ends. Cass and I each dipped our spring roll in one of the sauce dishes, took a bite, and then gagged. We put our napkins to our mouths and each spit out a little chunk, slowly chewing the rest, valiantly trying to get it down.

Oblivious, Jack chomped on his spring roll. "Decent enough, I think. Maybe next time I shouldn't leave the wrapper in the water so long. I think it's a bit soft. What do you think?"

"Maybe a bit," Cass said, coughing.

"But it's very tasty." I added.

If you like eating dental floss.

The main courses weren't much better, but at least we didn't gag and the spicy sauces helped with the mushy consistency. The water, too. Cass and I gulped down long glugs after every bite. After dinner we congratulated Jack on a great first effort. I started to help with the clean-up, but they wouldn't let me.

"Just sit down, and I'll fix you an after-dinner drink," Jack said.

"No thanks, I'm so tired it would just knock me out."

"So, why not just go to bed?" Jack asked, carrying the dishes to the sink. He began scraping the plates. "Maybe this wasn't so great." He frowned, then started laughing.

"You went the distance, all those complicated dishes you made." I smiled. "You'll only get better."

"That's right," echoed Cass. "It's not like putting a TV dinner in the oven."

"I guess so." He smiled, then turned to me. "You should go lie down, Annie."

"I will, as soon as I call Mrs. Meldon. I've got to get that over with."

I went upstairs and called information for Palm Springs. They did have an "L. Meldon," but the number was unlisted, so I called the hospital to see if they could get it from my father. The floor nurse was the same guy who'd been at the desk when my father had been admitted and he thought the easiest thing would be to check my father's cell phone contact list.

"We lock up the patient's valuables and I'll check for you when I get break."

"Thanks, I really appreciate it." I gave him my phone number and then lay down while I waited for him to call me back. I couldn't remember experiencing exhaustion like this except when Mom died. My arms and legs felt like they were weighted down with concrete. Daisy lay on the floor beside me and I was too tired to even reach down to pat her head.

It was several hours later when the nurse called. He'd found Mrs. Meldon's number on my father's cell, but now it was close to eleven, too late to call her, and I went back to sleep, too tired to even get out of my clothes.

The first chance I had to call her was the next morning when I was in my office between patients, and it seemed to take a few minutes before it registered with her just who I was.

"Mrs. Meldon, this is Annie Duppstadt calling..."

"Yes?" she said, formally.

"I'm Alex Gunther's daughter, we met at—"

"Oh, of course," she said, perking up. "Hello Annie."

"My father wanted me to call you—I'm sorry I've got some bad news, he had a stroke the day he came back from Palm Springs and—"

"Oh, no—"

"He's at Swedish Hospital, but he's pretty alert and wanted you to know."

"Oh my. Oh that's terrible...oh what a shame...." Her voice trailed off. "I'm just so sorry to hear this." There was a long silence, and then she asked, quietly. "Is there much impairment, much damage?"

"His speech has been affected and his right side is weak, but the doctor thinks it's possible he could make a good recovery. He'll be transferred to rehab soon."

"Please give him my love and please let him know how sorry I am, and if you can give me the address of the hospital, I'll get some flowers off before I leave. I'm flying out in the morning to my home in Hawaii, but I'll call as soon as I get there to see how he is."

Mrs. Meldon's flowers, a huge extravagant bouquet of spring flowers in brilliant colors, were on the windowsill when I stopped in to see my father after work. The room was dim and his eyes were closed when I came in. I wasn't sure if I should stay, but he must have just been dozing because he opened his eyes and lifted his left hand in a slight wave.

"Hi Dad." I pointed to the bouquet. "They're very beautiful. From Mrs. Meldon?"

He nodded, but didn't smile.

"When I spoke with her this morning, she said she'd be going to Hawaii tomorrow and she'd call after she got there. And she said to send you her love."

My father looked quite glum. He didn't try to speak and I didn't attempt any conversation. And there didn't seem to be any point in staying. I'd done my job: shown up and delivered Mrs. Meldon's message, and I left a few minutes later. The visit was short, but of course, not sweet. It never would be with him. But at least he hadn't been nasty and that was the bottom line.

I was still exhausted. The past two days, I spent what little energy I had at work with patients, and then crashed as soon as I got home, falling into bed, where I'd sleep for hours. Creative energy was out of the question and I didn't how long it would be until I could get back to my painting. I was pretty sure it would have to stay on the back burner until things stabilized with my father, until I knew what was ahead for him. But I would get back to it, no matter how long it took. I'd never let my fears stop me again.

Friday after work, I went to the hospital and met with the social worker and was relieved that everything was on schedule for my father's transfer to rehab. It gave me a lift, and instead of taking a nap when I got home, I took Daisy for a walk.

I loved walking with Daisy; I found her obliviousness to all that was happening somehow comforting. The wind had scattered the few remaining blossoms of the cherry trees and they were strewn in the street like pink confetti. A squirrel darted across a lawn and I had to hold tight to Daisy. It stayed light so much later as we neared summer; the sun didn't set now until close to nine, but the evening was cool and I was glad I'd grabbed a sweater. Some kids, who looked about eight or nine, were kicking a soccer ball in the street with their dad, and I smiled watching them. They reminded me of Jack with Cass and Ian at that age.

When Daisy and I turned the corner and headed down the block toward the house, I was surprised to see both Jack and Cass in the drive. My station wagon was in the driveway with the back gate raised. I wasn't sure, but from where I was, it looked like they were loading something in the car. I was confused; I didn't remember Cass saying she wanted her stuff out of the basement yet.

Then I got closer. I couldn't believe it. It was my painting. My meadow painting. They were loading my painting in the car!

"What are you doing with that?" I shouted.

"We're taking this to Vashon," Cass said, calmly.

"What?" I threw up my hands, dropping Daisy's leash. "You can't do that!"

"Right after you left, I got a call from Martha Jane Morrison," Jack said, cheerily. "She said they were hanging the show tonight and they'd left a space for your painting next to Jane Doe and John Deere. Those can't be people at the studio. I know Vashon's weird, but that's a little too odd." Jack smiled. "She was delightful, just like you said. And then Cass got here and—"

"I can't have mine in the show." I interrupted, feeling frantic. "It's not done!"

"It's done enough. We're going to hang it with the others, Annie."

"Oh, Jack, didn't you tell them it's not done?" I reached on the ground for the leash, completely flustered.

"We know that, Mom. She told Dad they'd make a note on the title that says 'work in progress.'"

"What title? I don't have a title!"

"They gave you one, a temporary title, just for the show. Come on, get in the car. Daisy, too." Jack opened the back door and Daisy hopped in. "Annie, we're going." He held open the passenger door for me.

The whole foreground was a mess: What were they thinking?

"Mom, get in," Cass said from the back seat.

I shook my head. "Look, let me just go in the house—"

"We don't want to miss the ferry," Jack said. "Come on, Annie."

"I have to get my purse!" I went in the house and up to the bedroom where I'd left my purse on the chair. This was ridiculous, but I was too tired and felt too depleted to continue to protest. I got my purse and went back downstairs and locked the house.

Jack held the door open for me and put his hand on my shoulder as I reluctantly slid in the seat.

I wasn't sure how I felt about being railroaded like this. It was a big enough hurdle just to think of showing my painting at all, let alone not having it done. "What are we doing about dinner?" I finally asked.

"Martha Jane suggested we all eat on the island after the show is hung. She said she's bringing stuff to snack on to tide us over."

Dear Martha Jane, she thinks of everything. She even

gave my painting a title, for heaven's sake. My curiosity finally got the better of me. "What's the title?" I asked.

"Title?" Jack backed down the drive.

"Of my painting—you said they gave it a title."

"She said it's called, 'Three Steps Forward, Two Steps Back,'" Jack said.

"I bet Martha Jane made that up." I sighed and then I began to laugh. 'Three Steps Forward, Two Steps Back.' Of course that's the title." I turned to Jack, then to Cass in the back seat. "Actually, " I said with a sigh, " I am glad you'll be meeting Martha Jane and Fred."

"They wanted to know how to list your name." Jack said, as we came to the stop sign at the end of the block.

"For what?"

"I don't know, that's just what she said."

Listing my name? I didn't want to sign my name to the meadow painting until I finished it. And I would finish it, I reminded myself again, no matter how long it took.

I tried to imagine what kind of spin Fred and Martha Jane would put on having an unfinished piece in the show, knowing they'd want to reassure me. I thought about it for a while and figured they'd probably say it was something like having a staged reading of a play. I tried to accept that it would be okay, although I felt pretty tentative about the whole thing, to say the least.

But there was no hesitation when it came to how I'd sign my paintings. I closed my eyes and smiled. It was easy. I didn't even have to think. I had known for years. I would never use the name Gunther, even though my legal name was Anne Gunther Duppstadt. On everything I did, my mother's name would be there.

"I can tell them how to list my name when we get there."

"How?" Jack asked.

"Anne Kuroda Duppstadt."

When we reached the dock at Fauntleroy, the sun was setting and by the time we drove on the ferry, the tip of the red arc dropped behind the Olympic Mountains, turning the jagged peaks to the shade of purple I loved. Against the lavender sky, Puget Sound became violet, pink and silver like the iridescence within a large shell. It was so beautiful, I wanted to paint it. Everywhere we went, I would always bring pastels and canvas paper. To all the places we might travel.

Near the dock in the bay by Lincoln Park, I saw a small sailboat, its sails gold and pink in the evening light. The engines revved, and I smiled at Cass in the rearview mirror, who gave me a thumbs up. Then I reached for Jack's hand as the ferry moved slowly away from the dock and headed for the island.

EPILOGUE

ANNE KURODA DUPPSTADT

Anne Kuroda Duppstadt didn't begin painting until she was in her sixties, studying with Frederick Weiss for several years at his studio school on Vashon Island, Washington. She has exhibited widely in the Northwest with solo shows at the Silverwood Gallery, Vashon Island, Washington; Blue Creek Gallery, Walla Walla, Washington; the Roby King Galleries, Bainbridge Island, Washington; and the Foster White Gallery, Seattle, Washington. Kuroda Duppstadt's Phnom Penh Series brought the first national attention in North America and her work was exhibited at the La Fond Galleries, in Pittsburgh, Pennsylvania; the Theodore Evans Gallery in Hudson, Ohio; the Roger Lewis Gallery in Halifax, Nova Scotia; and the Welch-Shanaman Gallery in Vancouver, British Columbia. Known for her unique use of color, and the juxtaposition of contrasting colors found in ukiyo-e prints, Anne Kuroda Duppstadt's work has found a wide audience in Japan in the past decade. Now, still painting in her eighties, she is preparing for the Pacific Rim Painters Exhibition, which will be held at the Kumagai Museum, Honolulu, Hawaii.

READER'S GUIDE TO
THE LOVE CEILING

AN INTRODUCTION TO
THE LOVE CEILING

In the laundry room, I unfolded my easel and set it up next to the aging washer and dryer. Then I went back to the furnace room where I'd set the cedar case and I brought it in, putting it on the shelf over the washer between a box of detergent and a bottle of bleach. I brought the meadow painting down last and propped it on the easel next to the washer and dryer. The overhead light was weak and the painting was dark and poorly lit.

I sat on the clothes hamper across from the painting, folded my arms across my knees, put my head down and just wept. I thought about my father's studio, the entire carriage house, the space my mother so valiantly guarded for him.

I didn't hear Jack come in.

"Oh honey." He put his arms around me. "Come to bed."

"I'm beginning to think this whole thing is futile," I wiped my eyes with the back of my hand.

"Come on, let's go up and get some sleep." He took my hand.

"There is a glass ceiling for women, Jack," I stared at my painting in the dim light next to the washer and dryer. "And it's made out of the people we love."

Set in the Pacific Northwest, *The Love Ceiling* tells the moving story of sixty-four-year-old Anne Koroda Duppstadt, a woman who struggles to follow a life-long dream of becoming an artist in the face of the needs of her thirty-two-year-old daughter, her husband's resistance to face retirement, and the hurtful legacy of her father, the famous artist Alexander Gunther. In this funny and touching exploration of a long marriage and the conflicts that arise both in retirement and in parenting adult children, a major theme in *The Love Ceiling* is creativity and the pull between family and self-expression central to women.

The roles of a woman in her sixties: wife, mother, grandmother, art therapist, and artist are richly explored with complexity and depth. It is the story of a woman, a daughter, a long marriage and a journey into creativity

QUESTIONS FOR DISCUSSION

1. When Cass returns home and Annie has to give up her studio she says, "There is a glass ceiling for women and it's made out of the people we love." What do you think she means by this? Do you agree with Annie? What about the constraints for women imposed by society?

2. Both Jack and Cass refer to Annie's work at Woodside as "her little part-time job." Do you think this is a reflection of how society in general views women who work part time? Do you think Jack and Cass each have different reasons why they characterize it this way?

3. Annie and Cass disagree about the concept of unconditional love. Why do you think Annie becomes annoyed when Cass brings it up? What are your thoughts about unconditional love? Do we have the right to expect it from another adult? Annie thinks love has conditions, the condition that every effort will be made to treat the other with kindness and respect. Do you agree with her?

5. Annie talks with her friend Martha Jane about Jack's fear of retirement, and his fear of losing his identity without his work. Do you think fears about loss of identity occur in women who have had careers outside the home? Martha Jane refers to women feeling invaded when their husbands retire. Do you think this is a common fear? Are women likely to worry about feeling "taken over" when a husband begins spending a lot of time at home?

6. In spite of Jack's growing acceptance of Annie's commitment to art, Annie still struggles with feeling she should get home to make dinner for him every night. Do you think this feeling is typical for women Annie's age or women of

any age? For women who experience this sense of obliga-
tion how do you think it might influence their creativity?

7. How does what we learn of Annie's mother Akiko make
her seem different from Martha Jane Morrison? How much
of a role do you think culture and the history of Japanese
Americans may have played in Akiko's personality? In what
way do you think it might be difficult for women to learn to
stand up for themselves when they've had a timid mother?

8. Annie was born with talent but her father's abusive
behavior robbed her of the confidence to believe in it. Do
you think she could have overcome her self-doubt without
Fred's encouragement and Jack's support? Do you think
creativity can thrive without encouragement?

9. Jack feels threatened when Annie tells him about wanting
to work at Fred's studio. Do you think this is a reflection
of Jack's personality or the fact that he's struggling with his
own career? Or do you think it reflects a fear that arises naturally for most people when a person's spouse or a partner
moves in a direction that doesn't include him or her?

10. Cass tells Annie that she felt she wasn't allowed to
fail, and when she compares Annie's expectations to the
expectations Mrs. Choi had for Lena, Cass thinks Annie
expected her to "have it all." She was expected to have a
great career, travels, adventures, marriage and children. Do
you think Cass was accurate in assuming this? Did femi-
nism bring a pressure on young women from their mothers
or society to have it all? Do you think it's possible to have
it all?

11. When Annie remembers her first marriage she talks
about the classic but doomed dance where a woman chooses

to pair with a person who psychologically resembles a parent with whom there has been a conflicted relationship, and it always turns out badly. Do you think Cass was influenced by her family relationships in her choice of Richard? Do you think Cass should have tried harder to make the relationship work when Richard wanted her back?

12. Annie thinks men aren't as well equipped to care for young children as women, and would "like it both ways" when it comes to marital fidelity. Martha Jane thinks women adapt better to retirement, and that their ability to have close friends helps them. Do all these women have an overly negative view of men? Do you agree with them on any of their conclusions? Is there a generational difference in how they see men and women?

13. Annie realizes that she won't be able to help her father until there is a reckoning. She then decides to confront him because she assumes it might be more painful not to. Do you think she did the right thing?

14. Martha Jane says there can't be forgiveness without deep remorse on the part of the person who has caused injury. Do you agree? How much do children owe their parents?

15. The epigraph, which precedes the novel, is a quote from Anaïs Nin: "Then the time came when the risk it took to remain tight in a bud was more painful than the risk it took to blossom." What does this mean to you? Does it apply to Annie's situation?

JEAN DAVIES OKIMOTO is an author and playwright whose books and short stories have been translated into Japanese, Italian, Chinese, German and Hebrew. She is the recipient of numerous awards including *Smithsonian* Notable Book, the American Library Association Best Book for Young Adults, the Washington Governor's Award and the International Reading Association Readers Choice Award. A member of PEN, she lives on an island in Puget Sound.